T0018501

TEAR

a novel by
ERICA MCKEEN

Invisible Publishing
Halifax & Toronto

For my mother, Michelle, and for Sophie

© Erica McKeen, 2022

All rights reserved. No part of this publication may be reproduced or transmitted in any form, by any method, without the prior written consent of the publisher, except by a reviewer, who may use brief excerpts in a review, or, in the case of photocopying in Canada, a licence from Access Copyright.

Library and Archives Canada Cataloguing in Publication
Title: Tear / Erica McKeen.
Names: McKeen, Erica, author.
Identifiers: Canadiana (print) 20220247919
            Canadiana (ebook) 20220247978
            ISBN 9781778430060 (softcover)
            ISBN 9781778430077 (HTML)

Classification: LCC PS8625.K4185 T43 2022 | DDC C813/.6—dc23

Edited by Bryan Ibeas
Cover and interior design by Megan Fildes | Typeset in Laurentian
With thanks to type designer Rod McDonald

Invisible Publishing is committed to protecting our natural environment. As part of our efforts, both the cover and interior of this book are printed on acid-free 100% post-consumer recycled fibres.

Printed and bound in Canada.

Invisible Publishing | Halifax & Toronto
www.invisiblepublishing.com

Published with the generous assistance of the Canada Council for the Arts, the Ontario Arts Council, and the Government of Canada.

"But my form is a filthy type of yours, more horrid from its very resemblance."

— Mary Shelley, *Frankenstein*

PROLOGUE

If you sit on the living room couch and look out the living room window, you can see the road, Ford Crescent, stretched out like a grey elastic band from the point on the left where it begins to the point on the right where it bends out of the eye and into the temple, cut off by the straight line of the window frame. This is one road of many in the city of London, Ontario, named long ago after that larger London in England—one curve of many in the neighbourhood of Medway, named also after that larger Medway.

The surrounding neighbourhood is University Heights. It's called this because of the university sprawled just a few blocks away, close enough to keep this cluster of houses from having its own identity, its own name.

The public school on Ford Crescent is also called University Heights. If you look out the window at the right time of day, you can see kids scuffling back or forth along the road with backpacks the size of their torsos, puffy hats and coats in winter, brightly striped running shoes in spring. You can't see the school itself—it's hidden by the houses at the turn in the road. These houses are mostly ranch-style, built in the 1970s and '80s, nearly forty or fifty years old. New compared to other neighbourhoods in London—compared to Old North or Old East or Old South, which form, in chunks, the central portion of the city. New, but without that feeling of freshness. No flawlessness, nothing too sharp or perfectly white. These houses sink lazily into the earth, peeking out from beneath heavy lids. They see each other from across the street but don't actively watch. They're sleepy and unassuming, appearing to mimic one another—out of habit, perhaps, or a lack of effort. They all have one- or two-car garages and driveways. They all have front yards with a scattering of trees sticking up like fingers. They are houses made of brick, with small front porches, small concrete steps leading up to these porches, with skinny makeshift gardens, shingled roofs, and limp eavestroughs.

But they aren't identical. They aren't what people call cookie-cutter, like those houses rapidly constructed in the ever-expanding northern part of the city, eating farmland so fast they have cornstalks in the framework of their walls. Not like the houses in Masonville, where the mall is as necessary as the gas station and grocery store, where the fields are so close you might smell hay on the breeze. These houses in University Heights, tucked between Sarnia Road and Oxford Street, Western and Wonderland, have differentiation. An extra window here, a bulging dining room there, a side entrance, a metallic chimney, red bricks, white bricks, brown bricks—but none so unique that these differences are notable. These houses were not built identically, but they were constructed as if from the same corner of one person's imagination: an imagination clogged with square windows and walls, pavement and fake hardwood and carpet.

One house, 48 Ford Crescent, blends in with the rest. It is one floor with a two-car garage, perhaps the least noticeable house on the street, the most congruous—except in autumn, after the leaves have fallen from the tree in the front yard; except in summer, after a few long weeks of spasmodic rain; except in winter, after the snow tumbles down around midnight and isn't slush by morning, but stays and clumps and pushes against the garage door and front porch, swallows the garden. At these times the house departs from conformity: the leaves remain unraked, the lawn unmowed, and the snow unshovelled.

This is because 48 Ford Crescent is a student house. Students, the house's neighbours reflect, have an intrinsic disrespect for houses. Whether it's their age, their drinking habits, their having too much money or not enough, students don't know the delicate nature of houses: the thinness of walls, the see-through quality of ceilings. This is simply a pause for them in a larger moment of transition. They'll learn about houses later, when they see their years billowing out ahead of them like bubbles expanding underwater. They'll learn that to keep a house quiet, to keep it covering you at night instead of crushing you, hours of dusting, wiping, scraping, vacuuming, spraying, flushing, and scrubbing are required, like a pagan god requires prayer, requires sacrifice. The house wants sweat in dedication, it wants time and muscle strain and money to remain untroublesome, to remain still and quiet and blind.

So the leaves rot on the front lawn, the snow grows an icy crust on the driveway, and the summer grass grows up long and spiky. The neighbours smirk. Student house. Around Christmas they see a string of lights framing the living room window; they see the black lip of a couch pushed up against the wall. In the evening the blinds are drawn. They see a bloated shadow or two pass behind the bright slats.

The house keeps its eyes shut, its mouth shut. The house is sleeping.

╫

The house has a dark-shingled roof. It looks black even in full summer sunlight. It's rough on fingertips, on kneecaps, if you climb onto it from the hedges that line the backyard, which you might do, which a grown person can manage if she stays close to the trunks of the hedge growth. The branches are thin and bendy. They tear off, soft like green tongues on the inside. Watch the eavestrough. It's already leaning off the edge of the roof, catching more leaves than rain. It's already rusting—it rattles in the wind.

Climb over the roof to the other side. Down below is the front face of the house. It's made of grey and white bricks. A concrete porch with wrought-iron railings juts out from the front door. A paved path extends from the porch and joins with the concrete driveway. One large window cuts through the brick—the living room window.

If you look closely you can see the smudgy outline of a face in that window. It blends with the reflection of trees, the road. The face looks blue in the layering of sky and skin in the glass. Sometimes it looks grey.

Lean closer. Here's the cheekbone, the eyebrow, the long bend of lips.

This is Frances. Frances James.

Her eyes are tilted, are minutely too far apart. Her hair is frizzy, almost curly, as if run through with static. She has freckles on her nose. In her lap is a bundle of fingers, clustered up, perhaps too tightly, the knuckles bent, the knuckles white. She sits on the couch, which is pushed up against the wall, and watches the world outside the window. It's morning and cold outside, so cold she can feel it through the glass. She watches the children as they walk to school.

These children rake up a memory: a memory of red shoes on her feet, of brown tiles beneath the shoes.

She stops it there. Stops the memory and fills herself up with breath. Her lips droop slightly, drop toward her jawbone. Frances strengthens the knot of her fingers, digs her toes into the floorboards. She feels the vertebrae in her neck creak as she turns her head, hears the children's feet clop like echoes on the other side of the glass. She turns away from them and presses her hands into the seat of the couch to lift herself.

Little red shoes and brown tile beneath these shoes, she thinks, and in her mind she jumps from tile to tile, avoiding the white lines between. Her body is small and easy to move. Her brain is simple and fluid.

But when Frances looks down, she sees socks instead of shoes, floorboards beneath the socks. Her body is tall and stuttering. Her skull feels swollen and heavy. She has the taste of blood on her tongue: she's bitten it, cut it open in her concentration, her jumping. But where was she jumping, and to what? A silence curdles up from the cracks in the laminate flooring. The living room is quiet around her. The house is quiet. Her roommates are gone, in class at the university, and she is alone and curled up inside herself. The walls are very thin, she feels, she can feel the wind through the wallpaper.

Frances sees the little red shoes—hanging as if by their laces in front of her eyes—as she moves through the kitchen to the basement door. She moves through the basement door and down into the basement, to her bedroom where the window looks out onto the backyard, away from the street and the children.

She closes the door behind her.

In four months, she'll be finished university, gone from this house. Frances closes her eyes and imagines herself invisible. She lies down in her bed and unrolls her invisible toes.

PART ONE

SLEEP GUT AND SLEEP ROT

ONE

The basement was dark in a blinding way, in a thick, physical way. It pressed on Frances, on her hair and clothes and skin. It snuck into her nose, climbed like a beetle into her ears, clung to the wet corners of her eyes. The darkness was a paste along her tongue. It was phlegm that she spat into the sink and urine that she pissed into the toilet. The darkness was the palm of her hand, spread out and invisible in front of her eyes. She knew only by wiggling her fingers that the hand was there, by the texture of skin on air.

By touch, she knew she existed. Here was the blanket on the bed, sweat-stiffened linens on her back and legs. Here was the rug in the hallway weaving up between her toes. Here was the cold laminate flooring, the tile in the bathroom, the metal framing of the stairs. The wood at the end of her bed, which she reached with the curve on the bottom of her foot. Here was the wall and door frame, the bedroom door—streaked, she imagined, with oil marks from her fingertips as she dragged them along to find the way.

By hearing, she knew she existed. She heard the rain outside her window, the thrum of a car far away on the street; heard the muffled turn of Ky, her roommate, in the bed overhead; heard the flush of the toilet, the spurt of the faucet, the shush of midnight footsteps, the quiet slug of her own breath moving in and out of her mouth. She heard the house settle and waken—sounds so subtle you could only hear them in darkness, darkness as thick as this, a shuddering and stretching, sighs and wood popping, brackets cracking.

Sometimes she would raise her head and think, *What brought me here? And what about here and why?* She wasn't a remarkable person, and this house, she knew, was no different. The day she'd moved in, when she and her mother drove up and down the street, around the neighbourhood, she noticed that this house was only one of many just like it. When they swung onto Ford Crescent, Frances didn't recognize this house in particular. Not even when her mother stopped the car in front of the yard—not until she saw the metallic number pinned above the garage doors, 48, did she believe this was it.

I'll get lost coming home from school, she thought. *I'll get lost taking the garbage out to the edge of the street.*

But she only said, Mom, do you notice anything strange?

And her mother said, What do you mean? Looking past Frances, she scanned the white-and-grey-brick house, the paved driveway, and trimmed front lawn. What do you mean? No, nothing. Nothing strange.

Frances nodded and said, Me neither. I can't see anything unusual.

And she thought, *I'll get lost putting my shoes on at the front door.*

Frances lay in bed and watched her toes waving near the wall. They were plump, nails trimmed, skin almost blue in the layers of moonlight pushing through the window. Below her toes, making them wiggle, making them wave, were her feet, blue-veined, soft-looking, and white, the bottoms of them as soft as the white bellies of mice. Below her feet were her ankles, and attached to these, her legs. Her legs were roughly outlined, prickly from a week without shaving, disappearing up into a pair of unwashed sweatpants. The rest of her body lay mountainous in her view: dips and folds of fabric, the movement of lungs expanding, the unexpected bending of joints. She breathed and felt herself breathing. She lay in bed, in her bedroom, and watched the ceiling. She counted the walls.

####

Frances moved up and down the long basement hallway, all in darkness, all in the dense, wet darkness that stuck to the roof of her mouth and the insides of her eyelids. It was a small space for a body to move in. But she moved there anyway, back and forth, from the laundry room door to her bedroom, past the kitchenette and staircase and bathroom, sitting sometimes on the couch against the wall, staring sometimes at the bookshelf, each ledge stuffed full with books like rows of discoloured piano keys. She touched the books with her fingers, pressed them as if to play them but never read them. The darkness was too thick to read in, her eyes were too slow in blinking. With her fingers, she touched the pages and tried to reassemble the jumbles of black scribbles that used to be words.

Frances touched floorboards and door frames and countertops. She touched the sink in the kitchenette, the sink in the bathroom, the toilet bowl, and the bathtub beneath the shower. She stood on the couch, her desk chair, to touch the ceiling. Frances touched the basement blindly, the way you rummage through the hair on the back of your head in search of a wound when you feel pain. In search of bleeding.

Frances found dust in the basement. She found rough dust balls and tangles of hair, dried-out shells of dead insects, and the serrated edges of torn-off toenails. She didn't find bleeding. She didn't know if she was hurting, or if she was looking for the source of hurting. She felt the slow, blank hollow before a hurt. She felt the cold, tugging ache that hides just behind pain.

The basement wasn't a place for a body to move. But a mind—Frances found space there, her mind found space and roamed. The darkness, the loose and billowing shadows, that blackness, was deep and thick and sweet like jelly in her head, a conductor better than water for her thoughts. She wandered through it, wading back and forth, down the hallway and back, from her bedroom to the laundry room door and back.

If she slept, she didn't remember sleeping. If she dreamt, she didn't remember her dreams.

✝✝✝

Her grandparents' house was on the outskirts of London, in Nilestown. It wasn't really a town but more an intersection of roads with houses on each corner, and her grandparents' house was even farther past this, out into the farmland and forest.

When she lived there with her mother, up until the age of six, her grandparents lit lanterns outside on summer evenings, and they would all sit on the back porch, facing the backyard, looking out into the trees beyond. And when the time was right, when the sun lowered just so, when the crickets held their breath, when the wind fell off and only occasionally lifted the leaves in the trees or shifted the blades of grass in the yard, her grandfather would pour a glass of grainy homemade wine and tell ghost stories.

Frances would sit in the space between her grandfather's knees, wrapped in an oversized sweater, and listen. There were stories of corpses crawling out of the earth, of old crypts in the forest long covered by moss, of houses with secret rooms, of sleepwalkers walking out of bed and down the road to the river, where you could still hear them gurgling if you listened hard enough, where you could still feel their hair on the bottoms of your feet if you went swimming in the water, where—

Stop now, that's enough, her grandmother would say, rocking in her favourite chair. You're scaring her.

Frances would look up from where she sat on the porch, holding her toes in her hands.

Her grandmother's mouth was a hard line, there were hard lines all over her face. She rested her arms on the chair's armrests and pushed with her feet, up and down, the lobes of skin on her neck hanging into her shirt collar like dough, her hair strung back in a grey braid.

Stop now, she would say, that's enough.

Oh, come on. Frances's grandfather shifted in his seat. They're just stories. Are you scared, Frances?

Frances shrugged into her sweater, into her hands, which held her toes.

You're scaring her, said her grandmother.

And what's wrong with a little scaring? What's wrong with that?

Frances's grandfather had thin legs, scarecrow legs, and scarecrow hair, all frayed out like straw under his hat. His eye sockets looked swollen, and his nose was a large ball beneath his skin. His hands, blue and bony, rested on his knees, then fidgeted up to his stomach, under his armpits, arms crossed.

What's wrong with that?

You're putting ideas in her head, said her grandmother.

Oh, pah! That's what heads are for. What are they for but to be filled with ideas? What are ideas for but to be put in heads? Pah! He unhooked his arms and scratched his left temple. He grumbled something, his lips bubbling, the words hardly leaving his tongue.

Frances, what do you think? asked her grandmother.

Frances shrugged.

Her grandmother sighed, dragging her eyes to where the candle burned in the lantern on the table. Ideas are different with Frances, she said.

Frances looked up at her grandmother, but her grandmother didn't look back at her.

Her grandfather sighed, as if in echo. Well, I don't know what you mean by that, he said. Besides, I hadn't even gotten to the best part. Not the scariest part, but the best.

That's fine, said her grandmother. No more.

But there was more. The next night, and the night after that, always to a point, always until her grandmother raised a hand or raised her voice. Said, Stop now, that's enough. All through the summer with the lanterns and the trees and the smell of homemade wine, and sometimes through the winter with the fireplace inside, the shag carpet on the floor, blankets, a book on her grandmother's lap, and the same wine.

In this way Frances became accustomed to stories with no endings, or stories that stopped without conclusion and started abruptly into another. She didn't complain. She liked it this way. A collage of characters, events, of places and plans, all mixed against the backdrop of her grandparents by the lanterns or fire.

The spell would break when her mother returned home from her shift at the restaurant, sweaty and greasy to her hairline. Frances, off to bed, she would say, and in five minutes Frances would have teeth brushed, pyjamas on, and be upstairs under the covers, listening to the voices of her grandparents and mother downstairs, like the rumblings in some deep volcano. She would watch the dark room spiral around her eyes or study the strands of moonlight shifting through the curtains. And wait for her mother to join her.

ǂǂ

There's something living here with me. I'm not alone down here.

Frances had these thoughts at night, one of the first nights after one of the first days that she stayed in the basement and didn't go upstairs. Whether it was really the first night, or whether it was the second or third or fourth, she couldn't remember. She knew only that it was near the beginning.

Many things are lost in recollection. Many things are smudged and moved around. This feeling, however, would never leave, not for one second, one breath—this idea that something was living there with her. That she was not alone. The thought traced its cold fingers on the underside of her skull, trickled down her spine, found its way into her shoulders and hands, her thighs and kneecaps and toes.

Frances woke to this thought, surfaced to it, and found herself standing in the middle of the basement, in front of the stairs, cold in that section of floor at the bottom of the stairs, uncertain how she had gotten there. Her feet were bare, her hair hung in greasy clumps around her face, the sweat under her arms and around her neck was cold. She wore pyjamas that were poorly buttoned in the front. Behind her was the shadow of the kitchenette, built up against one wall, and behind that, the deeper shadow of the bathroom door. She could see the shape of the couch and bookshelf, the rectangular rug on the floor and the rectangular hollow of her bedroom doorway. To her left, hanging loosely over her like an arm hangs out of its socket, was the staircase, running up into the darkest dark of the basement. Although she couldn't see it, she knew the basement door stood at the top of the stairs, and she knew the kitchen stood behind it. She knew this like she knew that inside closed cupboards there were shelves and inside closed books there were words. Above her, beyond the basement door, was the rest of the house—the street, the city. The world.

But at night, when you awaken standing in the middle of the basement, barefoot and sweating, in the dark and dark and dark, it's easy to believe that there's nothing past these walls but packed dirt. That you are deep, that you are buried, that to get out you would have to dig, that you would have to claw and scrape until your fingernails grow ragged and your bones start to show, and then and only then would you find something different, some passageway, a piece of light.

Only then, with your clothes ripped, your hair fallen out of your skin, and your brain slipping out of your ears—only then would you find something different than this.

The light by which Frances could see, the light by which she could make out the couch and the bookshelf and the shadow of the kitchenette behind her, came from the window in the bedroom. She put her feet in front of her body and followed this light. She moved through the bedroom doorway, trailed her fingers across the desk, her books stacked beneath, and sunk onto the mattress. She sat with her knees pressed together, thinking she should lie down and sleep. But the light from the window felt good. The moonlight filled her head, flung up thoughts, felt good.

TWO

In the world of childhood, all things are visceral, immediate, extreme. What Frances could see, touch, taste—that was what she knew. Her head, in memory, was a hurricane. She was a pair of eyes, a nose, and two ears. She was a groping skirmish of thick fingers pushing through the grass.

Frances sat in the grass in her grandparents' backyard, searching for ants between the blades. Every so often she found one, as small as a moving dot of dirt, and she plucked it up and put it in the palm of her hand. She liked to watch it explore this new environment, the swells and cliffs and wrinkles of her skin, the sloping valleys in the creases of her palm. Every so often she picked up an ant too quickly, too imprecisely, and smeared its body between her fingertips. When she did this, she thought of her own body, her own bones, her own hair and teeth and skin. From above, from the view of an airplane or bird, she wouldn't look much different than the ant, not much more than a smear on the map of long backyards, farmland, and forest rolling off toward the city.

She smeared the ant into a thinner layer on her jean shorts. She couldn't think so far beyond herself. She knew only what was near her. She knew she was alone in the yard. She knew in front of her were her legs and her bare feet; behind her was a row of sunflowers, planted in the garden by her grandmother; to her left was the forest, the trunks of the trees jumbled close together, their leaves whispering, the wrinkled whorls of their eyes and eyebrows hunkered down against the sun; and to her right was the house and the back porch. In the kitchen window above the porch was the occasional darkened shape of her grandmother's head, watching Frances between washing dishes, sweeping the floor, and preparing dinner.

It was summer, warm, and Frances was coming up on her first year of school. Her limbs were thinning out, her hair was long enough for her mother or grandmother to put up in a ponytail, and she was gaining scabs on her knees and the heels of her hands, gaining bruises as she gained speed, climbed trees, learned to catch ladybugs but stay away from wasps. She had learned the letter *F* for *Frances* and she left it everywhere, imperceptibly, the tip of her finger tracing that sign of her identity into floor mats and walls, her kneecaps and T-shirts, the bathwater and ribbed seams of bed sheets.

She was tracing this letter *F* into the grass when she heard gravel crunch in the driveway. She looked up, momentarily bewildered by time, thinking from the sound that it was evening and her mother was arriving home from work. From where she sat, she could see the back of the vehicle around the side of the house: it was black and polished, small, sitting low against the ground. Frances heard the sound of a door opening, saw the long protrusion of a leg, a brown shoe. A man stood in the driveway. He almost walked to the door without noticing her, but then stopped, seeing her.

Looking at her.

He wasn't anyone she had met before, but he looked at her like she should know him. He had honey-coloured hair, oily and swept back over his head, forward-sloping shoulders, and glasses pushed up against his eyes. His hands were small and frozen in fists. His limbs were long, the lines of them invisible beneath his clothing. He had shadows under his cheekbones.

Frances hooked her fingers into the grass on either side of her, anchoring herself to the ground.

Hello, said the man. He had a strange, resonant lilt to his voice, his vowels deep and long. He took two steps forward, a jagged hurriedness to his movements.

Frances didn't answer.

Frances? he said. He moved closer.

Yeah, said Frances, that's me. She watched him watching her. Frances swallowed and turned away. She traced an *F* along her shinbone.

Frances, he said again. He knelt beside her and looked at her toes sticking up from her feet. He reached out as if to touch one, as if to pluck it up like she plucked up the ants, and hold it dismembered in his hand. She flinched as his fingers approached, and he twitched backward, retracting his reach with a frown, his brows furrowed and confused, as if he had forgotten himself, as if he had lost some thought he had extended along with his hand. From this distance, Frances could see close up the pointed tip of his nose, the individual spikes of hair growing on his jaw and around his mouth. From this distance, she could smell him—a cologne that stung like hot spices in her nostrils. She could hear his breath as it worked its way in and out of his mouth. She could hear his clothes shifting as he moved. From this distance, she could see that his eyes were blue.

Frances, he said, and looked again toward her toes. It's good to see you. It's been—

I'm catching ants, Frances cut in.

Catching ants? He laughed. His eyes went thin when he laughed, like cracks in his face. What do you mean?

I mean I'm catching them and making them mine. I'm keeping them so they won't go away. She paused, looking at the tan curve of his forehead, the straight and hulking bone of his nose. Who are you? she asked.

Oh, he said. He scratched his head. Well—

A bang behind him sliced his voice apart. Frances's grandmother stood on the back porch, her hands dripping suds from the dishes and her grey hair tangled across her face. Frances couldn't see her expression, but she knew what it was from the way her grandmother held her arms: stiffly, away from her hips, her fingers curled at the ends of her hands. She knew by the way her feet, jammed into slippers, were spread apart and immovable, block-like, as if they had grown roots into the porch.

Excuse me, her grandmother said. Excuse me. The moment she spoke, her feet uprooted. She came down the porch steps and into the grass. Excuse me.

The man stood, stretching tall above Frances, and stepped away. He held up his hands. I'm sorry, he said. I didn't mean—

Her grandmother squinted at him, inspected him, suspicious, perhaps, of the spotless, sharp cut of his clothing, of the scooped-out hollows in the centre of his words. She folded her arms across her chest.

What do you want? she asked.

I'm Peter, he said. I'm Peter.

Her grandmother's eyebrows lifted. The tight weave of her arms loosened. Peter? She stared at him. Jeanette's Peter?

He shrugged, buried his hands in his pockets.

Does she know you're here? her grandmother asked.

The man shook his head.

Okay, okay. She won't be home until after dinner. Would you... Her grandmother's eyes dashed around the backyard, falling briefly on Frances's face. Would you like to come inside? I'll make tea.

The man nodded. Sure, he said. Of course.

Frances, said her grandmother, you stay here.

Frances watched them go up the porch steps and into the house. She saw the shadow of her grandfather hovering in the kitchen behind them. She saw the door close, heard the click as the door closed, and then she was alone in her own body, back in the backyard, the wind playing tricks and joining with the sounds of the forest to make words, the birds dancing around the sunflowers. In her lap were two handfuls of grass that she had pulled from the ground. There was dirt beneath her fingernails. There were red marks on her hands where her fingernails had dug into her palms.

She stared at these new indents, these new ridges on the map of her skin. Then she rolled onto her stomach and began combing through the grass again, searching for ants.

#

That summer was the last summer that Frances went shoeless. In the fall, her grandmother bought her running shoes for school. Frances got to pick the colour: bright red. She already had sandals for hot sand at the beach, for going inside restaurants and shopping malls; she had boots for the rain and the cold. She didn't have running shoes and she didn't understand why she needed them. When she asked her grandmother about these shoes, why she needed shoes for running, her grandmother explained that on the playground and in the classroom these shoes would act as protectors. More sturdy than sandals and completely covering her toes, they would keep her from getting hurt.

Hurt by what? asked Frances.

Her grandmother bunched her lips together and thought. Hurt by gravel, she said. By stones. By other kids' feet. By accidental sharp things lying around.

Like pine cones? asked Frances, thinking of the pine cones she had stepped on in the forest behind the house.

Her grandmother nodded. Like pine cones. But maybe even sharper things. Maybe even glass. She saw Frances's expression and said, Don't worry. These shoes are your protectors. Protectors and attackers. You can kick balls farther, run faster. How do you like them? How do your toes feel?

If Frances had known the word, she would have said, *Suffocated*.

After a year at school, a year of closed-toe shoes and closed doors, of small windows and sharpened pencils and the stiffness behind the initial powder of blackboards, Frances would come to associate bare feet with open air, with a green world of grass, forest, and gardens. The world of shoes was a world of tile and pavement, of wooden desk and chair legs, of piles of pebbles beneath plastic and metal playground equipment. A tough, scratching, polished, hurting world. A hard world. She knew, after entering this world, that she was growing up. This was what getting bigger meant. A layer of fabric and rubber around her feet. Protection and defence. Run faster, jump farther, come home with soft feet and toes, calluses cradled away by socks and soles. Learn about laces, how to tie a knot. Pull it tight.

Frances learned to play and wander and enter forests with shoes. She learned to feel naked without them.

###

In her bed in the basement, Frances looked down at her bare feet. She wiggled her toes.

###

You know that man, her grandmother asked later, after everything—after Frances had grown cold outside and she had tried to come in, after her grandfather had chased her out again and then picked her up and swung her over his head, after he told her to count all the clouds she could see in the sky, all the birds that went by, after she finished counting and found him gone, after the man came out and touched her head, touched her shoulder and left, backing out of the driveway in his shiny black car, after she watched him go down the road and disappear, after she came inside to her grandparents talking on the living room couch—after dinner, after everything. Her grandmother said, You know that man who visited this afternoon? You remember him?

Frances nodded.

This is very important. She held Frances's shoulders. I don't want you to tell your mom about him. She would be very upset. You don't want to make her upset, do you?

Frances shook her head.

Okay. It's very important. You have to remember not to tell your mom about that man. Do you understand?

Frances nodded.

Say that you understand.

I understand.

Thank you, Frances. And I'm sorry.

She hugged her.

╫

Frances learned later, much later, that her parents met in university. It was the first time her mother had left home for longer than a week. She went to Toronto. She was eighteen. Frances's father was twenty-seven and a PhD student. He was the teaching assistant for her mother's first-year political science course, and he held very generous office hours. Her mother was pregnant by January and back home in Nilestown by May. She started work as a server in a nearby restaurant, the highest-paying job she could land.

Frances's mother told her father about the pregnancy, but neither of them told the university. When Frances was born at St. Joseph's Hospital in October, her father was proctoring a mid-term exam.

Any mention of him flung her mother into silence. When she heard from an old university friend that he had received an assistant professor position at the University of Toronto, she stayed in bed for five days, took to scratching her wrists until the skin tore, nearly lost her job. Frances remembered playing with Lego on the carpet while her mother lolled, half-conscious, up on the mattress. She sang songs to make her mother happy, coloured pictures and taped them on the wall with help from her grandfather to make her mother happy. She knew intrinsically and from the very beginning—from the moment of conception, perhaps—that her mother wasn't happy.

卌

On the second day of her first year of school, Frances came home and asked why she lived with her grandparents, why she didn't live alone with her mom. All the other kids lived with their mom and dad; nobody lived with their grandparents.

Her grandfather replied, You're lucky. You've got it better than the other kids. There's more love for you here. There're more people to love you here. Wouldn't you miss us if you left? Wouldn't you want to come right back?

Frances answered, Yes.

She didn't ask the question again, not out loud, and within a year it became irrelevant: she and her mother moved with her father to a townhouse in North London.

She wouldn't ask the question again, not even in her head, until she was older, a teenager, and her father was gone. But by then she knew the answer. By then she had witnessed her mother in the house alone, had seen how she forgot about dinner, slept too much or too little, avoided the shower. Frances would think back to that first year at school, to her grandfather standing in the living room with his arms open, saying, *Wouldn't you want to come right back if you left? Why would you ever want to leave?*

THREE

Frances remembered sitting up in bed.

She was little then, back in the Nilestown house. It was night. She shifted to the edge and dropped onto the hardwood—dashed to the door, which was open a crack, letting in light from the hallway.

She had been listening to the sounds of the house, listening to the snippets of whisper from somewhere below, waiting for her mother to come upstairs. She grew less tired as she lay. She rolled, fidgeted, counted her breaths, tried to find faces in the shadowy shapes on the walls. She couldn't bear it. She had to tell her mother, her grandmother and grandfather, how unbearable and impossible it was, that she was growing less tired as she lay.

So she sat up in bed. She shifted to the edge, dropped onto the hardwood, and dashed to the door.

Her feet were soft on the hallway carpet. They made a chorus of soft creaks in the floorboards beneath. From her grandparents' bedroom came the similarly soft sounds of her grandfather getting ready for bed: dresser drawers sliding closed, a closet doorknob turning, blankets lifting, the crack of a book opening.

Frances went down the stairs.

She would have walked right into the kitchen, opened the door, and plunged into that white light, rubbing her eyes with her fists, perhaps, or pouting, slurring her words, saying, Momma, come to bed. But she stopped before the door, pressed herself into the wall. She had heard her name, *Frances*. Her name, *Frances*, when they thought she was upstairs sleeping. Her name passed back and forth between her mother and grandmother like an old photograph for inspection. She heard the seriousness, the slow, monitored pulse of their voices, the care with which they picked and presented their words. Frances put her fingers in her mouth, pushed her cheek against the wall, and listened.

Later, she would have trouble remembering the specific words, and what she did remember she didn't understand. Not at the time.

There was talk of Peter—Frances thought vaguely of the man she had met in the backyard a couple weeks before—and then talk of Frances's mother being unkind, even cruel. Her mother snapped back, her words raw at the edges, sharp. There was talk of money, her mother complaining of only enough money for one room in her parents' house, enough space for a bed and dresser, living like a teenager, taking on the voice of a teenager as she pleaded with Frances's grandmother.

Her old life, she said—and Frances remembered these words—her old life hanging like a snakeskin from her, a shell she couldn't shake off. Everything I thought my life could be, said her mother. Her voice was almost a whine, melodramatic. Everything I imagined it would be.

Then they spoke again of Frances. And Frances's grandmother asked why her mother hadn't had an *abortion*.

In the hallway, Frances tried this word in her mouth, silently, moving her tongue around her fingers. *Abortion.* This was a strange word, an unknown word, a clinical word. *Abortion.*

What, get rid of Frances? asked her mother. No. Never. She's more real than anything else. But sometimes...sometimes, God, I wish she weren't.

Weren't what? asked her grandmother. Real?

It would be easier, wouldn't it? Fuck.

Frances flinched at the word, the hard and bad and forbiddenness of the word.

What am I saying, said Frances's mother. I need to go to bed.

Frances heard the screech of a chair pushing away from the table. She turned and raced up the stairs, her hand still in her mouth, biting hard on her fingers until she reached her bed and dove, headfirst, into the blankets.

†††

What, getting rid of Frances?
What,
getting rid of Frances?

†††

No. Never.
No. Never.
No. Never.

†††

Cold and alone in the house on Ford Crescent, Frances went up the basement stairs and stood by the basement door. She placed her hand on the doorknob and thought of the food in the kitchen, the food she should prepare and eat in the kitchen. But her stomach felt numb; her tongue was a lump in her mouth. She was tired, so tired down deep in her body, in the hollow, quiet spaces of her body. There was a grating pull in her lungs as she breathed, a dull, sleepy strain in her muscles as she moved. With her hand—cold—on the doorknob, she thought of the food in the kitchen.

Later, she thought. *Later. Maybe in an hour, maybe in ten minutes. Later.* She would go up later into the kitchen and into the light—weak, winter light straining like her muscles strained—through the kitchen and living room windows. She imagined that light and then shrank from it in the same way a worm retracts in the hardness of sunlight while exiting the earth.

It had been some time, an immeasurable amount of time, since Frances had been upstairs. The basement was cool, the basement was dark, the basement was familiar, the basement was not yet uncomfortable. She would stay down in the darkness for now. It was better, for now, down in the dark. She was tired, she would stay downstairs to rest. Her hunger wasn't strong enough, wasn't important. She would come back later.

Later, she thought—her hand on the doorknob, she didn't turn the knob—*I will come back later.*

Jeanette—Frances's mother—grew up in the city. Frances knew this. She knew that her grandfather was a public school teacher and that her grandmother stayed home. She knew from bedtime stories, passing remarks, and tidbits of information dropped like bread crumbs from her mother's and grandparents' mouths, that they'd had a house with four bedrooms and a big backyard, that they lived near a park. She knew the three of them were an unconventionally small family for the time, that her grandmother had tried and was unable to have more children after Jeanette.

What Frances didn't know, and would never know, were the daily, intricate details of her mother's early life. She didn't know, for example, that her grandmother told Jeanette often, so often that Jeanette remembered it as a staple in her childhood, that she was enough—smart enough, strong enough, kind enough, pretty enough—for five children, seven children, ten children. She was enough and could do everything and more than her imagined siblings might have done. Unburdened potential: she had it, she felt it. She excelled in school, at sports, in friendships. She entered competitions, learned humour, grew daring in her successes, avoided failure.

Jeanette had clear skin, straight A's, and the full attention of two parents. What did it matter that skipping a grade in elementary school slipped her timeline slightly out of joint? What did it matter that she had a temper, and sometimes got angry enough to throw chairs, start rumours, or burn her scalp briefly but purposefully against her hair straightener? What did it matter that she sometimes found her fingertips tingling, brushed her teeth until her gums bled, that she looked in the mirror and found her expression unfamiliar? What did it matter that Jeanette occasionally had nightmares in which she walked into her house and found strangers living there, found a different girl sleeping in her bed?

Frances knew that her father—Peter—was born in Berlin. She knew that he moved with his parents to Toronto when he was three years old, a transatlantic voyage meant not only to teach Peter fluent English but also to jump-start his father's career. His father bought a factory that produced bearings from a retiring family friend, made more money in his first year of business than he had in his entire life, and split from Peter's mother before three years had passed in Canada. He had his millions and Peter had his fluent English—the endeavour was, all in all, a success.

Frances knew that Peter and his mother moved back to Germany when Peter was six years old—to Cologne, where his grandparents lived. What she didn't know was that Peter spent his first two weeks there dizzy. He had trouble breathing, struggled to recognize a world his mother expected him to remember. She lived bitterly. His mother never mentioned his father's name, and when he paid for Peter to visit Canada during the summer, she refused to drive her son to the airport. One afternoon while his mother napped upstairs, Peter had to call his grandparents to ask the favour.

Frances didn't know much about Peter's father. She didn't know his house in Canada was luxurious, complete with high ceilings, a Jacuzzi in the bathroom, and arcade games in the basement. She didn't know he had a cleaning lady and three cars and a fridge full of beer specially imported from Germany. She didn't know he worked seventy hours a week and that so many of the rooms in his house were empty.

She didn't know that Peter, wedged between these two worlds, felt guilty and also triumphant about the ease with which his father lived. The further he moved into his teenage years, the more time he spent with his father in Canada—or, rather, alone at his father's house. He made friends with the neighbourhood girls, who liked his accent and his dad's outdoor pool, liked the classically European nonchalance with which he smoked his cigarettes. He let them stay late but never the whole night. He liked his temporary life there, the dreamlike quality of his days and evenings. He despised going back to his mother during the school year, the dim and dull afternoons, the tired conversation and dragging hours.

When he completed his master's program at Humboldt-Universität zu Berlin, he applied—on what felt simultaneously like a whim and an eventuality—to the University of Toronto for his PhD in political science. It was, he decided, the inevitable outcome of his split life that he should come back, once more, to Canada. He didn't approve of the phrase *meant to be*, but this was the closest he had come to it, and when he finally arrived in Toronto, he experienced a feeling that he concluded must be happiness.

Frances didn't know any of this.

〜

Jeanette first saw Peter in a political science seminar on utopias and dystopias. He sat at the front of the classroom, his hair a tousled mess at the top of his head, and when the professor introduced him as that year's teaching assistant, he raised a hand but didn't turn to face the class. He wore a dark blue blazer and khakis. He took notes steadily throughout the lecture, hardly looked up. Jeanette didn't see his face.

Peter first saw Jeanette at the end of class close to mid-term season, first semester. She had a question about a mark he'd given her on a recent assignment. He had to run, he was busy, always busy, he explained. Could she visit him during his office hours the following day? She had dark eyelashes, dark eyebrows, and dark hair. She wore a dark red sweater. Her lips, he noted as he left the room, were precisely the same colour.

#

I'm not supposed to do this, Peter said.

Jeanette sat in a chair on the other side of his desk. It was the second time she had visited him in his office that week. The weather was getting colder and, out the window behind Peter, Jeanette could see students rushing by with their heads down, chins tucked into scarves, pushing against the wind. Behind her, the door to the office was closed.

Do what? asked Jeanette.

I'd like to see you, said Peter. His voice was low—broad and resonant in the middle of his words. He looked at her lips, the red-wine colour of her lips. I'd like to drink wine with you, he said. I want to see you drinking red wine.

His words were slow, measured, stiff as if rehearsed. Or overused. Jeanette unintentionally blanched, her body shuddering; in the same moment she hid the shudder by jerking her chair closer to the desk. She imagined them at a restaurant together, red wine and candlelight, dark hardwood floors and light-footed waiters bowing minutely, whisking away platters, a scene she had witnessed a thousand times in movies but never in real life. A table with white tablecloth between them instead of this desk. A meal between them, food small-looking on large white plates, luxury that Peter could—probably—afford. The waiter swinging by, nimble as a dancer, to refill the wine, and Jeanette, fumbling in her large, dark-wooded chair, her underage ID a rock in her pocket.

Jeanette blinked. I'm eighteen, she said.

Peter laughed, a bellow that rolled up from his chest. I'm not asking you out to dinner, he said. He laughed again, hard and sharp.

Oh, said Jeanette.

I'm asking you to drink wine with me. I'm sorry, did you think I was asking you out to dinner? Come to my place, we'll drink wine. It's simpler, he said, and as he said this there was still a glint of laughter in his eyes. I bought this bottle recently, forty-five dollars. I don't usually splurge, but—

Okay, said Jeanette. She could feel, distinctly, the shape of her body in the chair, the hard edge of her tailbone digging into the wood. She drew her arms closer to herself. Okay, she said.

Good, said Peter.

Okay, said Jeanette again. Okay.

His apartment was small by Canadian standards: a bachelor with a kitchen in the corner, a bathroom, one closet, a bed that took up the majority of the living area, and a coffee table crowded with books and empty bottles of gin. There was a desk pushed up against the wall; it doubled as a dining table and was guarded by a slumped black chair. The place was the opposite of his office. It was untidy and careless, with clothes on the floor, a jumble of shoes by the door, notebooks and

CDs, discarded gloves, thin European-style scarves and cigarettes, a tall box of tea, chocolate wrapped in tinfoil from his last visit to Germany that he would offer her later, and postcards on the kitchen counter displaying various pictures of Cologne Cathedral. He had left the room this way purposefully. Messy but not dirty, cluttered but clean-smelling, vacuumed, a facade of vulnerability, proof of trust.

I've been busy, he explained, as he always explained to women who bore witness to his apartment. Horribly busy.

But Jeanette, holding her elbows in her hands, was looking past the room and out the glass door that led onto the balcony. In the distance were the hulking shapes of other apartment buildings dotted with similar glass balcony doors. Between these buildings were long rectangles of sky.

They talked for a while. They watched TV. They listened to music and he told her about Germany, how the bread tasted from the bakery in the morning, how the Rhine looked and smelled, how the trains sounded as they rolled out toward Switzerland and Austria and Belgium. Jeanette listened. They drank his forty-five-dollar bottle of red wine. They kissed. Talked some more. Had sex in the light coming through the balcony door. When it started getting dark, he rode the elevator with her down to the lobby and pointed the direction back to the subway.

The next day, when she had a question during the break in the middle of class, Peter suggested Jeanette visit him later in his office. It was the first time she would make love in a public space—she considered it public despite the jacket they hung over the small square window in the door. She could hear professors and students mulling by in the hallway, could hear doors opening and closing, people greeting one another or locked in quiet conversation, a keyboard clacking in the adjacent room. She could almost hear, somewhere deep within the walls, the slow rumble of a lecture steadily proceeding—she thought of Peter with his head bent, taking notes that first day in class—and she felt, as Peter flattened her against the side of his bookshelf, that she was somehow making love to the university itself, that it was moving inside her, that it touched her with practised fingers, that it dissolved her skin, dissolved her vocal cords, until the soft sounds she made were no different than the outside sounds passing through the covered door.

Jeanette cleaned herself up using the tissues Peter kept in his desk. She went home to shower and to sleep and to wake and to cry, inexplicably, as she warmed up leftovers in the microwave for dinner.

#

She saw him sporadically, on weekends or after class. She visited him during his office hours. They went to boutique coffee shops, wandered by the lake, and spent hours lounging in his bed by that glass balcony door. Or rather, she lounged, while he sat up against a pile of pillows or at his desk, reading books and writing papers, looking occasionally over at her, looking her over, telling her things and liking how she listened, like a child in the blankets, warm flesh, comfort, in his bed.

#

She phoned to tell him she was pregnant. It was late afternoon and she didn't want to wait until she saw him at the university the next day.

The conversation was short, his words incisive, as brutal as a hammer striking upright fingers. Was she certain? Had she been to the doctor? Would she keep it? How far along?

She drifted somewhere above his tone, failed to register the meaning behind his words, and when she hung up the phone she wrote him off as naturally in shock, naturally concerned. She spent the evening thinking not only of what she would say to him the next day, but thinking further. Her world at this point was still expanding, her imagination blooming. She saw him coming home with her to London, landing a job at the university or one of the newly constructed office buildings downtown. She saw them with the baby and a little rental house, visiting her parents in the near-countryside on the weekends. She saw the baby becoming a toddler, learning to bike on the road outside their house, drawing with chalk on the driveway, Peter mowing the lawn. She saw him asking her to stay in Toronto and her accepting, relenting; their tiny apartment; holding the baby on the subway, severe and wary with strangers; taking classes at the university, perhaps, part-time; their baby in the bathtub, babbling, bubbles on its head; Peter cradling it on the balcony and herself staring out, as wide-eyed as the baby at the lights in the evening, the other apartments glowing; getting a sitter and going to restaurants; the baby down by the lake, downtown; visiting her parents in London on holidays; the baby on the airplane, taking the trip finally to Germany.

She saw it all and couldn't unsee it. The visions grew hard like a scab in her mind, and when she went to see Peter the next morning in his office, it was already happening, years unfolding, before she opened the door.

I've been thinking about it all, he said as she sat down. He was behind his desk, fingers drumming his kneecaps, a hard glint in his eyes. All night I was thinking, he said.

Yes, she said.

I've decided it's not so different from my thesis, he said. The relation of psychology to culture, the creation of identity, the single identity of society, the predictability of people.

Your thesis? asked Jeanette.

She felt suddenly tired. Worn. The sleepless night caught up to her. She felt the weight all at once of her skin on her bones, her clothes on her body, and her backpack, shield-like, on her lap.

Yes, he said, my thesis. Let me explain, because it does warrant some explanation. As you know, I'm writing about how people learn explicitly from their parents and teachers, from public law and private household rules, but also and arguably even more so from implicit observation and a feeling of security in sameness, in being a *man of the crowd*, so to speak. And so culture forms culture, society forms, mirrors itself, reproduces and clones indefinitely, and we all become impressions of each other, archetypes—this is how archetypes are possible in the first place. Do you understand?

I understand the concept, yes, said Jeanette.

Well, what I was thinking is that we fit, you and I, very neatly into this theory of impressions and archetypes. What are you, for example, with your dark hair and brown eyes, your white skin and healthy weight and intellectual apti-tude—what are you but a model of female middle-class ambition? What am I but a young academic immigrant? There are fewer examples of me, I suppose, but still enough to make me an archetype. Is it so strange or so spectacular, is it so *revolutionary*, that we should get together and make this mistake, both of us feeling, however implicitly, disad-vantaged—a woman and an immigrant, respectively—and becoming power hungry because of it, and hungry for each other because of it?

Think about it, he continued. We aren't so different or new. You could be any female first-year student, me any male PhD candidate. We're impressions. Copies. Clones. We are placeholders. And this baby could have been anyone's baby. Is this our child, or rather a child birthed from a certain combination of events, a certain collision of unknowing participants, unaware of the larger stage production in which they play parts? Is this really my baby and your baby, or the baby of any undergraduate and PhD student, any man and woman? A classic story, a classic outcome! An old dance being danced on and on. What is this baby but one more addition to the dance? It's almost beautiful, really, almost pure. Unarguable, like Puritans and their predestination. Our actions being pulled along by eternity's puppet strings, and we mute and staring as we experience it all but control nothing and roll on to the next, the next, and the next.

Jeanette left with robotic steps. Numb. Not able to feel her limbs or the skin on her fingertips, her thumbs—not able to touch anything or think a thought that didn't turn translucent and melt away.

My name is Jeanette, she said into the mirror that night. Jeanette James. But she didn't believe it, not fully, and when she reached for her face, she came up against glass. The mirror was cold on her hand.

#

By the end of April, when she finished exams, she was almost four months pregnant. Her body was heavier, her stomach beginning to stretch, her limbs and feet thicker, her mind thicker with the weight of it all, far enough along that the pregnancy—the baby—was real, that it was all really happening. And yet not so far that anyone noticed if she wore loose sweatshirts, if she complained about not getting enough exercise, about the weight she had put on since high school.

She told her friends and professors that her parents weren't doing so well with their money, their health, that she might not be back in the fall, that she was needed in London, had unavoidable obligations. She repeated these excuses, fabricated reasons for her eventual disappearance until no one asked after her or expected her, until they hardly saw her, until she was already gone in their minds, invisible in the hallways. Until even she believed for moments at a time—bright, floating moments, fleeting moments—that her parents actually were sick or out of money, or both, and that she was going home to care for them.

She woke many mornings from dreams—dreams in which her stomach was flat and all her excess fat had vanished, in which every movement was light and easy, and her pregnancy had disappeared—in the same way she had as a child, the nightmares drained from behind her eyes when her mother pulled open the curtains. Waking now to similar sunlight, her dreams only dreams but still vivid, her stomach firm and growing, her eyes sometimes tearful, sometimes dry and frozen. Waking and hearing *Momma*, and not knowing if it was her calling for her mother to open the curtains and chase the nightmare away, or if it was her own child calling from inside, calling to be acknowledged, recognized as palpable, persistent. Real.

FOUR

In the summertime, when Frances's mother had the day off work, she, her grandmother, her grandfather, and her mother went to the beach. Squishing into her grandparents' blue car, they stuffed shovels and umbrellas and buckets and towels and sunscreen into the trunk and tucked a cooler of sandwiches and juice boxes between Frances and her mother in the back seat. They took country highways around the city and listened to the radio. Frances watched for horses out the window, for tractors rumbling across fields, for old barns with gaps in the wood planks of their structure like pulled teeth, leaning sideways across the sky.

Frances and her mother were salty with sweat, warm beneath their armpits and knees, as they pulled into the beach parking lot. Frances stretched as she slid from the car, felt wobbly on her legs, tested the toughness of the gravel with the toe of her sandal. Her mother made her hold a bucket and shovel, and she teetered toward the water with her arms full of colourful plastic, tripping on lumps of sand, eyes steady on the water—the waves, the white froth along the shore and above the sandbars. She spread out a towel with her grandfather, who squinted against the sun and promised to bury her in sand up to her neck, her elbows at least. Her grandmother scrubbed cold sunscreen into her shoulders and warned her about going too far into the water. She was four. She couldn't swim.

A couple hours later, sand under Frances's nails and in each nostril and dotting every eyelash, the sandwiches eaten and the juice boxes pressed flat, her mother asked her if she would like to walk down the beach to look for shells. Frances liked shells in the same way she liked ants. They were small and fit into her hand. She liked the way they lay open, fan-like, in her palm, as open as an eyeball with the lid peeled back, or else closed and spiralling down into shadow, throwing out the tiniest whistle, the tiniest breath, back at her, when she blew into them.

After Frances had found ten shells, which she could hardly keep in the cage of her fingers, her mother stopped to look out at the water. Frances nearly collided with her thigh. She jerked back and lost one shell as it rolled off her pinkie finger and into the lurch of a wave sucking at her feet.

Momma! she cried, lunging for the shell and losing three more as she bent down. Momma!

Quiet, Frances, her mother warned.

They were alone on that stretch of beach, and the silence of the oncoming evening dug itself into the spaces between the waves. Frances looked up at her mother. Her hair was pulled into an elastic behind her neck, her shoulders pulled forward, her arms crossed, and her elbows pulled into her hands. Her whole body seemed to lean toward the water.

Frances tugged at her mother's sundress with her free hand, the other clenching the remaining shells until she felt them bite her skin. Momma, she said, Momma, my shells.

Go get them, said her mother, as stiff as stone beneath Frances's touch. Can't you see them? She pointed toward the murky, sand-spun water near the shoreline. Frances spied two spots of white rolling under the current.

Momma, she said.

Go get them, said her mother. You're afraid to get wet? Go get them.

Frances released her mother's sundress and put the six leftover shells in a pocket of sand above where the water touched. Then she turned and strode in up to her ankles, kicking around for the shells.

Where— Frances began, but her mother cut in, her arms crossed again, looking out over Frances's head.

Farther, her mother said. I can see them, just a little farther.

Frances was up to her knees, wading with her hands hanging down into the water. The afternoon heat still clung to the inside of her skin, and the water felt good on her limbs.

Farther! her mother called.

The water was up to her waist. She couldn't see the shells, couldn't see her feet, only a brown liquid mist where her body broke the surface.

Farther!

Her mother seemed very far away on the shore, her figure dark against the long grass rising up the hill behind the sand. Frances looked up at the beach homes, hunched and rectangular in front of the sky, their glass eyes gaping, glinting orange. The water slid into her belly button.

Farther!

Frances walked until the water touched her armpits, her arms spread like airplane wings on either side, until something touched her ankle, a soft and slippery something. She saw a shadow under the water, darker than the dark sand, faster than the seagulls dashing through the air down the beach, and she screamed, Momma! Momma!

Her mother called, Frances! Farther! I can see the shells out just a little farther. Kick your feet.

Frances screamed, Momma, and felt the slippery something again, this time against her kneecap, against the inside of her thigh. She saw the shadow and kicked—kicked!—bucking her body sideways and submerging herself, feeling bubbles with her toes instead of sand, feeling water and sand and her hair in her eyes, water and sand and her hair in her mouth. Her shout was lost in the lake, stuffed down her throat. She flailed and felt the shadow swim up right beside her face and look at her, but she didn't want to look back, didn't want to see it, so she crumpled up her eyes and closed her mouth, drifting and turning quietly in the water, the shadow inches in front of her eyelids, she knew. Looking and blinking, she knew. She knew.

And then she was pulled from the water. Her mother was dragging her to shore. Frances's mother—her sundress soaked, hair down across her chest and neck, breathless— sat in the sand, lugging Frances up between her knees.

It was just a little farther, she breathed. Just a little. You could've done it, she said. And the sun went down against the water, and the water tossed itself up like vomit against the beach. You could've done it, I saw you. You could've reached.

━━━

As a child, Frances often dreamt that her mother was very small; it was a dream that recurred all the way into adulthood. It surfaced frequently, shouldering into her mind as she slept. In the dream, her mother was small enough to fit in one of the plastic toy boats meant for the bathtub, small enough that her voice was a squeak, that Frances couldn't hear her speaking. Small enough that, if the boat tipped, her mother would fit down the drain.

Frances always woke sweating from these dreams, and she would turn to touch her mother, large in the bed beside her. Even now, in the basement, she would turn for her mother and instead touch the wall, the expanse of empty bedsheet, the cold texture of midnight air.

FIVE

Frances was hungry. It was nighttime and she was hungry.

She left her bedroom and went up the stairs. She wanted to go into the kitchen, but she hadn't ventured beyond the door at the top of the stairs in a while, in such a long while that she couldn't recall the time that had passed, not in regular measurements. She couldn't remember minutes or hours or days, but she could remember events, slippery mirages behind her eyes. She remembered coming downstairs of her own volition. She had slept, or wandered near sleep, had wandered—of her own volition?—for what seemed a very long time. This she recalled in syrupy bubbles of memory, of dream.

Now she was hungry. But at the top of the stairs, when she tried the door, she found it locked. Or she thought she tried the door, and she thought she found it locked. She looked for the deadbolt, whether it was pulled into the slot. She couldn't see it. She couldn't remember this door having a deadbolt, but she knew it must be there. She knew it must be there.

Frances leaned her forehead against the door and felt her lungs stretching steadily beneath her rib cage. She fumbled through a series of thoughts, wondering who had locked the door and why, wondering how long it had been locked. Wondering how long she had been in the basement with the door locked above her head.

She tried the knob again; she couldn't open the door.

She didn't try the knob; she didn't open the door.

She pushed and banged; she thought she pushed and banged.

How long had she been in the basement with the door locked above her head?

She didn't open the door.

She called the names of her roommates. She started to scream.

She couldn't open the door. She didn't open the door.

Her roommates didn't hear her. Her mouth didn't open. She didn't scream.

She didn't open the door.

She breathed. She started to sob.

She went back downstairs to sleep.

One evening, out on the back porch, Frances's grandfather told her a story about a woman who was so tired of walking back and forth from the grocery store, of walking up and down the aisles to get food, that she cut off her own feet. But she could still move around the house in a wheelchair—until she got so tired of wheeling here and there, of washing dishes, doing laundry, and wiping counters, that she cut off her own hands. Nobody understood, and she got so tired of explaining herself that she cut out her own tongue. She got so tired of the questions that she cut off her ears, and so sick of the expressions that she cut out her eyes. And she sat there in silence and stillness and nobody knew if she was happy or sad, if she regretted it or thought about how things could have been otherwise. Nobody could even guess.

Frances asked, How could she cut off her tongue if her hands were gone? How could she cut out her eyes?

Frances had tried the basement door maybe a hundred times, a thousand times. Ten thousand. It was bolted. Turn, click, the latch opened, but the deadbolt above was solid and stiff—she swore there was a deadbolt, solid and stiff.

She moved her hand with the doorknob—she thought she moved her hand with the doorknob—and pushed. Turn, click. Turn, click, turn, click. She sat at the top of the stairs and tried this, over and over, until her head spun with the noise—turn, click—until her jaws creaked with the noise—turn, click—until her body ached with the noise—turn, click. Turn, click, turn, click, turn, click. Until her dreams reeked with the noise, rotted with it. Turn, click. She sat on the stairs and tried again, pushed her fingertips through the space beneath the door. Turn, click. She banged on the door—she thought she banged on the door, she didn't bang on the door—turn, click, heaved a shoulder, a hip, a foot against it, turn, click, screamed into it, scraped her nails against it—she thought she screamed, scraped her nails, she didn't—turn, click. Nothing replied but silence and darkness and stillness. Nothing but hairy, thick silence filling up her ears, that thick darkness in her eyes and in her mouth, that thick stillness lying down across her arm and her hand as she turned—as she thought she turned—turn, click.

+++

Frances heard the turn of a body upstairs, the turn of a body in bed. Ky slept in the room directly above hers. Ky was probably sleeping now. Katie and Reese, her other roommates, were probably sleeping now. Frances thought of standing on her desk chair and smacking the ceiling. She thought of screaming.

She pulled the blankets up closer to her chin.

+++

Frances was whole and breathing in bed, naked in the wide square of moonlight coming in through the window. She pulled the blankets up over herself. She hid her face. She couldn't remember the moon rising, and she couldn't remember taking off her clothes. It was late, she was tired, that was all. She hadn't slept, she couldn't remember sleeping, that was all. It was only the moon. *Only the moon*, she told herself, *only the moon*. But lately things that were usually commonplace, insignificant, like the texture of walls, the taste of water, the blankness of sleep, had taken on new, prowling shapes.

A few days ago, maybe forty-eight hours, she had found the basement door locked. She'd left the problem until morning, went back downstairs to sleep, but morning didn't come. Not that she knew of. Neither did sleep. So she walked the hallway, or stood under the water in the shower, and counted the seconds, counted minutes, but never hours. Hours slid then bloated then disappeared. The texture of walls, of water, the blankness of sleep, what she could remember of it, were suddenly important, harsh and static.

A couple of days, forty-eight hours; that was her best estimation. She had screamed and they hadn't heard her, the sun had never come up, and she couldn't count hours. So she lay and watched the moon, walked the hall, tried the door, the bolted door. She couldn't see the bolt, but she was sure it was there.

SIX

Frances woke up hungry. She had never felt so hungry in all her life, never so worn, so deflated and old. She looked down at her legs and touched the skin there, pinched. She looked down at her stomach, her breasts, and her arms. Pinch, pinch. The same. This was how it was for her. She had been the same weight, a hundred and forty pounds, since the age of fifteen. But now, lying in bed, she felt flat and thin, as if her skin had nothing but veins and bone beneath. Her stomach was a mouth. She could feel its tongue stretching up her throat like a chunk of food she couldn't swallow. But when she touched herself here, pinched there, she was the same. The hunger wasn't so urgent, after all.

Still. She sat up in bed and pulled off the blankets, set her feet onto the floor. She kept no food in her bedroom, none even in the kitchenette—those cupboards held only cleaning supplies and extra pots and pans, bowls, cutlery, an electric kettle, and a rice cooker. Doubles of what they had and used upstairs.

Frances grabbed a sweater and a pair of pyjama pants from the floor; they smelled of must, of old sweat. She held the mouth in her stomach shut as she moved through her bedroom, through the basement, up the stairs, all in darkness. Up the stairs, groggy and rumpled, thinking of milk and maybe a slice of cheese, she almost tried to open the door. Then she remembered it was locked.

Frances stepped back. She wondered why she wasn't afraid, wondered where that feeling had gone.

※

Frances woke up at the top of the stairs, sitting with her back against the door. She turned and tried the doorknob—she thought she tried the doorknob. It stuck.

Ky? she said, her voice dry, her tongue as thick as a tumour in her mouth. Katie? Reese?

✳

Frances dreamt that she turned the doorknob and opened the door. She dreamt she walked into the kitchen and found bread in the cupboard. Then she went to the living room and sat on the couch. She spoke to Ky, who was reading a textbook in the recliner. She had trouble putting the bread in her mouth. When she tried, it turned into crumbs, and Ky said, Are you really going to leave it like that?

Like what? asked Frances. She looked down in her lap. She was covered in bits of bread, and she said, Like Hansel and Gretel. I'll make a trail.

Ky stared at her, and Frances stood and hugged her arms all the way up to her ears and looked out the living room window, which showed an evening sky, one bird sitting on the telephone wire, the lawn hidden under snow, the tree on the lawn bare of leaves, and the street empty without kids or cars. Frances said, The sky looks pink for January. The sky's rarely pink in January.

It's February, said Ky. Frances, it's February.

Frances pulled her shoulders up into her ears. She bent to eat the bread off the carpet, where it had fallen.

Ky was gone. Frances didn't see her leave, but she knew in the way of dreams that she was gone.

Frances sat and looked out the window, watching the bird shiver in its feathers.

✳

Frances woke up at the top of the stairs.

+++

Frances woke up in bed.

+++

Frances woke up face down on the basement rug.

+++

A long while ago, when Frances was still living with her grandparents, her grandfather told her a story about an old tree.

Her mother was working a closing shift and wouldn't be home until past midnight. Frances was used to falling asleep alone, but she didn't like that she might wake up in a couple of hours alone, that she might wake up many times alone.

This wasn't the first time Frances's mother had worked the closing shift. When Frances wouldn't settle, when she fidgeted and squirmed and whined, her grandmother—who hated useless talking, filling silences, who struck down the idea of storytelling with a cutting gesture of her hand—would come and sit by Frances while she grew sleepy. She would sometimes, when Frances begged her, tell some tidbit of family history or an anecdote about the weather that morning while Frances was still in bed, how the forest looked behind the house before the sun came up. Usually, however, her grandmother would just sit quietly with her hands in her lap, and Frances would listen to the near-silence, to the sound of wind, of cars moving outside, of her grandmother's slow and methodical breathing. She would match each breath with her own, filling her lungs and then letting go. She would count each exhalation until she fell asleep.

But on this night, a long while ago, Frances's grand-mother was out of town visiting a friend, and it was her grandfather who sat by Frances's bed. And as Frances lay awake without even a trace of tiredness in her eyes, she asked her grandfather what sleep was good for, why she had to do it, what was the point when it just felt like wasted time.

Her grandfather told her a story about an old tree. The tree's name was Mr. Sleep. Mr. Sleep had not always been an old tree. He had been young once, too. And when he was very young, not much bigger than a sapling, still twiggy and a little bent, with only a smattering of leaves in the summer and a far lean in the wind, a little girl who had been up to no good, and who was hiding in the forest on account of this, came and stuck her mischief between the sapling's branches.

Her mischief, said Frances. What's that?

In this case it's her skull, said Frances's grandfather.

Her skull!

Well, not *her* skull. The little girl had found a baby rabbit the week before and captured it and kept it in a box. She tried to care for it but didn't do it right, and the baby rabbit died. The girl didn't know what to do. So she buried it in the garden, in secret, but the dog dug it up and shook it to pieces. So the girl took the head, which was really by this time only a skull, and brought it into the forest, found the sapling, and stuck the skull between its branches, understand?

Yes.

The sapling, Mr. Sleep, grew very fast because he had deep roots. Instead of pushing the skull out like most other trees would do, he grew around the skull and grew up high, and put so many layers of wood and bark between the air and that secret spot of bone that no one would guess he was hiding something, or rather helping something stay preserved and quiet and dead. You would only know if you rapped just right with your knuckles on the tree's wood—

you might hear a hollow echo, because deep in the tree, in the skull, was an empty pocket, where the air was stale and old, filled with the smell of dog tongue and patterned with little girl fingerprints.

And the thing about this tree, Mr. Sleep, was that he could be any tree. He didn't look any different. He wasn't the oldest, although he was very old, and he wasn't the tallest, although he was very tall. Mixed in as he was with all the other trees, you would never know he held a tiny skull, a baby rabbit's head, unless, like I said, you rapped your knuckles just so, or—or, yes, you could wait.

Wait for what?

You could wait until Mr. Sleep died and fell down. Then you could chop him up and look inside. Because you can't see his rings, the number of years he's lived, until he's old and dead and the wind pulls him down or lightning cuts him in half.

Her grandfather continued in a whisper. You would find the skull, the bone. It's as old as Mr. Sleep, it has just as many years encircling it, but it's protected. It's small and polished and unused.

Frances pawed a hand over her eyes and yawned. Is that it?

That's it.

You didn't answer my question, Grandpa. Why do I have to sleep?

Aren't you tired, Frances?

I guess a little. But why do I have to?

Shhh...

SEVEN

Frances was lying in bed in her sweater and pyjama pants. She couldn't remember the last time she had slept, so she thought about sleep. She thought herself into sleep. Or thought up something similar to sleep, made it up like it was a game or story: these are the rules and these are the players. This is what the sleep will give and take. This is what the sleep will leave behind. I will lie here until I sleep. Everyone has to sleep, eventually. I will lie here until I sleep.

When Frances looked in the bathroom mirror, she saw her mother. She had never looked like her mother before. No one had ever told her she looked like her mother, not even her grandparents, who had known Frances's mother in all her stages, from toothless to toddler to woman. Frances had never seen it before, not once in a photo or video, not in a recording of her voice or a tic of her expression. Where her mother had flat dark hair, Frances had lighter, almost amber-coloured curls; where her mother was round, Frances was thin; where her mother was short, Frances was tall, gangly, a little bony around the joints; where her mother was sallow, Frances had colour.

But now Frances saw it. In the bathroom mirror, she saw it. The room was dark, layered up to the ceiling in shadows—only by the moonlight coming through the window in her bedroom and falling into the hall could she see anything. And what she saw was her mother, just returned home from work, her hair matted to her head like a soccer field's grass matted underfoot, her body undefined beneath her T-shirt and dark jeans, her tired hands holding the strap of her bag, her face—this is what Frances saw in the mirror—her face, punched in and pale, puffy here, sunken there, with wide-set eyes and a pointed chin, her lips pouched over her teeth.

But was her mother's chin really that pointed? Were her eyes that wide-set, the hollows beneath her cheekbones that pronounced? This was Frances's face, after all, and what connected it so intimately with her mother's now was merely its exhaustion, the lines around the mouth and swabs of charcoal under the eyes. In her sweater and pyjama pants, she could be any build. She could be slim and long like she normally was, or she could be short, almost squat, with round hips and shoulders like her mother. She could be anyone, but it was her mother who she saw.

This woman in the mirror, her mother, her mother—who was she? Frances had spent the first ten years of her life trying to reach her, and the second ten trying to escape. Now she dove into that glass, that reflection, and wondered, who was she?

First and foremost, her mother was work. Her mother was sleep and work. In her earliest memories, when they lived with her grandparents in Nilestown on the outskirts of London, Frances saw her mother as a mirage—a flurry of movement on the stairs or in the kitchen—leaving in the morning after breakfast and not returning until long after dinner.

Frances remembered her mother as cold in the morning. Her flesh was cold as she scrubbed her face at the bathroom sink and shoved a toothbrush into her mouth. Her hands were cold as she ate her cereal at the kitchen table. Her feet were cold as she pulled on her shoes and hopped out the door, throwing Frances a wave, if she was lucky, as she left.

But Frances's mother was warm in the evening, her skin oily and soft. Off to bed, she would say as she entered the living room or sidled up to the back porch. Off to bed, and Frances would go. Twenty minutes later her mother would step into the shower, and ten minutes after that she would fold herself into bed beside Frances. This was where Frances had her, knew her—in bed. Her mother was warm in bed. Her skin was warm. Her hair, still wet, was warm. Frances shuffled between her arms and felt her breathe. She registered when she fell asleep—this was really where Frances had her, in sleep. Sometimes she would turn and watch her mother's face, watch the muscles relax around her eyes and mouth, the clump of skin falling with gravity around her neck. This was how Frances knew her mother: in the binary of rush and freeze, the collision of work and sleep—two different displays of dedication, two different kinds of absence.

In her later memories, when they moved with her father to the townhouse in North London, Frances's mother was groggy in the mornings, indirect in her intentions, fumbling. She misplaced things, sung off-key, forgot mid-sentence what she was saying. In the afternoons, after school, she was snappy, her words crunching as they made contact with Frances's ear; she whipped dinner up in the oven or on the stovetop, wiped counters, swept floors, made phone calls, and caught snippets of the news and weather reports that played on the TV. She rarely worked when Frances's father lived with them, going into the restaurant maybe two or three times a week. She slept with Frances's father instead of with Frances. She didn't like going outside. By evening she was cold, as cold as she used to be in the mornings, and she wrapped herself up in blankets on the couch, watching game shows or whatever TV drama or comedy fell on that day. *Desperate Housewives*, *Medium*, *Malcolm in the Middle*. She sat quiet and motionless, expressionless, seeming hardly to see the screen.

Frances's father would go in sometimes and sit with her, pulling a blanket up over his knees—he was only cold up to his knees. Sometimes Frances would sit, too, shoved between them or alone on the floor. She would pull a blanket up around her feet—she was only cold up to her feet.

But Frances's mother, cold everywhere, sat holding her elbows tightly in her hands, as if her arms might fall out of their sockets, sat holding her eyes open as if they might fall out of her head if she relaxed. She kept her mouth in a long, straight line, as straight as her spine, showing nothing, giving nothing, letting nothing enter in.

Her father would throw an arm around her mother's shoulders and exhale. Frances, on the floor, would lean back against the couch and encounter her mother's toes, small and hard as the knots on a tree. The toes didn't pull away or soften, but pressed like stones into her shoulders.

Momma!

Mooommaaa!

Frances could hear someone calling, she could hear someone sobbing. The voice sounded like retching, like a guttural pull deep from the stomach. In Frances's ear the voice felt like retching. She could taste bile on her tongue.

Momma!

It was the wail a baby lets out after hitting its head, a slam so hard the skull vibrates, a moment of breathlessness, then choking, a gag—

It was the squeal a pig makes as its throat is cut.

Mooommaaa!

Frances opened her eyes. Her hands were flat on the floor. She was crawling, crawling around the bedroom, her shoulder dragging along the wall. Her fingers were chalked with dust. Her eyeballs felt swollen, as if gravity had pulled them a little from their sockets. Something in her mouth was bleeding; she could taste the thick metal flavour of blood. Her throat was hot and throbbing, as if stripped bare on the inside. It was raw from screaming.

Screaming? Had she been screaming? She had heard someone calling, she could hear someone sobbing. It sounded like retching. She could taste bile, blood.

Had she been screaming?

Frances leaned back, pressing her hands into her knees, and raised herself to her feet. She was unbalanced; she reached out for her desk. Her shoulder was numb from sliding along the wall. She swallowed the blood in her mouth.

Momma, she croaked, trying the sound. It was foreign, wrong in her gums and teeth, like a pocket of burs in her mouth. Her tongue swiped out across her lips.

She found her way to the bed.

Momma?

Frances was small under the blankets. She felt almost small enough to curl up on the pillow and call it a mattress. Her mother had just crawled in. She was adjusting herself, pulling at her twisted pyjama legs, getting the blanket just right under her arm, the pillow just right under her head. Her hair was wet. Frances could smell the damp. She could smell the fruit from her mother's shampoo. And something deeper: the warm, scrubbed scent of her mother's skin, the absence of sweat, grease, and garlic from the restaurant, swept off by water and soap and the rubbing of a stiff palm. Her mother's hands had muscles nearly as tough as bone. Her veins ridged up like blue worms. Frances watched her long back, her shoulder lifting as she inhaled.

Momma?

Her mother grunted.

Mom?

Frances, her mother said, I'm tired.

Frances put a hand on her mother's back under the blankets. Her fingers circled the lumps of her spine.

Frances, her mother said, you're going to keep me up. Do you need to sleep with Grandma and Grandpa tonight?

Frances pulled her hand away. She put her fingers in her mouth.

You should be sleeping, said her mother. Aren't you sleepy?

No, said Frances through her fingers. She watched the grid pattern the light from the window made on the wall. It was yellow from the street light. At its edges she could see bunches of shadows made from the leaves on the trees outside. They swung with the wind, but it wasn't a wind so strong that she could hear it in the walls or rushing up the rooftop. She thought of rain, the sound of rain. The clock high up on the wall ticked, and she imagined it was rain, slow and regular rain; she thought of thunderstorms and how sometimes during storms her mother rolled over in bed to face her, how she pulled Frances to her chest and stomach, and Frances wrapped her arms around her knees and stayed very still, very warm, very focused on the sensation of her mother's hands on the top of her head, in her hair, or cupped around her toes. Sometimes like this, buried under the sound of rain and wind, the gurgle of thunder, Frances would bury herself deeper, further, pull the blankets over her head and pretend she was still tucked away in her mother's tummy, like her mother told her she had been, like the pictures from her grandmother's album showed her she had been.

This is you, her grandmother said, pointing at her mother's bloated belly, her mother leaning back against the kitchen counter, her hair shorter, hanging just below her earlobes, and a softness, an excess of flesh, around her chin and neck that Frances didn't recognize.

That's Momma? asked Frances.

Her grandmother nodded. And this is you.

Where?

In her tummy. Right there.

How?

You were very small. Right there.

Frances held the photograph and touched her mother's belly with the tip of her finger. Under the blankets, under the storm, she thought of this picture and imagined herself still tucked there, warm and small in the dark. And now as the clock ticked she thought about rain. She watched her mother's shoulder above the blanket, the trail of her damp hair falling down onto the pillow.

Momma, she whispered.

Her mother flinched, a jump of flesh beneath the blankets and pyjamas.

Momma?

What, Frances?

Frances reached out to touch the tips of her mother's hair but stopped halfway, her hand spider-like, frozen on the bedsheet.

Frances, what?

What's that noise? asked Frances.

What noise?

It's ticking.

The clock?

Frances nodded but didn't say anything.

Is it bothering you? Is that why you can't sleep? I can take it down.

No, said Frances. She raced her fingers back into her mouth. It's okay.

Go to sleep, said her mother. Close your eyes. Pretend they're windows and shut them up. Go to sleep.

‡‡

Frances, said her mother's voice from the hallway. Frances.

The voice was a whisper, short and sharp, full of air. It cut through the black silence beyond Frances's bedroom door.

What, Mom? Frances mumbled, sitting up and feeling, distantly, the weight of the blankets fall around her waist. She forced herself from the bed. The floor was cold on her feet.

Frances, come here.

Her mother was crying.

Frances, Frances, please.

Frances followed the sobbing out into the hallway. It was almost too dark to see the couch and bookshelf, almost too dark to note the emptiness of the space beyond the bedroom, the narrowness of the walls. Up ahead the sobbing fell in hiccups down the stairs. Frances dragged her fingers along the wall as she moved.

When she reached the bottom of the stairs, the wall fell away from her hand. Above, two voices collided and overlapped. She realized she had been wrong. It was, as she thought, her mother calling her name. But there was another voice crying, a small and familiar voice—as intimate as a cupped hand against the side of her head, as soft as an exhalation in her ear.

Frances stood at the bottom of the stairs and felt that old chill crawl over her, felt the cold climb up her skin, the prickle like wet, dappling fingertips on her shins and forearms. She squinted upward, trying to discern the shapes huddled by the closed basement door. Her mother was hardly more than a shadow on the windowless landing, bent with her hands on her hips. She was in profile, standing sideways and leaning over a second and deeper shadow pressed into the corner where the walls met. This second shadow was shaking. This second shadow was crying.

Mom? said Frances. She started up the stairs. Mom?

The second shadow froze, its blurred shape solidifying like stone into the corner. It stopped crying.

Frances? said her mother. Frances? What's the matter?

Nothing, said Frances. Nothing. She couldn't stop staring at the second shadow, the figure—she could see now that it was a figure, with little arms wrapped around its little knees, little eyes peeking out, white and shiny, through its hair.

Nothing now, Frances was saying. I'm okay now. I've been stuck down here for a while. I don't know how long. I was wondering where you were, Mom. I thought you'd forgotten about me. I thought—

Frances, said her mother. Her voice was harsh, hard, clotted with fear. What's wrong? What are you staring at?

That girl, said Frances, and the little shadow spoke at the same time, matching her words. They looked at each other. The shadow produced a finger to point down the stairs; Frances pointed up.

She's looking at me, said Frances.

And the little shadow spoke back: She's looking at me.

Who? said Frances's mother. Who are you talking about?

That girl, Momma, said the shadow. She's coming up the stairs. She's looking at me, Momma. Please make it stop. Make it stop, said the shadow, please Momma make it stop, please Momma, please Momma, please Momma—

###

Frances woke at the top of the stairs, crouched, her back pinched in the corner where the wall and door jamb met. She was mumbling, Make it stop, make it stop, please Momma, make it stop. But down below there was nobody, even through the darkness she could see there was no one. Her mother wasn't there, it was quiet, and her eyes ached from crying.

Momma, please, she said, make it stop. She's looking at me. She's looking at me.

She rocked on the stairs.

Make it stop.

EIGHT

In the quiet of night, when the house was dark inside and out, Frances sat at the top of the basement stairs waiting for the basement door to open. She pressed her forehead against the door and imagined the kitchen on the other side. She listened to the electric buzz of the refrigerator no more than ten feet from where she sat. She imagined the contours of the kitchen, the cupboards and countertops, shelves and sinks. She grabbed the skin of her belly and pulled, pulled, pulled until her hunger pains were dull, slow, and inconsequential.

When the darkness wasn't so dark, when the moon outside had a face, things were better. When the moon was more than a slit above the hedge in the backyard, when it at least had a rounded, pocked cheek, when it had eyes, when it was looking down at the house and through Frances's bedroom window, things were better. Frances left the basement door and went to her bedroom, up onto the dresser and into the window, really into it, pressed her whole face against the glass. In the light from the moon's pocked cheek, she could see the length of the hedge, milky shadows among its branches. She could see the snow on the grass, in clumps where the ground rose in clumps. She could see the top of the maple tree from a neighbouring yard, its bark warped and naked, moving in this or that wind, knuckles knotted, its twigs like pointed fingertips. Frances put her hand on the glass and felt the frozen air through the frozen window. She felt it down to the bones in her fingers. Sometimes she dozed, curled on top of the dresser in a swatch of moonlight. Sometimes she dreamt.

✚✚

Three girls lived in the house besides Frances. Katie, whose full name was Katrina; Reese, whose full name was Rhaeesa; and Ky, whose full name was Kaya. None of them had known each other before university, but Katie and Reese had been roommates in residence, and Ky might as well have been, considering the amount of time she spent in their room. Frances had lived down the hall. She knew the girls by sight, not by name.

She was convinced they didn't know her at all, not until the end of first year. Frances was holed away studying for exams when Ky knocked on her door and announced they needed a fourth, someone to fill the empty bedroom in the basement of the house they were planning to rent. Frances, who hadn't thought about where she would live next, who assumed she would go back to her mother when she ran out of money, nodded and said, Okay.

She met the girls outside the Rec Centre on a Wednesday to do a final walk-through of the house. They crossed Western Road together, and as they were passing the 7-Eleven, Frances tried to introduce herself. Reese grabbed her arm and said, We know.

They told her their names. Then they chatted about exams, professors. People Frances had never heard of. A boyfriend from Mississauga. Kittens someone's sister had found.

Ky walked in front, following the map on her phone. She was petite, pale, with eyes nearly as dark as her hair— half-Japanese, she later explained, but she couldn't speak a word of the language. Her father worked at a law firm in downtown London. Katie and Reese followed behind Ky, shoulders together. Katie was white and had a wide face, wide eyes and a wide mouth. You could see her gums when she smiled. She wore ripped jeans, a dark T-shirt, and three piercings in each ear. Her dad was a dentist, her mother a yoga instructor, and her brothers—all three of them— were living in Toronto. That's where she'd go when she graduated, she figured. But she wasn't thinking about that yet. Not at all. As for Reese, she liked to giggle. She was thin, loose in her joints when she walked. Dark-skinned, dark-eyed, dark-haired. She wore large, clear-rimmed glasses and chipped nail polish on her fingers. She never mentioned her parents.

They rounded the corner onto Ford Crescent and followed the same curb that the elementary school kids followed, single-file and quiet now as they counted the numbers on the houses. Ky stopped in front of a dark cement driveway. Number 48. A man stepped out of a car parked on the road and shook each of their hands.

They went inside.

Some of the rooms were near-empty, others crowded with roughly used furniture: a bookshelf sagging out from the wall, scuffed mattresses on metal bed frames, chipped side tables, bent lamps, laundry hampers, dressers, desks.

The boys are moving out soon, said the man. Ignore the mess. The place itself is sound. And don't worry, we bleach everything before the new group comes in.

Ky nodded, slightly stupefied. Katie and Reese peeked into the closets and out the windows.

The living room was large, the kitchen spacious, and the backyard private, surrounded by tall hedges on all sides. The basement stairs were steep, but the basement itself was roomy, the bathroom newly renovated and the washing machine in the laundry room newly replaced. A cold cellar. Closets. And Frances's soon-to-be bedroom, empty but for some dead spiders curled up in the corners. Currently, nobody lived in the basement.

On the way back upstairs, Frances paused. She thought she had felt it on the way down but now felt it for sure. There was a patch of cold air at the bottom of the basement steps. She looked around for a vent in the ceiling or floor. She reached her hand up the stairs to feel for a draft.

It crawled over her, like a prickling under her skin, pressure in her lungs. Cold, deep cold. Cold that made the roots of her teeth ache.

You okay? asked Ky. The girls looked at Frances, then looked at each other. The man stopped halfway up the stairs.

Can you feel that? asked Frances. Right here.

Reese stepped in front of Frances and giggled. I don't feel anything, she said.

Katie and Ky came to the same conclusion.

It's cold, said Frances. Right here.

Cold? said the man. He came back down the stairs and waved his arms over the spot. You feel cold?

Only here, said Frances. She traced the place as a circle with her finger in the air. Freezing.

Maybe it's haunted, said Katie.

Reese giggled.

Haunted only for Frances? said Ky.

It's not haunted, said the man.

Maybe someone died here, right in this spot, said Katie.

The man sighed. No one died here, he said.

Maybe someone's going to die here, Katie chirped.

The man stared at her. I can check the ventilation, he said, make sure everything's in order. But really, it's probably just—he glanced at Frances—an air current, or maybe you're not feeling so well.

I feel fine, said Frances.

All right, said Ky, her eyes dashing around the group. I think I'm ready to go. Katie? Reese? Frances?

Yup, said Katie.

Reese giggled.

They followed the man upstairs, Frances the last in line. She looked back before she switched off the lights at the top.

NINE

Somewhere deep inside her body, somewhere deep inside her hunger, Frances was wound in a tight ball. Her legs moved her around the basement and her chest breathed. She went to the bathroom and came back to bed. She drank from the kitchenette faucet in long, straggling swallows, her hair falling into the sink, clotting the drain in inky, blood-like bulges, in dark, stringy clumps.

She walked and she breathed and she swallowed—she did all of these things, but not really. She didn't choose to move her limbs or tell her chest to breathe, didn't choose to go to the bathroom or sleep, she didn't choose to drink. That was all her body, her hunger. Frances was deep inside, watching it happen, watching her shadowy reflection in the mirror as she lost all roundness in her cheeks, around her hips and ribs, on her shoulders. The skin holding her breasts thinned. Her joints—knees and ankles, elbows and wrists—looked swollen and inflated. She had knuckles on her toes. This she had never known—she had never known she had knuckles on her toes.

Those knuckled toes and her hunger often led her up the stairs to the basement door. She leaned against the door, leaned into it as you would lean into a human embrace. She dragged her fingertips across it, her nails scraping and bending, and she didn't even try the handle, didn't try the handle, because she was tired of that empty feeling when she pushed and found resistance. She was tired of calling for Ky, calling for Katie and Reese, calling for her mother.

She had bruises on her hands from banging—did she have bruises on her hands? They were sore, nonetheless—raw patches on her feet from kicking—did she have raw patches on her feet? They were tender, made her wince, nonetheless.

Her fingers were red and pruned where she had sucked them, sucked them as she slept because her mouth was hungry for anything, for the taste of skin and sweat. She had scabbed-over slits on her palm and the meat of her thumb where she had bitten, where the skin had broken so easily, where she had licked and sucked and lapped.

She had stood by the open kitchenette cupboards and stared at the cleaning supplies and wondered what she could drink. Windex and bleach and dish soap and vinegar. She tried the vinegar and vomited, and her vomit smelled like pickles. Then she tried the vinegar again, and this time she kept it down. Over the next two days, or maybe it was a week, or maybe a couple of hours, she finished the jug of vinegar. She cut it open and licked the plastic. Then she went to the bookshelf and began tearing pages from books and putting them in her mouth. She chewed them until they turned to pulp. She chewed them until she could swallow them. She chewed them until she could taste the ink. She thought about eating the rug, about ripping apart the couch, but instead she sat down and fell asleep there, or at least she fell into dreaming. She forgot about her hunger for a moment, her stomach was quiet for a moment; her mind was dark and blank for a moment, and her heart was silent and her blood stayed calm.

Whenever Frances reached up to scratch her scalp or rub behind her ears, a clump of hair came back with her fingers. She remembered when she was younger and her mother had taught her how to stick her hair to the shower wall so it wouldn't clog the drain. Like this, she said to Frances, who was small and naked in the shower, like this. When you're finished using the conditioner and your hair comes out in your hands, stick it up like this, and keep it there until you're done. And her mother put her hands in Frances's hair and pulled conditioner from the roots to the tips, and her fingers were warm and careful. Frances remembered how the shower was hot on her forehead, on her chest and legs, how she'd closed her mouth and her eyes and felt her mother's hands on her head and in her hair, warm on her neck, careful on her neck.

⫫

Do you remember that boy? Frances said, looking into the bathroom mirror in the dark. Her reflection was huge and slouching, her hair matted, her face like a lump of clay, mashed and twisted and shadowed.

Do you remember him?

She thought once again about little red shoes and the brown tile beneath those shoes. She thought of jumping over the white lines between the brown tiles.

Do you remember him? What was his name?

⫫

It was 2003, the summer before Frances started second grade. It was the first summer she would spend away from her grandparents, and the first summer she would spend with her father. She was six years old.

Frances remembered how the townhouses in North London were all exactly the same. She remembered standing in the parking lot while her parents unpacked the car. She remembered looking down the row of houses, growing dizzy at that long length of connected white stucco, those uniform black front doors, the windows patterned, just so, like *Tetris* blocks falling in unison against a white backdrop. The front lawns were not really lawns but slivers of grass rolling from the townhouses to the road. And the road was not really a road but a series of places to park your car. They had a special place for their car, Frances's mother pointed out, with a number painted in yellow on the cement that was the same as the number on their house. Frances spun around, looking at all the other cars and all the other yellow numbers. She saw on the opposite side of the road another line of townhouses reflecting theirs, as if through a mirror. Each with the same grey front step leading up to the door. The same charcoal roof tying the whole building together like a long, sloping hat.

Frances? Frances! Come on, said her mother, pulling a box from the trunk of the car and hoisting it onto her hip. Help us with something, bring something inside. She grunted as she pulled the box up higher and headed for the front door.

But when Frances went around to the trunk to grab what she could—the lip of the trunk was above her waist and the boxes too far back—she saw a boy approaching down the sidewalk. He was taller than she was, with mud-coloured hair, flat mud-coloured eyes, and a tough, round nose. His lips were wide and full—red as if he had been biting them— and Frances could see veins under the skin of his neck. He wore scuffed jeans and a T-shirt that hung down past his waist. His arms looked minuscule, breakable, in his sleeves. He was barefoot.

The boy drew closer, then stopped. They looked at each other. Frances imagined the open trunk of the car behind her, imagined crawling in and shutting the lid and lying in the quiet dark to stop his looking. She didn't. She stood and looked back until finally he said—

Hi.

Hi, said Frances.

I'm Jasper, said Jasper.

I'm Frances, said Frances. She reached up to hold her elbows in her hands.

Jasper pointed. I live over there.

Frances followed the direction of his finger, but all she saw was the long line of townhouses: nothing to mark it as his own, no differentiation except the numbers nailed up beside the doors.

He paused for a moment, looking at her.

I was hoping for someone like you, he said. He moved forward and leaned against the side of the car, twining his fingers together. When the old guy moved out, I was hoping for you.

For me?

Someone like you.

What do you mean?

I don't know. A kid! There aren't any others around here. And that old guy gave me the creeps.

The creeps?

He was missing an eye, okay? And all his teeth were fake. I could smell him out the window if he left it open.

Jasper pointed to Frances's townhouse, up to the second-storey window.

Smell him? asked Frances.

Yeah, it was sour, Jasper said, reaching up to hold his nose. Like vinegar. His lips were permanently purple. Permanently. And his fingertips, too. My mom says he made his own wine.

What happened to him? asked Frances. Where did he go?

He didn't go anywhere, said Jasper. He died.

Oh, said Frances.

My mom says he was sitting on the toilet.

He died on the toilet?

That's where they found him.

You mean, he was...he was *going*, you know, number two—she held up two fingers to clarify—when he died?

Dunno, said Jasper. I just know he was naked, from tooth to toe.

Tooth to toe?

Mm-hmm, that's what I heard.

But—

Frances's mother swung around the end of the car, saying, Frances where are you, I thought I told you—and nearly ran full into Jasper. Oh, she said, jerking backward, away from the unexpected boy leaning against her open trunk, staring at her daughter. Oh, hello. Frances's mother pulled a hand through her hair. Who are... She tried to hold the boy's attention, tried to shift instinctively between him and Frances. Do you live around here?

Jasper glanced at her absently. He raised his hand to point.

Well, that's nice, isn't it, Frances? She leaned over to pull another box from the trunk. A friend in the neighbourhood. But I'm sorry, she said, looking down at her daughter. Frances is a little busy right now. You'll have to play another time.

Jasper frowned, shrugging. That's all right, he said. He plunged his hands into his jean pockets. My mom's probably wondering where I am anyway.

Good, said Frances's mother. What house, again? I'll have to come by and meet her.

Jasper pointed.

Well, okay, said Frances's mother, squinting at the row of houses. Okay.

Jasper blinked twice at Frances. Then he turned and walked down the street.

Frances's mother looked after him. Strange boy, she said. What was his name?

Jasper, said Frances.

Strange name, said her mother. She lifted the box she had pulled from the trunk. Come on now, she said. Grab something and get inside.

⸻ ✳ ⸻

Frances remembered moving out of her grandparents' house to live in North London, a transition that happened slowly and then all at once, like a shoulder being twisted in gradual increments and then popping out of its socket.

After the first time Frances saw him in her grandparents' driveway, her father visited twice more while her mother was away at work. He brought Frances presents from Toronto—sweets that she promised to eat before her mother got home—and sat with her grandparents in the kitchen or living room, talking about his job at the university, his probable tenure in the years to come, how he only lectured three days a week and the commute would be easy. He talked about everything he could give Frances, everything he wished he had already given her.

What's changed? asked Frances's grandmother. Why now?

I've changed, said Frances's father. I've grown up. I was an idiot before, and I was scared. What else can I say? I miss Jeanette. She was the only one who ever cared about me. I feel a responsibility for my daughter. What else can I say?

What Frances and her grandparents didn't know, what they would never know, was that Frances's father had throughout the past year experienced stomach pain—a shocking, startling stomach pain that spread down his thighs to the soles of his feet and left him sweating, cold, shaking after every meal. After a trip to the doctor and an ultrasound, a polyp was discovered on his gallbladder, large enough to be cancerous. He spent months planning for surgery—without his parents around, without anyone he trusted to help him, he would have to recover in his apartment alone—and imagining at night, in bed, always at night in bed, that the cancer was spreading, although his doctor had assured him this was impossible. After a final, preliminary ultrasound, it was found that the polyp had disappeared, seemingly swallowed up by his body. The surgery was cancelled. The polyp had been, probably, a lump of residual sludge, never really a polyp at all. But here was

Erica McKeen

still this fear of the cancer spreading, and he would awaken often at three o'clock in the morning to silence and darkness, imagining the incisions and the stitches, and recovering in his apartment alone.

Frances's grandmother arranged a dinner date between Frances's mother and father. Her mother wore lipstick. She came home late, and when she slid into bed with Frances she shook as if she had been crying; she was cold, she rolled and fidgeted. The next day she saw Frances's father again, and again the next week. One evening he came over with flowers, and they all ate together in the dining room. He tried to play with Frances on the floor, tried to hold her in his lap, tried to make her laugh, but she clung to her grandmother and grandfather, even her mother, staring perplexed at that man across the room, that man who had suddenly appeared in the driveway with his brown shoes, who had touched her head, asked her why she caught ants, looked at her eagerly, with care and caution and expectation, who reached, tentatively, for her toes.

That's your father, her mother explained. That's your father.

That's your father. Go give him a hug.

That's your father. Be nice. Frances, smile.

Frances, let go. Frances, you're hurting me. Frances! Stop it! That's your father, don't be so rude.

Frances!

In late spring, her mother came home sobbing from a date with her father. Her grandmother rushed forward, saying, Oh no. What happened? Oh no.

Frances's mother took the tissue her grandmother offered, blew her nose, and smiled. She knelt by Frances, held her shoulders, but when she spoke she looked upward and spoke into the air. Her words lifted and hung in the space between their faces, the words weightless things, dead and empty like the shells of cicadas. Frances shivered.

We're moving in together. Frances, we're going to live with your father. It's all okay now. Her mother pulled her into a hug, crushing those weightless words between them. It's all okay now. It's all okay.

※

They found a townhouse on the north side of London, not too expensive but in a good neighbourhood. A safe neighbourhood, close to good schools, a shopping mall, grocery stores, bus routes, restaurants, a large expanse of forest that in the coming years would be chopped down and developed into more houses. There were fences around the townhouse property, a playground for kids. The walls were thick enough between the houses that you couldn't hear what your neighbours were watching on TV, couldn't hear their coats rattling on the hangers in the closet or the movement of their beds.

Frances's father rented a condo in Toronto near the university. He commuted back and forth, spent Monday to Thursday in Toronto lecturing, holding office hours, and drafting papers, then Thursday night to Sunday in London writing emails, finishing the papers he had started earlier in the week, and reading.

If Frances's mother ever vocalized her desire for him to spend more time in London, her father would speak critically and wonderingly of the notion of *home*, of the possibility of physical belonging, of the nature of presence in general. And he would remind her, however gently, of everything she had to be thankful for.

※

They were brushing their teeth in the townhouse bathroom on that first night. The bathroom was on the second floor, empty but for the toothpaste on the counter and a roll of toilet paper on the windowsill. Frances's father was downstairs watching TV. Voices from the news channel tumbled in from the hallway.

Frances stared at the toilet.

Her mother spit into the sink. Something I can't see? she asked. Looks like a regular old toilet to me.

Huh? said Frances. She stood on tiptoe to spit like her mother.

The toilet. What're you looking at?

The old man who lived here before, said Frances. He died on that toilet. Naked.

Frances's mother, who had been rinsing her mouth, turned off the water. She almost laughed, but when she saw Frances's expression, the laugh warped into a frown that rippled across her forehead.

Jasper told me, said Frances.

That boy who lives down the street? Her mother put down her toothbrush and looked at Frances through the mirror, setting her mouth into a hard line. I don't know why he would tell you that, she said slowly, because there was no old man living here before us, and he certainly didn't die on that toilet.

But Jasper—

Forget Jasper. We met the previous owners. They were a married couple, young. Something like your dad and me.

But you're not married.

Her mother sighed. Besides that. All I'm saying is, there was no old man. No one died here.

Really?

Really.

But later in her bed, the first time alone in her own bed, Frances imagined the old man on the other side of the wall, with purple lips and purple fingers, one eye missing, skin with vinegar pressed into its folds, and plastic teeth pressed into his mouth. She thought of her mother frowning into the mirror, and she thought of the townhouses mirrored outside, the road running between them, and she thought of a purple-lipped man in each of those houses, sitting naked on each of the toilets.

###

Do you remember that boy? Frances said, looking into the bathroom mirror in the dark. Her reflection was huge and slouching. What was his name?

###

When Frances first went into Jasper's townhouse, she knew that it belonged only to his mother. She didn't know how she knew this—she was too young to understand the significance of details, the leftover clues from the habits of women and the lack of clues from the habits of men—but she knew it.

She asked, Where's your dad?

Jasper shrugged. Dunno.

You don't know?

I dunno!

You don't know your dad? Frances asked. She wanted to say something more, about how she hadn't known her dad until a year ago, about how she still didn't know, not really, who he was, about the way his hands felt when he tried to hold her, the way his lips felt artificial in her hair. She wanted to say something more, but the words were incomprehensible and stuck in her throat. She swallowed them into her stomach.

Sure I know him, said Jasper. I just don't know where he is. He used to...he used to live here with us. Now he's not allowed.

Frances stared at him. Why's he not—

Jasper was already halfway up the stairs. Come on! he yelled down at her. I've got Lego!

⧶

Frances's mother spent that summer babysitting Jasper and taking infrequent evening shifts at the restaurant. With Frances's father around to help pay rent, she didn't have to work like she used to. Frances didn't know what to do with her mother hanging around their house, with her expounding on the soap operas she was watching on TV or complaining about the dirt Frances left on the floor after trekking through the kitchen with her shoes on. So Frances went to Jasper's house most days. His mother worked in the morning and afternoon—she was a waitress like Frances's mother—so they could watch TV however long they liked and turn the air conditioner up when they came in hot from outside, as long as they checked in with Frances's mother every few hours.

The walls of Jasper's townhouse were covered in weird artwork: paintings of breasts and dead bodies, red vines crawling up a white cottage, a cavity in a tooth close up, an upside-down motorcycle. Most were his mother's, Jasper explained, but some were from her friends back in university. The carpeted staircase leading up to the bedrooms teetered with stacked books, so many that you had to dodge between them as you walked. Everything in the living room was furry with dust except the couch, where Jasper and his mom watched movies. The dining room table was cluttered with painting supplies and dishes from last night's dinner. The curtains in the kitchen were yellow, the dinnerware was mismatched, and Jasper's pet bullfrog looked out glumly from its aquarium on the counter.

Often they went out to the playground behind the townhouses. They liked to play hide-and-seek, for hours sometimes, just the two of them. They liked to climb trees, peek at passersby over the fence. The playground behind the townhouses had a jungle gym and monkey bars and a tire swing. They liked to sit with their legs dangling down the middle of the tire swing, competing over who could pull the chains harder, who could make the swing swing farther. Frances would laugh, squealing as her little fingers wrenched the metal links. Jasper never laughed. His mouth was like a smooth cut in his face, his eyes soft like rounded stones. He always had to win, pumping his arms and legs on the swing. After accepting her defeat, Frances would sit gliding with her hair in her face and the sound of traffic from over the fence in her ears.

Jasper had clusters of freckles on his cheeks and nose and a dark ruddy quality to his skin that made him look as if he had been scrubbed hard with dirt. His brown hair skimmed his forehead and the tips of his ears. The brown of his eyebrows and eyes made Frances think of swamps, of the mud at the bottom of bogs. His shoulders, always hidden beneath his shirt, were so pale they were almost blue, in contrast to his freckled face. Frances saw them only once as he threw off his shirt in his bedroom, changing into a sweater. They were nearly translucent. Bald, skinny, laced with veins.

They were playing hide-and-seek. Frances was out by the jungle gym behind the houses, looking up into the trees. Jasper liked to hide in trees. He liked to tuck himself into bushes that looked too small to be tucked into. Frances had learned to search beneath bags of garbage in garbage bins. She had learned to check beneath all the barbecue covers on the neighbours' back porches. She had learned to imagine Jasper's body in various folded positions, to think of all the places a body could fit, to think of all the places a body couldn't fit, and then to think again.

Once, Jasper had stripped off the latticework bordering his back porch and crawled underneath. He had emerged, when Frances called for him, soaked in mulch and mud from last autumn, smelling like earthworms and the deep rot of old leaves, his hair and skin stained a darker brown, dirt stuck in his eyelashes.

Once, when there was construction on the road between the rows of townhouses, Jasper had ducked beneath the caution tape and climbed down a ladder into a half-open manhole. He had mimicked Frances when she called for him, teasing her, whistling. When she finally found him, he was looking up at her from the sewer, water up to his ankles, large eyes reflecting the sky above, large lips split in a larger smile.

Once, he had discovered an unlocked minivan parked on the road and hopped inside, crawled through to the back. While Frances was searching for him, the owner got in and drove all the way to the grocery store and back without noticing the boy tucked behind the seats. When he was finally able to escape, Jasper found Frances sitting on the tire swing, her voice a little hoarse from calling his name, chunking up the dirt below the swing with her heels. She laughed as he told his story, but it was a weak laugh, a quiet laugh. It had been hours since the start of the game.

Now she was out by the jungle gym, looking up into the trees. They were full and glossy at this time of year—it was mid-July—and the green leaves were so stark and shiny that they looked coated in wax. It was impossible, from a distance, to see a figure balanced in the branches. But from below, through the spiderweb of wood, it was easy. Frances wandered from trunk to trunk, feeling that Jasper was watching her and laughing silently, knowing he would tell her later how close she had been, how she had looked but not looked hard enough, how she had just missed him.

She had checked all the usual spots and a few extra, had wandered up the front of the townhouses and down the backs, had even scuffed her feet through the dusty stones under the jungle gym, wondering if it were possible for Jasper to have buried himself beneath it, when she heard the growl of traffic on Adelaide Street, not far behind the fence bordering the property. She saw a cluster of sun-streaked clouds moving across the sky, and she felt an open emptiness all around her—not a quietness or a stillness, but an emptiness, like a hole deep in her stomach—bringing with it the knowledge that Jasper wasn't there.

She thought about calling out his name to be sure, or at least to cut the quiet in her head, but to call out would be a humiliation in the face of the feeling of emptiness so thick around her. She thought about going to the tire swing and waiting. She thought about going home—it would be dinner soon anyway, she could see her mother moving in the kitchen behind the sliding glass door of the townhouse—but everything felt impossible except to approach Jasper's front door, to knock, which she did, and wait for the answer.

Jasper's mother wasn't home; she wouldn't be home until evening. Frances had met her only a couple of times, and she wasn't expecting to meet her now. She especially wasn't expecting the person who did answer the door: a man dressed all in black, with scars on his forearms and hair the same mud colour as Jasper's. He had a foggy look in his eyes, like he was only half awake, and Frances had to step back when he reached to touch her hair, almost catching a curl between his fingers.

What then? he said. His voice was higher than she expected. It had gravel in the back of it, like a dog has a growl hunched up in the raised fur along its spine.

Jasper, she said.

Jasper, he repeated. His hand still hovered between her hair and his hip. She watched his fingers twitch.

Is Jasper home? she asked.

Jasper, he said. Sure, Jasper. He's upstairs.

The man looked from her curls down to her red running shoes, then moved aside to let her in. The smell as she went by was nothing she could recognize—the smell was putrid and sweet, so sweet it pulled at her stomach. Her nose felt thick and full of oil.

He watched her as she went up the stairs.

When Frances knocked on Jasper's bedroom door, she heard no answer. So she opened the door; he was sitting across the room on the carpet, his back tucked up between the nightstand and the side of the bed. His knees were pulled to his chest, wrapped in his arms. His fingernails had cut slivers into his bare calves, and his eyes were large, balls of brown and white staring, staring, and not blinking ever, at the place where Frances entered.

Is he gone, whispered Jasper. It was a whisper full of phlegm, cracking out from his throat, from the dry edges of his mouth. Is he gone?

All Frances could think was that Jasper wasn't hiding. All the places to fit his body, all the possible contortions and covers—in the closet or under the bed, behind the door or under the blankets—and Jasper wasn't hiding.

Jasper who was so good at hiding, only sitting and watching and waiting.

TEN

Jasper. The boy's name was Jasper. And the minute she remembered the boy's name—how could she have forgotten it?—she heard something outside the bathroom: a soft tapping, a slow scraping. The sound was irregular but deliberate, like a tree branch swinging in the wind and rapping a windowpane. It was simultaneously muffled and hard, like a knuckle knocking drywall, the bony point of a fingertip tap, tap, tapping. Frances turned from the mirror, from her slouched reflection, and moved into the hallway, to the bottom of the basement stairs.

She assumed the tapping, the scratching, was coming from the door upstairs. This was where she, after discovering it locked, had herself tapped and scratched—where she waited in the dark, in her hunger, for a sound in response, for a voice or footstep. For a finger mimicking hers, like that figure in the bathroom mirror had, a finger striking as she struck, fingernails scraping as she scratched.

But as she ascended the first few steps, she heard the tapping come from deeper in the basement. A slow, methodical tapping, like a clock or bomb ticking—and between the tapping was the soft scrape and scratch like a fingernail dragging. She looked down at her own fingernails and saw them ragged and dark.

She went back down the stairs and followed the sound to her bedroom, the tap, tap, tap—looked for it under the bed, in the closet, through the window. No, no, no. The sound was muffled as if through a barrier, a basement door, a wall.

She found it in the wall behind her desk.

She shoved her desk aside, toppling a pile of school books stacked beneath it, and threw her hands against the wall, searching for the sound. The soft thick thump, the soft sick thump, the scratch and tap, the scrape, the drag. She searched with her fingertips, the soft pads of her fingertips, for the sound. She pressed her ear into the paint, pushed her skull there until she felt pain.

She found it in the wall. She found it in the wall. She found it in the wall.

ELEVEN

One of Frances's first memories of her own townhouse was of her father outside the front door, a cigarette in one small, pale hand. That was what she remembered most about him, her father, more than the sharp angle of his nose or his eyebrows, as furry as a cluster of pipe cleaners on his forehead: his small, pale hands. His nails were trimmed and shiny. His palms were soft. And between his lips hung the cigarette, smoke trailing up from its glowing tip and merging with the shadows in the dark.

Frances watched him from the upstairs window, the hallway window. She was barefoot and in her pyjamas, which were poorly buttoned in the front, her hair damp from her evening shower. And here was her father, whom she had met only a handful of times before moving to the townhouse, smoking a cigarette out in the cold, while she was warm inside with her forehead against the glass, her mother already sleeping. It was quiet in the house. She watched her father blow smoke into the air, she watched him reach up and put a hand through the smoke, wiggling his fingers until it dissipated. She wondered when he would come inside.

She fell asleep there, in the crook of the window frame, with her shoulder against the wall, and on his way to bed her father found her there and picked her up and brought her into her room. She half woke to him carrying her, one small, pale hand under her knees, another around her shoulder, and she felt the cold still in his shirt and the rumple of cloth on her chin, and the smell of cigarette smoke hanging from his breath, and she fell back asleep against him.

When she woke, she thought, *Where is he? He was just here holding me.*

But it was hours later and the sun was coming softly through the blinds, and she was alone on her pillow. She tried to smell it in her hair but couldn't, that cigarette smoke. She tried to remember what it felt like for him to touch her, but couldn't. She went to the window in the hallway and looked down, but the space by the front door was empty save for the grass and the stone step. She listened and heard him snoring through the wall.

At breakfast her mother asked, What time did you get to bed?

Frances was young, almost too young to put herself to bed, but her mother was tired, always tired, and couldn't stand her daughter's late-night protestations.

Frances lied. She said, Eight forty-five.

Is that true, said her mother. She looked at her father. Did you see her light on when you came in?

Her father took a bite of his bacon, tore a chunk out of his toast. Her light was off, he said. She was sleeping. Not a noise when I came in. Not a sound.

Frances looked at him, his nonchalance, and thought maybe she really had gone to sleep at eight forty-five in her bed, instead of later by the window, watching him from the window. Because she couldn't remember what it felt like for him to touch her. She couldn't remember at all.

╫

In the basement, Frances listened, from her bed, to the sound in the wall. The tap, tap, tapping in the wall.

╫

There were four rooms on the second floor of the townhouse. There was Frances's bedroom, her parents' bedroom, the bathroom, and her father's study. Her father's study had two large windows looking out over the playground and the trees and Adelaide Street beyond the fence. Below the windows was a wide, wooden desk, and along the walls were bookshelves—the only bookshelves in the house besides a small one in her parents' bedroom. The bookshelves in the study were so tall and packed so full that Frances was afraid of them falling when she looked up at them. They seemed to loom out from the wall: rows of textbooks and novels and non-fiction hardbacks, stuffed together like oversized teeth in a small mouth, towering, leaning over her, leering.

It wasn't often that Frances was allowed in the study. When her parents first went through the townhouse and discovered that only one bedroom of the three had a lock on the door, her father immediately arranged for his desk to be brought to that room. Her mother didn't argue—it wasn't often that her mother argued—and by the time Frances arrived on move-in day, that morning in July, the study was already a fully functioning office, her father's furniture having been brought earlier from Toronto. His desk was already between the two windows, his chair pushed up under the desk, his bookshelves hunched against the sides of the room like large, dark-wooded sentinels, his rug on the floor, and the framed certificates of his bachelor's, master's, and doctorate degrees hanging on the wall.

The rest of the house was empty, echoey, with an openness that Frances found exhilarating—there was room to run around and dance, corners to sing into and no place to hide. By contrast, her father's study seemed not comfortable or complete but like a rotten pocket at the top of the house, like a stuffed and clotted cavity that had dug itself deep into a molar.

Her father kept the study locked when he wasn't in it. Frances decided he must keep the key in his wallet or briefcase, because she'd looked for it once when both her parents were out of the house. She looked in all the drawers and cupboards, all the closets and cubbies. She looked behind curtains and in shoes and under her father's pillow. All she found were clusters of dust, grey and laced with static like tiny storm clouds. All she found were lost paperclips, elastics, loose hair, and strange smells.

Her father kept the study locked when he wasn't in it, and he wasn't in it for much of the week. During his time in Toronto it was locked, and on Thursday and Friday evenings, when Frances came home from school, her father spent his time downstairs labouring joyously over her mother's homemade dinners, smoking cigarettes, and falling asleep early with a book tented open on his chest. On Saturday he read books in the living room, watched TV, and did errands according to Frances's mother's instructions: I need milk and pasta from the grocery store. The car is low on gas. Frances's father would rise, rigid, like a marionette pulled by strings. Sometimes he invited Frances to come with him, and she would sit in the back seat, silent, watching the city flash by through the window, the news on the radio flooding past her ears. Sometimes she stared at her father through the gap in the headrest, counting the unshaven hairs on the back of his neck. Sometimes she put her hand on her chest and felt her heart beat loudly, felt it rear up into her mouth as they neared their destination. Her father always held her hand as he helped her out of the car.

For six days of the week, the study door was locked. It was tall and hard, as unrelenting and unfeeling and unresponsive as a wall. Frances pressed her palms against it if her mother wasn't around to see, pressed her ear against it. Tried the doorknob. Sat with her back against it. Waited.

What she was waiting for, she didn't know. What revelation she expected to find on the other side of that door, she didn't know, because she had been in her father's study before.

On Sunday afternoons and evenings, when her father had lectures to prepare for, articles to read and articles to write, other work to catch up on, he would unlock the study door and seat himself at the desk. If his work wasn't too pressing—if he was, for example, going over well-rehearsed notes or recording the day's events in his journal—he would leave the study door open. Frances would wait at the threshold, hanging from the door frame, and, after watching him for a moment, she would approach from behind, silent and breathing carefully, and stand beneath his leaning bookshelf, and wait for him to look at her.

When he found a place in his work to pause—when his shoulders dropped and his arms relaxed against the sides of the chair—he would turn and raise his eyebrows at her, looking from the twist of her topmost curl to her socked toes pushing into the rug.

Frances, he would say in his deep thunder rumble, the scooped-out vowels from his German background creeping into his voice and the twitch of a smile on his lips. Frances, I'm very busy.

Frances would lace her fingers behind her back and nod.

This was the part she played. She knew it well. She knew which face—meek—to make. She knew to tilt her forehead forward, to sway, as if pushed by the back-and-forth teeter of a breeze, to not form one syllable, one sound, in the dry and trembling pocket of her mouth.

Frances, her father would say, if you want to stay here you'll have to be busy, too. Do you need a chair? A desk?

She would shake her head and point to the rug. The rug was just fine, the rug was always just fine. She liked the feel of the fibres as she ran her fingers through them, the warmth on her calves as she sat cross-legged in the middle of the rug that hid the hardwood. Besides, there was no chair for her in the room, no desk.

Frances heaved a book from one of the shelves and sat down to pretend to read, balancing the heavy halves of the book on each thigh, her finger tracing unintelligible words, her father turning back to his work. She watched him then as she watched him sometimes in the car, the steadfast and focused back of him. The upright and muscled wall of his back, the trunk of his neck, the sandy crop of his hair. The stiffness in his wrist as he wrote.

Sometimes, Frances wrote, too. She journalled, mimicking her father, scribbling jumbled jargon on scraps of paper on the floor. Her father watched her, laughed at her. He bought her journals of her own, and as time passed she learned to write properly, how to hold her pencil properly and erase her mistakes and spell—properly. She learned also to record the day's events like her father and reflect on the week in its long and tangled entirety. She learned to recognize failure and laziness, lack of motivation. She learned to improve herself, to record in pencil these improvements. She learned to measure time in writing, in paper, on the lines of a page—to lock down memories as solidly, as definitively, as locking a door.

TWELVE

A tapping in the wall, that was what had woken her. She woke to blindness, complete blackness. She woke gasping, choking, thinking in a scream: *Run. Run as far and as fast as you can.* But her limbs were frigid and stiff. There was nowhere to run, and her body knew it before her brain did. Still she sat, convulsing, *run*, blind, unbelieving of the tap, tap, tapping in the wall.

Unbelieving, in her bedroom that was so black she was blind, could feel the sweat cooling on her skin, the sheets twisted around her legs. She could be in any bed. She could be small again, in Nilestown, her mother's body sleeping somewhere to her right. Or mid-size again, in the townhouse, the sound of her father's snoring drifting down the hall.

Blind, and her bedroom so black that she sunk, finally, into numb torpor. She thought, almost as a reassurance: *There is nowhere left to run.*

╫

The tapping continued throughout the night and into the following day. But what were night and day to Frances? Where was the release of dawn, the transition of time? Frances sat in darkness, on her bed, listening to the tapping. She found herself tapping on her skin in response, her fingers fluttering along her calves, shins, and knee bones, her thighs and stomach, the flat plane of sternum between her breasts. She crossed her arms and tapped her shoulders, tapped the sides of her head. She tapped her body because if she tapped the wall—when she ever thought to shift out of bed, along the floor, and tap the wall—the sounds from the other side stopped. The sounds stopped, the tapping and soft scraping stopped as if something had stopped to listen just as she listened, stopped to press its ear just as she pressed her ear. As much as she disliked—was made uncomfortable by, wanted to cut out her eardrums because of—the tapping and scratching, as much as she disliked those noises knocking around her bedroom, knocking around her head, the silence was worse. The silence after those noises, the silence, the blankness expanding in the wall against her hand, was worse.

The knowledge that something was listening back was worse.

Jasper was Frances's first and very best friend. Living in Nilestown with her grandparents, she had never had a friend like him before, never someone in such close prox-imity, never someone who needed a playmate as badly as she did, who had no siblings and absent parents, who knew loneliness like he knew his reflection: naturally, intimately, like a shadow sewn onto his feet.

Jasper had a handful of friends from school, of course, but in the summer he only saw them once every couple of weeks. Frances heard their names—Will and Ben and Nathan—and heard of their adventures: how their parents built them tree forts, put sprinklers under their trampolines, made homemade popsicles, how they watched movies with surround-sound speakers in their basements.

She understood, intuitively, both why she would never be invited to play with these friends—they were boys and she was a girl—and that she should not feel threatened, not feel envious. Because Jasper made it clear that his time with her was different, that he loved her differently, in the rapid and total way that children love. This difference was obvious, almost elemental, in the way he rang her doorbell in the morning without smiling or talking, but watched her as she put on her running shoes. This difference was evident in the seriousness with which he spoke to her, the secrets he told her, and the care he gave in saying goodbye to her each afternoon.

###

Jasper was Frances's first and very best friend.

###

Jasper described it as a flower growing out of your ear. It started as a seed in the centre of your brain. Your brain was like soil and your skull was like hard rock, pavement maybe, on top of the soil, and your ear was a crack in the pavement. The seed would grow and find this weakness in your skull and squiggle out into the air, outside of your head. This flower could be beautiful outside of your head, and it could even drop seeds of its own that would fall to the ground and roll with the wind and wedge somewhere and sprout. So even if your first flower got old, limp, died, and fell out of your ear, this new flower would keep growing, disconnected from you, unrecognizable, perhaps, to you.

This was how Jasper understood *ideas*. This was how his mother had described them when he asked her about *ideas*.

Even after his explanation, however, Frances didn't know what Jasper meant. If she thought of ideas herself, she imagined them as sunspots: bright, suspended momentarily, impressed in sepia behind the eyes, and then gone.

###

You're my friend, said Jasper. Just mine.

They were sitting together on the tire swing, Jasper on one side and Frances on the other, with their legs hanging down the middle. Jasper's legs were just long enough for his toes to touch the dirt, and he pushed the two of them lazily off the ground, twirling the swing in circles, moving in slow, oscillating rotations. Beside them was the playground, standing up against the trees and the fence and the sky. Behind them—or rather behind Frances and in front of Jasper, because of the way they sat on the swing—was the long row of townhouses, a series of sliding glass doors and small glass windows.

What do you mean? asked Frances.

I don't know if I should tell you.

Tell me what? What is it?

Well, Jasper said, I don't know if you'll believe me.

What? asked Frances. Tell me.

Well, Jasper said, pulling on the chains and leaning back to look up at the sky, before you came here there was no one. During the summer I didn't have anyone. He turned the swing in a stomach-churning twirl, his hair slanting across his forehead. So that lady down the street—Mrs. Norton?—she had to take care of me while my mom worked. And she smells like cheese, her whole house smells like cheese. And she has three cats that I don't think she potty-trained, so it just smells like pee and cheese.

Frances snorted, clutching the chains. Pee and cheese?

Yeah, he said. It was bad. He kicked off the ground, sending the tire swing flying, nearly vertical. But anyway, he said as they coasted backward, rocked forward, that doesn't really matter. What I'm telling you is that there was no one. And I wanted someone. I thought about it every day. I thought about my own friend, just for me. I thought about you.

Me? asked Frances. She saw the world in dizzying swipes of colour at the corners of her eyes. She felt her hair tickling at her chin and the backs of her cheeks.

Yeah, he said. You. Someone like you. Someone kind of different from me. Maybe different hair, different skin, different clothes, like your red runners, that sort of thing.

Maybe with different eyes. And lots of questions because I like finding answers to questions. Then you showed up and you're exactly what I thought. You've got the red runners and the curly hair. You play hide-and-seek even though you never find me. And you ask lots of questions.

I do?

Yeah, you do. So it's just that—I think you're *my* friend, just mine. Who knows, he said, squinting at her, a pinch that could have been a near-smile in the corners of his lips. Or it could have been a grimace of concentration as he propelled the swing, a grimace as he laid out this concept for her that he barely understood, that wafted murky in the shadowy sections of his mind. A joke maybe, a serious claim maybe.

Who knows, he said. Maybe I thought you up.

Thought me up? asked Frances. While he was speaking, she had noticed an ant crawling on the inside of the tire swing, and she watched it disappear behind one of Jasper's knees. I don't get it, she said.

I mean that maybe I made you, he said, tapping the side of his head. With my brain.

Frances frowned down at his knees, searching for the ant, wondering if it had crawled up his shorts—hoping maybe that it had crawled up his shorts.

That's dumb, she said. That's just dumb. If you made me up in here—she tapped her head like he did—then how did I get out? How am I right here? Right here, she said, squeezing the chains of the swing, swinging her legs in the open circle of the tire. Right here.

I dunno, said Jasper. He shrugged and pushed off the ground. It's like magic maybe. Like a magic trick.

Magic tricks aren't real, said Frances. They're not real like real magic.

Jasper shrugged. I dunno.

They're not, said Frances. She had a shrillness to her voice, an angry whine that Jasper had never heard in her before. If she were standing she might have stamped her foot. As it was, she could only grip the chains, her legs hanging loosely, her spine heavy with gravity as the swing passed the lowest point of its arc. She felt oddly frantic and simultaneously deflated.

They're not real, she said again. They're not.

⫫

Was she sleeping? Had she been dreaming?

Frances lay curled on the floor. The mattress on her bed had become too soft, cradling her body, lulling her into sleep. She needed a hard surface, definite pressure on her limbs, her back and stomach and forehead, a strict, stiff barrier between herself and unconsciousness. Because it couldn't be real, this tapping in the wall. It had to be in her head. She listened for it there as a physical reverberation, a tapping on the inside walls of her skull. She heard it there, inside, knocking around, vibrating her eyeballs in their sockets, but only as an echo of that outside noise, that tapping in that real and hard bedroom wall.

Was she sleeping, had she been dreaming?

She surfaced to the cold floor against her cheek, to the sound of the tap, tap, tapping, the scraping and scratching. She pulled a pillow off the bed and over her ears. Through the stuffing and fabric, she could still hear the tapping. If she went into the hallway, into the bathroom, or to the top of the stairs, she could still hear the tapping. Muffled, dull, quieter as she moved away from her bedroom wall, but still at the back of everything, all her movements, in the spaces between her thoughts. The tapping, the scratching. A grinding now that was growing louder. Hunger ground in her stomach and she pulled her knees to her chest, a barrier between the floor and her torso, pressure against her abdomen that didn't silence but kept shut the mouth that her stomach had become.

Was she sleeping? Had she been dreaming?

She remembered Jasper across from her on the tire swing, tapping the side of his head with his finger, Frances lifting her hand to mimic him. *It's not real*, she thought, but the tapping continued. *It's not real*, but the tapping continued.

Inside Jasper's head were razor-edged, scissor-edged, sharp-edged thoughts. He often said things that made adults upset. He often observed things that adults liked to keep hidden and would mention these things days or weeks later in order to shock and embarrass, in order to—whether he knew it consciously or not—remind adults how weak they were.

All his life, Jasper had seen adults, in fury and hysteria, struggle for control. The teachers at the front of the classroom, for example, or the parents at his friends' houses, his own house, asking or yelling, in every way pleading—saying please come write on the board, stay after school, turn off the TV, pick up your socks from the floor. Other children witnessed these commands, these outbreaks, and saw power. But Jasper saw weakness. He saw opportunity and vulnerability, even if he couldn't describe it in these words. He saw, in these moments, the rabid wildness behind the adults' eyes and knew they were no different from him, no better than him. Except for his own father, whose wildness was true wildness, he thought of adults only as larger, bumbling bodies of fear.

Because he knew the secret, one he had learned from his father: that he didn't have to listen to anyone. There was no real control—and certainly not as many consequences as he had been promised.

The school had dark brown tiles running up its hallway. Frances hopped from one to the next. The white cracks between the tiles were deep, stretching to rivers in her mind, white waters gurgling, albino fish emerging that she didn't recognize. In her red running shoes, she hopped.

Her mother walked beside her. Together they moved past the rows of hooks outside the classrooms, past the classroom doors and their long, skinny windows looking onto empty desks and empty chairs, their full bookshelves and full walls—maps and posters and the ABC's, occasionally a teacher writing something on the blackboard or flipping through papers at her desk.

But Frances saw none of this, heard nothing. Not the overhead lights buzzing as they brightened the hallway, not the measured step of her mother by her side. She saw only the brown tile beneath her feet, heard only the smack as her running shoes landed where she aimed them. It was eight o'clock on Tuesday morning, the Tuesday morning after Labour Day weekend, and fifteen minutes before the start of school.

Her mother stopped walking. Here, she said, I think this is it.

But Frances was already four hops away down the hall, arms splayed for balance, knees bent. Brown tile to brown tile. The white fish were hungry in the cracks, nipping at her heels. Was this playful biting? Frances couldn't tell. She couldn't see the size of their teeth.

Frances! her mother called. Come on. Come on.

In two steps her mother was behind her, grabbing her arm. Two taps on the door and they were inside. Two steps more and Frances was up beside a large wooden desk, as high as her chest, and her mother was talking to the teacher, who had pink feet tucked into shiny black shoes, who had nylons reaching up her legs into her skirt. Her mother was saying, This is Frances, she's the new student, she's a little shy, she's never changed schools before.

Yes, said the teacher. We talked on the phone. No problem. The transition's always hard, but everything will be fine and easy after a few days. Right, Frances? Isn't that right, Frances?

Frances had her eyes on the intersection between the white classroom floor and the teacher's black shoes. Her mother shook her arm.

Say hello, Frances. Be polite.

That's your father, thought Frances. *That's your father, go give him a hug. Frances, smile.*

Frances, said her mother. Say hello.

Hello, said Frances.

There was a pause, an open moment of silence, and she knew they were looking at her, looking right at the top of her head, right where her hair parted down the middle and curled out on either side. She imagined the white line of her scalp where they looked, saw fish jumping there. Frances sunk her fingernails into her palms.

Well, that's okay, said the teacher. That's all right, you know. We'll get her settled, no problem. Just wait a couple of days.

Sure, said Frances's mother. Of course. Now, Frances, she said, kneeling down. She squeezed Frances's shoulders. She looked her in the eyes. Then she nodded stiffly, pursing her lips—affirming something, some confidence in her daughter's abilities, some notion of safety. She was performing, with a smattering of cliché gestures and expressions, the farewell ritual every mother should offer her child on their first day at a new school. And she was aware—she was quite aware—of the teacher watching from above. I have to go now, Frances's mother said, but you be good. You'll be great. I'll see you at the end of the day, and—she glanced up at the teacher, then back down at Frances—I love you.

Mom, whispered Frances, grabbing hold of her mother's shirt sleeve.

I'll be late for work, said her mother, standing. When Frances didn't let go of her arm, she yanked it away. It'll be fine, she said. Everything will be fine. She bent down and kissed Frances on the top of the head, on that white line between her sections of hair, smiled at the teacher, in two steps was in the hallway, and in two more was gone.

Frances looked up at the teacher. She looked up, at last, at the teacher. She saw the wide circles of the teacher's nostrils, the flabby chin, the concentration of beige foundation in the shallow wrinkles around her mouth, the little eyes socketed away, the hair done up in tight spirals, the skirt cinched at the waist, the lips fidgeting as if pulled by strings. Frances shrank back against the front row of desks, becoming smaller, collapsing into herself until she became, she hoped, invisible.

The teacher looked down at Frances. She seemed to look into her, through her. Frances felt as if she had been turned inside-out: raw, vulnerable, her organs hot, thumping, presented for examination.

It's all right, said the teacher in a low voice, cooing at Frances in her soothing, well-practised tone. There's nothing to worry about. Look, here's your seat. She pointed to a desk in the front row, tucked over by the windows. Outside, children were shrieking, running back and forth across the pavement. Give it a try, said the teacher. See how you like it.

Frances approached the desk. It was larger than her desk at her last school. It was made from solid wood, light brown in colour, with a deep cubbyhole for her books and pencils, her ruler and paper and erasers. All hers. Her name was printed on a piece of laminated cardstock, taped to the top of the desk: *Frances*. All hers. The chair was plastic, blue, the same colour as her T-shirt, and each chair leg had a tennis ball on the foot. The room around her was deftly organized, and Frances had a feeling of belonging, of things coming together at last.

All hers.

The teacher confirmed it again. This is yours, she said.

Frances sat in her chair and spread her hands over the top of her desk, swinging her legs. The fish she imagined swimming in the white floor were smiling now, rolling to the surface with wide, fleshy grins. If they bit, they bit softly, a nip with no teeth, a wet, sliding sucking of lips.

The teacher sat across from Frances in her own desk, taking papers from the drawers and clicking her pen. Are you excited? she asked. She jotted something down on the page in front of her. You must be very excited.

Frances nodded. She knew the correct answer was yes, but she didn't quite know what excitement meant, what it felt like. Was it this acid building up in her stomach as she waited for the bell to ring? This electricity, like tiny fireworks in her fingertips?

Hmm? said the teacher, who hadn't seen Frances nodding. She looked up from her page, suddenly stern, with a knot of muscle between her eyebrows, thinking, perhaps, that she hadn't been listened to, that she'd been ignored already, even before the bell rang, even before the class arrived, on this first day of school.

Are you excited? she asked again.

Yes, said Frances.

You're going to make so many friends, said the teacher.

Yes, said Frances.

The teacher looked at her watch, began fumbling with notes again on her desk.

Frances, thinking of friends, remembered a question she had wanted to ask for two days, ever since Jasper had said, out on the playground behind the townhouses: I wonder if we'll be in the same class. This thought had never occurred to Frances, that they might not be in the same class. Now it occurred to her every couple of minutes, thumping like a heartbeat in her ears.

Will Jasper be here? she asked. She found herself gripping the edge of her desk, her fingertips white.

The teacher looked up from her papers. Jasper? she asked.

Frances nodded, swinging her legs quickly now under the chair. He's my friend, she said.

The teacher studied Frances from across the span of their two desks—squinting, quizzical, as if she were inspecting the length of Frances's nose, the tint of her lips, every freckle on her face. Will Jasper be here, she muttered to herself, pinching her lips together. You mean, she said aloud, will Jasper be in this class?

Frances nodded.

Because he's your friend, she said.

Frances nodded again. Yes, she said. The teacher didn't know, Frances couldn't explain—Jasper was her first and very best friend.

Sweetie, said the teacher. There's only one Jasper that goes to this school. Are you sure he's your friend?

Frances looked down at the floor, at her red shoes swinging beneath her. She didn't know what this question meant.

Sweetie, said the teacher again. I only know one Jasper. Are you sure you mean Jasper? Not someone else? Are you sure?

Frances nodded. She didn't look up from the floor.

The Jasper I know isn't a very nice boy, said the teacher. Her lips bunched together. She crossed her arms over her chest. Not very nice at all. Are you sure you mean Jasper?

Frances didn't move. She tried to nod, but found she couldn't. She had somehow said something incorrect, something not allowed. Already, the teacher was angry. Already, even before the bell rang, even before the class arrived, on this first day of school.

Look at me, said the teacher. Look at me when I'm talking to you.

Frances stared at the floor, focused on her shoes swinging under the chair.

Frances, the teacher said. Look at me.

The bell rang outside, shrill and clanging.

The teacher stood, huffed, clucked her tongue, and went to the classroom door.

+++

Thirty kids in the class or thereabouts, so many trundling in—brown hair and black hair and blond, pink cheeks and tanned cheeks and freckled, T-shirts and long sleeves and tank tops—that Frances almost didn't recognize Jasper as he slid in among the rest. He came in near the back of the line, and when he saw her his face split open, smiling. He clapped his hands.

Quiet, said the teacher. Find your seats, please. Your names are on the desks.

Jasper was one of the first to sit down. He was in the front row like Frances, but across the room, near the door. The rest of the students took longer, squinting while they read the name tags on the desks, wandering, and all the while throwing looks at Frances, who had been sitting in the classroom before anyone else, whom they didn't remember or recognize, whom they thought for certain was new.

The teacher clapped now just as Jasper had, two quick smacks exploding between her palms. You have five seconds, she said, and started to count. The students scrambled. Soon they were seated and watching the blackboard where the teacher was writing her name, but also watching, Frances felt, somehow from the sides of their eyes, every twitch of Frances's muscles—the *new girl's* muscles—every movement, every breath and turn of her head.

She should have been invisible. This was how she always felt in a classroom: invisible. But instead Frances felt swollen and full, bigger than the seat she sat on. In the class there were girls much larger than her, with stocky arms and big feet stuffed into running shoes, white socks rolled above these shoes. There were girls taller than her, slimmer, and girls smaller, with petite noses, delicate fingers, and freckled calves that were smooth, finely haired, descending down into doll-like shoes. The classroom was filled, behind the uniform desks, with different sized and coloured bodies. Frances was in no way unique or noteworthy. Only her newness made her noticeable. And she hated her newness for making people look at her. She knew they were looking at her.

Inevitably, throughout class, there was whispering that the teacher again and again silenced, but again and again the whispering, like a hiss of constant wind. Whispering about her, she knew. Nudging, too—inevitably there was the shuffling sound of children nudging one another, the secret passing of notes. *About her.* She looked over at Jasper, tried to catch his eye, but he was distracted, bored, staring at a large map of the world on the wall.

When recess came, they rushed outside. All thirty of them, pummelling down the hallway and into the schoolyard—Frances behind the rest because she didn't know the way—then through a pair of glass doors and into the sunlight, concrete rolling out and breaking into a grassy hill, play equipment with stones at its base, bordered by planks of wood.

Frances stood for a moment by the door and watched the other students disperse, grouping themselves into twos and threes. It was scattered and hurried play, only fifteen minutes before the bell rang and they had to go inside for their next lesson. One clump of boys headed for the grass with a soccer ball. A hectic game of tag started between the portables, punctuated by shrieks. Marbles were unleashed in a root-riddled patch of sand around a tree trunk. Frances's class mixed with other classes, a dizzying number of children moving in high speed, like a fast-forwarded movie.

Frances, welded to the brick wall beside the door, her palms flat, watched the recess pass with a feeling of muck in her throat—a kicking, a bucking, in her throat.

She searched for Jasper, but she couldn't find him anywhere, not until moments before the bell rang to go back inside. Frances spotted him up on the hill: hair split and tossed away from his forehead, a giddy grimace, what couldn't quite be described as a smile on his face, leading three boys—three boys who must be William and Ben and Nathan, Frances realized. They kicked the grass and pushed each other and jittered with chatter—constant, inconsequential chatter—as they walked. These were the boys who Jasper visited sometimes in the summer, the ones who had trampolines and treehouses in their backyards. The ones who had surround-sound speakers in their basements. The ones whose mothers were at home every day of the year, who gave Jasper homemade snacks, fed him homemade dinners, and drove him back to the townhouses when it started to get dark.

The bell rang as the boys neared the school. A rush of children sprang at Frances, who still stood beside the door, their voices ringing with the sound of the bell, and she was nearly swept up in them, nearly tossed into the loose crowd forming and turned invisible, when out of the clambering bodies Jasper grabbed her arm.

Frances, he said, seemingly in earnest. Where were you? I was looking all recess, where were you?

In the commotion of children forming lines, frantically searching for their class, Frances didn't answer. She couldn't say, I was right here, I was standing right here. Right here, and you didn't see me. Frances saw, in the bustle behind Jasper, William and Ben and Nathan watching them, squinting and whispering, laughing, prodding another boy, two girls from the class and whispering. Raised eyebrows and laughing, glancing at Frances and Jasper.

Next recess, said Jasper. You and me, okay?

Frances nodded but didn't say anything. Pressed against the wall, fingertips still feeling the brick, nodding but not saying anything.

╫

Frances sliding from the bed. Frances pressed against the wall, fingertips feeling the paint, the drywall. Frances nodding and saying, Hello? I'm right here. Saying, I can hear you, hello? I'm right here.

╫

The next recess was lunch recess, a long recess. Jasper found Frances at the beginning, found her in the classroom and walked with her outside. He showed her the different sections of pavement, the secret alcoves by classroom windows, the poorly drawn hopscotch, the fenced-in electrical box, the out-of-bounds spaces between portables. He showed her the play equipment, the plane of flat grass up on the hill where older boys were again playing soccer. He showed her where the school property ended and turned into a public park, a vast field, a clump of trees they couldn't enter.

Frances followed him, nodding, breathing, thinking, *This is normal. This is okay, me and Jasper, just like home.* She saw but tried to not-see occasional groups of children watching them and talking, she knew, about them. Looking away when she looked at them, turning their heads, giggling. This was because she was a girl, she understood. Jasper was a boy and she was a girl—she understood.

She thought she understood.

Jasper seemed not to notice.

THIRTEEN

It was impossible that the second day could be harder than the first.

That was what her mother told her in the parking lot, as Frances sat in the back seat of their car wiping away the hot, swollen tears pouched in her lower eyelids with her shirt sleeve.

After school the day before, she'd been so exhausted that she fell asleep on the couch, waking just before dinner, disoriented and groggy. When bedtime came she couldn't sleep and instead knocked repeatedly on her parents' bedroom door, complaining of a sore stomach, until her mother came into the hallway and gripped her by the arms, shaking her, saying she didn't know what she would do, she would lose her mind if Frances couldn't stay quiet and in her bed. Frances cried until her eyes were raw, and only then fell finally into ragged sleep.

Now, this morning in the parking lot, her mother looked back at her from the front seat and repeated that the second day couldn't be harder than the first. That any animosity Frances imagined was just that—imaginary. Any distance she felt from the other students wasn't on purpose, but only born from unfamiliarity.

What's *animosity?* asked Frances. She hiccupped. What's *unfamil*— But she couldn't remember the rest of the word, not even enough to repeat it.

It was impossible that the second day could be harder than the first. But on this second day, as Frances entered the classroom, she felt surrounded by a large, infectious bubble. Students seemed to step back from her or dodge away, avoided even grazing her with their arm. But her mother had warned her that this distance was imaginary, so Frances walked steadily, unblinking, to her desk, her face warped in a tight smile: *I wouldn't want you to touch me anyway. I wouldn't want your fingers on my skin.*

Little red shoes, and the white tile of the classroom floor beneath her shoes. Frances spent the morning staring at her little red shoes under her desk—the scuffed white laces, her veins pulled like blue elastics across her ankle bones—and listening vaguely to the teacher at the front of the room.

During first recess, Jasper started a game of hide-and-seek, and twenty participating students fled to different corners, different secret spaces of the playground, disappearing amid the clatter of the rest of the school. Frances hid in an alcove by a classroom window and sat there, growing stiff and cold in the shadow made by the wall, until she was sure they had forgotten about her. She began wondering if they had started another game without her, continued wondering until the bell rang.

Only then did she join the others. Joined Jasper, who exclaimed that she was too good at hiding, too good to be found. Joined the others, who stepped back. She was sure they were stepping back from her, and that a smile passed between them, a dashing of eyes, as they did so.

Jasper, said Frances as they went inside, stretching on tip-toe to whisper in his ear. Why do they keep looking at me like that?

Like what? asked Jasper.

But she couldn't explain. Each time Jasper turned, the other students looked away, laughing.

But they could have been laughing at anything, Jasper reminded her, his own laughter building up behind his eyes. No one's looking at you, he said. You're making it all up in your head. Just forget it, Frances. Forget it.

Before lunch, Frances asked to go to the bathroom. She sat on the toilet looking at the scribbles on the back of the stall door, trying to decipher them. How could she not read them? She was nearly seven years old. She thought of the word, *animosity*, given to her that morning by her mother. She thought of the infectious bubble slopping around her body like an inflated wet suit. This was why the scribbles were difficult to read—this bubble was blurring her vision, creating a ringing in her ears.

The bell was ringing, signalling lunch recess. Frances jumped off the toilet, but by the time she had washed her hands and left the bathroom, the halls were already empty. She stepped on the tiles, little red shoes on dark brown tiles, avoiding the white cracks between. The albino fish had grown into piranhas, grown teeth as long as their bodies. They didn't swim but sat fat and floating, waiting for her to misstep. She turned and through the glass doors could see the other children as seriously as ever at play. She pushed out into the sunlight, past the teachers chatting idly, looking out across the playground. She looked for Jasper and couldn't see him, couldn't see anyone she knew anywhere, so Frances kept wandering, looking up into the play equipment, rounding a portable and finding—

A crowd of children from her class, ten at least, waiting for her. Or not waiting for her, not exactly, but if she came they would be ready. Jasper was among them, mid-laugh, his face dark and deep red as if rubbed with dirt. The children turned when they saw Frances approach, and all ten of them staring together morphed into a jumble of eyes blinking, Jasper's mixed with the rest.

At the front, three boys nudged each other, nudging closer. William and Ben and Nathan.

You check, you do it, the boys were saying, voices tumbling out from the jumble of eyes. No, you! You do it! Pushing each other, laughing sharp-barking, dog-like laughs. You do it! You check.

Frances felt muck bucking up in her throat again, but she managed to say, whisper-thin, Check what?

The tallest boy, William, stepped forward, hair sticking up like a porcupine and a space between his front teeth. He crossed his arms.

Check that you're real, he said. The other boys snickered. There came a nervous giggling, a shifting, from the group behind them.

That I'm real? echoed Frances.

Yeah, said Ben, gaining courage from William. We know you, you're Frances. Jasper told us about you, Frances.

Can we touch you to make sure? asked Nathan, and behind his eyes was an eagerness, a reaching. He stepped forward and reached toward Frances.

To make sure of what? Frances said, stepping back from him. She felt a shriek building up behind her tongue, felt words fall away, and a blankness like smoke enter her head. There was something too horrible in the thought of them touching her, of their unwanted and unfamiliar hands pressing at her body. At the age of six, almost seven, even the thought itself was unfamiliar: the thought—the possibility—that people could just touch her.

To make sure you're real, said William, the porcupine boy, reaching his hands, his fingers, toward her. Not Jasper's imaginary friend, like he says you are.

Where was Jasper now? Frances couldn't see. The bubble around her had blurred her vision, the bubble about to pop. She was unable to move, feet stuck in the dirt behind the portable.

The eyes continued staring. Frances heard a low sniggering, saw hands reaching, mouths open, awaiting the moment of contact between the boys and herself. The moment of collision—or the moment of passing through, the moment of proof that although the teacher had addressed her, introduced her, on the first day of class, that Frances wasn't real. That somehow she didn't exist, somehow she was physically present, visible but illusory. A mirage to put a hand through.

The boys, William and Ben and Nathan, stepped forward. Frances began to scream.

At least, she thought she was screaming. No one heard her, but she could feel the scream like thunder in her head. She felt the teacher looking at her—*Look at me, Frances, when I'm talking to you.* She felt her mother shaking her shoulders in the dark hallway of the townhouse—*I'm going to lose my mind.* All the tightness in her body from the last two days, all the tension built up in her like a taut elastic, came flooding, white hot, through her vocal cords. She screamed, but no one heard her, the scream like electricity, violent, in her body. Something inside her popped, snapped—the taut elastic snapped. It made the same sound in her head as joints popping. She became disjointed. She reached up and grabbed her hair, the two halves of her hair, and pulled them flat against her head.

William and Ben and Nathan, she said.

The boys paused, their hands faltering at the sound of their names.

Get back, she said. Get back! Don't touch me. Don't you dare, don't touch me! She closed her eyes and shrieked blindly—she thought she shrieked blindly. No one heard her, her vocal cords raw and shaking, and when the words came out they were hardly a whisper, an animal impulse against the thought of them touching her, an innate and prehistoric fear piling up inside her body. Don't you touch me or I'll pull out your eyes, I'll kill you, I'll kill you!

The boys dropped their arms and stared blankly, stepped back, but still Frances twisted where she stood, contorted, her voice louder now.

Don't you touch me or I'll kill you, I'll pull out your eyes and I'll cut off your feet, don't you dare, I'll kill you and I'll stuff your mouth with dirt, I'll take off all your skin, don't you dare, don't you touch me, get back!

In the silence that followed, Frances opened her eyes. More children had walked closer to look at her, a larger group had formed. A jumble of eyes still stared, but now these eyes also glanced at each other, bodies shifting, trying to move away. At the back of the crowd Frances saw Jasper, mouth open and unmoving, watching her even as the others pushed him, trying to move away.

Frances heard the sound of feet running on the other side of the portable—heavy feet, teachers running, following the crowd of students. She started to cry.

If you touch me, I'll kill you, she said. She hiccupped through her sobs. You'll be dead and you'll never see anything again.

‡

Her mother was there, outside the classroom, at the door, while the other kids pulled out their notebooks. Frances took her backpack and went into the hallway. The teacher followed behind.

Maybe tomorrow, the teacher said. Maybe try again tomorrow.

Her mother took her hand and led her out of the school, down the hallway, and over all the white lines between the brown tiles on the floor. Frances's feet moved too quickly to dodge them as her mother hurled at top speed into the parking lot, nearly dragging her, nearly lifting her off the ground.

You made me leave work for this? her mother said. She opened the car door and heaved Frances into the back seat, buckling her seat belt so quickly she nearly caught Frances's finger in the plastic clasp. They called me out of work for this?

Frances looked down at her red running shoes as her mother started the car.

A death threat, said her mother, really? Did Jasper tell you to say those things?

No, Frances said. She breathed in and her lungs felt ragged. Her eyes were still hot with tears. It wasn't Jasper, she said. She breathed in and her words hitched in her throat. It wasn't Jasper's fault.

Her mother looked at her through the rear-view mirror. She sighed. All right, she said. Okay.

###

Jasper came by after school and knocked on the door. Want to come play? he asked, his hands stuffed deep into his pockets.

Frances pulled on her running shoes and quietly followed Jasper back behind the townhouses to the playground. She shivered. It was a cold day, colder now in late afternoon, hinting in its bite, its slice, the winter to come. Jasper climbed up the jungle gym to the highest point, his hair flying up in the wind, and rested his hands on the safety railing. He looked down at Frances and pointed his finger directly between her eyes.

If the moon was falling to Earth, if it was going to fall right on your house, would you tell? he called down.

Frances squinted up at him. She could still feel an ache in her head, she still had some crying left behind her eyes, but her feelings had been numbed by cartoons and a tall glass of orange juice from her mother.

Tell who? she asked. Tell what?

If fifty pirates kidnapped you, if they were going to chop off your arm and kill your family, would you tell?

Jasper, said Frances. She couldn't help but laugh—a sharp, dry sound from her throat. She started to climb the play equipment, pulling herself up the metal ladder. The wind was heavy in the trees, she could see it up above her in the sky, splitting the chunks of cloud. The wind touched the back of her knees, wrapped itself around her ankles. Jasper, she said. I don't know what you're talking about.

Would you? called Jasper. He followed her with his pointing finger as she climbed. If a crowd of eagles swooped down and pulled out your hair with their claws, if the ocean rose up and covered the whole world, if—if—if your mom said she was going away forever, would you tell?

Frances had now reached his level. His finger pressed into her collarbone as she walked toward him. She stopped, pulled her hair out of her eyes where the wind had placed it, and crossed her arms over her chest.

They're called talons, she said.

What? His finger faltered, weakening against the stiffness of her bone.

Eagles have talons, not claws.

So what?

So you're wrong.

That's not the point. The point is, would you tell?

Tell what?

I can't say it. You just have to know.

That's not fair.

Yeah, it is. It's like a promise.

You told everyone I'm make-believe.

They weren't supposed to do that. They weren't supposed to touch you.

You told everyone I'm imaginary!

Not everyone.

Will and Ben and Nathan. And now everyone else believes it, too.

Well, aren't you?

I'm not!

Remember I thought you up?

That was a joke! That wasn't real.

But you remember?

Frances closed her eyes against the wind. She tried to remember their conversation on the tire swing that day, weeks ago, but she couldn't quite reach it in her mind.

Instead she remembered the first time they'd met. His bare feet by the car tire, his eyes looking out from beneath his tufts of brown hair. Dirt stains on his jeans. His fingers intertwined, braided together. Telling her he hated the old man who used to live in her house. Vinegar and purple lips.

Then she remembered Jasper in his bedroom with his knees tucked up to his teeth and his father downstairs. *Is he gone?*

She remembered Jasper looking out at her from the back of the crowd behind the portable, the only one not scared when she threatened them, the only one not moving, not looking away.

Frances couldn't remember anything before him. Her whole world began with that summer. The stories with her grandpa, the backyard that led out into the forest, the sunflowers in the garden, the bed she shared with her mother— they were all gone in that moment.

She wrapped her hand around Jasper's finger and pulled it away from her chest. I wouldn't tell, she said. Not even if the sun exploded, or—or it rained and rained forever.

Jasper raised his eyebrows. Not even if pirates snatched you up? Or the eagles?

Not even.

Not even if your mom said she was going away?

Not even. Not ever.

Jasper smiled a full, open smile, something she had only seen on him a couple of times before. The smile was a crack between his lips that split right up to his ears, a smile that showed pink gums and gapped teeth. He jumped and whooped and smacked her on the shoulder. Then he turned and flung himself down the slide, landing at the bottom and jumping again, jumping into a jig that tossed up dust from the stones covering the ground, whirling his arms around in the cloud that he made, and laughing, laughing, laughing.

Frances, thinking now of the last two days zipping away from her like a rewound movie, discovered the question that had been building in her like a balloon, building in her since the previous morning, when she had first met her teacher at school.

Jasper, Frances said. Jasper.

It was something she had thought to ask him at recess, something she had forgotten about until now. She followed Jasper down the slide, coughing at the bottom in the dust.

Jasper, she repeated. Jasper.

He calmed, kicking the stones once more to finish his dance. They burst up and rained on the slide, skidding down to settle in a pile near the bottom.

The teacher, said Frances. She doesn't like you. She says you're not very nice.

What do you mean? asked Jasper. He stuffed his hands into his pockets and walked off into the grass, coming to rest by a tree, leaning his shoulder into the bark.

She told me. She said, "He's not a very nice boy." Did you do something bad, Jasper?

Jasper blinked and shook his hair out of his eyes. I don't know, he said.

What was it? What did you do?

Nothing. It doesn't matter.

Tell me!

What if I don't want to?

Jasper.

It's stupid.

Jasper! Jasper, she said. Jasper.

Jasper sighed. Okay. Well, he began. And he told her quickly, distractedly, what had happened the year before. He told her, while looking at the ground, with his toe scuffing grass and digging into the earth, about his birthday and a surprise visit from his father, about how his father gave him a BB gun for his birthday.

A BB gun? Asked Frances.

It's like a fake gun, said Jasper. With little rocks instead of bullets. Little—pellets. It's like a fake gun that looks real but won't kill you.

Oh, said Frances.

So his father had given him a BB gun for his birthday. His mother didn't like it, his mother and father fought, the birthday cake was ruined—Jasper didn't say how the birthday cake was ruined—and Jasper ran upstairs to hide, vigilant in his bedroom, with his gun.

Jasper paused here in the story, his eyes dashing back and forth, a high-speed scanning of the grass, as if looking out a car window and seeing trees, buildings, road signs, other vehicles suddenly close, but being unable to catch them, hold them, with his eyes.

Frances imagined—in this space, this vacuum of non-speech—Jasper's mother and father in the kitchen downstairs with the ruined cake as he sat, maybe with his knees tucked up under his chin, limbs stiff like when they'd played hide-and-seek and she found him upstairs in his bedroom. She imagined him waiting, listening. What did Jasper hear? Frances imagined his parents arguing, what Jasper must have heard, how long he must have waited, but because she was a child she could not nearly imagine what Jasper had really heard, how long that waiting had seemed to him.

The next day, Jasper said, I brought the gun to school. It was a BB gun, it was a fake gun, it was a joke gun. It was supposed to be funny.

Here Jasper grimaced, almost laughed.

It was stupid, he said. I wanted to show Will and Ben and Nathan. It was supposed to be funny. I took it in my backpack. And I showed everyone at recess. And I told them it was real.

Like a real gun?

Yeah, like a real gun. I told them it was real.

That's all?

No.

No?

I took it out during the afternoon, after lunch. I asked to go to the bathroom and I went to my backpack out on the hook and I got the gun. And I brought it into the classroom and I pointed it at the teacher.

Our teacher?

No, a different teacher. Last year's teacher.

She was mean to you?

No.

Then why'd you point the gun?

I don't know why.

So she got mad?

Sort of. The other kids thought it was real, so the girls cried and some of the boys started yelling and saying it was real and telling the teacher to hide. So she did. She hid behind her desk.

And then?

And then I shot the wall above her head, and the little rocks, the—pellets—they just bounced off the wall and onto the floor. I thought it would be funny. I don't know. I really thought it would be funny.

Did anyone laugh?

Will and Ben a little, but that was only so people couldn't see so much that they were crying.

And the teacher?

She peed her pants.

What?

She peed her pants. It was all over the floor. She had to go home for the rest of the day.

And you?

I couldn't go home 'cause my mom was working. I sat in the principal's office.

That's kind of a stupid thing, Jasper. That's kind of a stupid thing to do.

I know. I really thought it would be funny.

And now the teachers think you're bad.

Sure, said Jasper, and the way he spoke told Frances he was done talking about his BB gun, that there was nothing more to say. He pulled a piece of bark from the tree and held it close to his eyes. He squatted with it between his hands. He brought it so close to his face that he brushed it with his eyelashes.

What is it? asked Frances. What are you looking at?

It's like a whole world, he said.

What is? Asked Frances.

He motioned to the chunk of bark. A whole world, he said. These bumps could be walls or houses. Sometimes you see ants and maybe they're living there. And maybe the tree's like this big, long planet stuck sideways in the ground.

Here, said Frances, let me look. I want to look closer.

Frances ran her hands over her bedroom wall, feeling with her fingers the minuscule ridges of paint, the pattern and texture of drywall. She was sitting on the floor. The tapping had stopped when she approached. There was now only a soft shifting, as of limbs being rearranged, from the other side. *A whole world*, she thought. She swallowed. She leaned back and sat against the end of her bed.

For a week after the scene behind the portables, her classmates looked at Frances differently, treated her differently. They looked at her the way you look at a frog you are about to dissect—with awe, curiosity, thinly disguised revulsion.

Jasper played with her at recess, alone, until one day, when William approached and jabbed Frances in the arm with his finger, then ran off yelling, She's real! Everyone, she's real! And Frances, relief coursing through her, relief that his finger had made contact with her skin, no matter the sting, ran after him in a wild chase, starting a game that would last for a month, punctuated always by a jab and declaration—She's real!

FOURTEEN

Frances dreamt she was eating what she thought was cereal, but was actually small, hard-shelled bugs. She dreamt she opened the cupboards in the kitchenette and found toads sleeping there—quiet brown lumps of breathing flesh. She picked one up and placed it on the back of her hand, and then it wasn't a toad but a swollen bulge under her skin. She pushed at it until it popped, and pus, brown as the toad, leaked out. It was oily. It dripped onto the floor. It smelled like vinegar.

⧼

There's something living here with me. I'm not alone down here.

⧼

Mice was what she should have thought, but she didn't think *mice*.

Mice were what lived in walls. Mice were what scratched in walls. Mice were what shuffled behind walls, rubbed their little bodies against walls, sniffed their brown or black or pink noses at walls. Frances didn't think *mice*. She thought bigger. She thought *dog, wolf, wildcat*. Because what lived in the wall felt larger, to her ears it felt larger. What scratched in the wall scratched louder. Frances didn't think *small*, she didn't think *mice*: she was sure that whatever it was, whatever scratched and shuffled, was too big to live in the walls of the house. It must have carved a space beyond the walls. And so Frances thought *groundhog*, she thought *rabbit*, because these were what tunnelled and tucked into dirt, what kept and slept in darkness. But even these were too small for the scratching. *Dog*, *wolf*, *wildcat*.

Frances sat back against the end of her bed and listened. She fell asleep there, and woke, and listened. The scratches were worse than nails on a chalkboard. They were like a finger tunnelling into her ear, breaking the drum, fiddling with the little bones in her head. They were like a finger pushing buttons in her brain. She sat and listened, watched the wall, studied the desk pushed off to the side, jammed up against the dresser, and watched the wall.

Listened.

╫

What? What are you looking at?

You always do that, that thing with your tongue.

What thing?

That thing. When you put your tongue up over your teeth.

I don't know what you're talking about.

It's when you're thinking hard about something.

Yeah, right.

Well, I promise you, you always— Right there! You just did it!

Like this?

Yeah! It looks like a brain underneath.

Underneath what?

Your tongue. It looks like a pink-and-blue brain.

Oh, quit it.

I promise you! Maybe that's why you do it when you're thinking. You got this other little brain, tucked away—

Oh, quit it, Jasper. Come on.

Well, what're you thinking about anyway?

I wasn't thinking anything.

Aw, come on, you've got to tell me.

No way!

Frances...

...

Frances, come on!

All right. Okay. I was thinking about...

⧣

In the basement, time collapsed. All the moments spent with her mother and grandparents at the Nilestown house—all the moments with Jasper, her father and mother at the townhouse, her elementary school days—collapsed with it. In a way, it was a gracious fall, a soft descent into chaos. Falling into this collapse of memory was as easy, as numbing, as death-like and complete, as falling into dream.

⧣

She remembered, in this collapse, the townhouse. Going into the kitchen on a Sunday afternoon to grab a glass of milk, her father gone to Montreal for the weekend to do a lecture at McGill, her mother upstairs napping. She heard a bang as she opened the refrigerator door. She turned, saw a red streak fall from the window: a bird, a cardinal. Frances ran out in her winter boots and pyjamas—she had been watching cartoons since morning—and as she flew out the back door, her vision blurred, her warm body hit the cold air like a hurl of hot wind. The snow was higher than her boots and slid down onto her feet, her toes. There was no breeze outside. It was still and frigid, and the sky was solid white from corner to corner.

She looked for the bird. A couple threads of red feather remained pinned to the glass behind her. In the yard the snow was flat and untouched except for a patch three feet away that threw itself up and over. The bird writhed, a flop of red wing breaking the air.

Frances approached the bird. It rolled and heaved, breathing raggedly, its one visible eye black and wide. Its wing was broken, Frances could see it bent and pinned under the bird's body.

As she watched, she saw that this was the only part broken. *Birds can still live with broken wings*, she thought, and she ran back into the house, kicked off her boots, dashed across the kitchen on frozen toes, found a box from the basement, padded it with T-shirts from her dresser drawer, grabbed her mother's mitten from its pair on the kitchen table, and went back out to the yard.

Jasper, having come in through the gate, was standing by the broken bird.

He was older now than he was their first summer and their first year at school together. Both of them, older now.

Jasper, she said, did you see it? It flew into my window.

I saw you, he said. I heard the door slam and I saw you in your pyjamas. He looked at her, almost smiling, as if at the thought of her—he must have been thinking of her—as a bird, too.

It's a cardinal, she said, staring down at the creature twisting in the snow.

It's dying, he said.

Maybe not. I've got a box set up in the kitchen, it's warm and it's dark. I've got a mitten here.

She showed her mother's mitten.

Its neck is broken, said Jasper.

No, said Frances, its wing. Birds can still live with broken wings. I've seen it on TV, and my mom—

Look, said Jasper.

When Frances looked, she saw that the bird's neck was indeed broken, snapped straight to the side, and that its chest was heaving more softly now, its wings still and sprawled like little flames, its legs bony and curled inward.

I've got this mitten here, said Frances. She played with the knitting along the thumb.

It's dead, said Jasper.

They kicked snow over the bird, and then Jasper went home. Frances stayed and pulled her mother's mitten over both her hands. She felt the snow melting between her toes in her boots.

She remembered that the sky was white from corner to corner, and she had been watching cartoons since morning. She remembered her house and her mother napping upstairs. She remembered the rest of the day.

As she turned to leave, she thought she saw a twitch in the snow. She paused and stared at the raised lump where the bird's body lay. It couldn't have been a twitch, because the bird had a broken neck, she had seen it, and it was dead. Jasper said so.

Frances wove her fingers together inside the mitten. In the same way, she wove the image of a bird—one with a broken neck, not with a broken wing—into her brain. She kicked one last clump of snow over the bird and went back inside.

※

She remembered, in this collapse, her parents yelling down in the kitchen while she tried to fall asleep. Lying in bed, listening to their voices through the walls.

It was late summer, 2007. Frances ten years old, soon to be eleven. Her father had announced that day that he was going to Germany. To visit his mother, it had been too long since he had visited her, he said, and also to lecture, a short stint, he said, an indefinite leave from U of T. He had wanted for too long, he said, to lecture at Humboldt-Universität zu Berlin, at his home university. It was an opportunity, an invitation he couldn't ignore. Four months only! One semester, a half course only! What more could Jeanette ask of him, he stammered. What more could he give?

What Frances didn't know, what neither of them knew, was that her father had been toying with the idea of leaving from the moment he arrived at the townhouse four years ago. The thought, caught in the back of his mind like a moth in a spiderweb, festered and ached, swollen, threatened to burst like a sack of blood.

It had always been obvious to him which half of his life was long-term—which half was real, substantial, and made a difference. He received recognition for his work in Toronto; he received promotions, awards, invitations. Pieces of paper he could frame and hang on the wall.

Whereas his life in London was vague, almost dreamlike, time passing lazily, hours stuffed with inconsequential errands, chores, and conversation, episodes on the TV, a voice buzzing out, incoherent, from the radio. The slow rhythm of domesticity.

Worst of all was Frances, always puzzling him—not on purpose, of course, not yanking at his sleeve or pant leg, whining, like he saw other children do, but keeping to herself, existing in her own world that he only occasionally caught glimpses of. Arranging the food on her plate before eating at dinnertime, for example, or meticulously tying her shoes. Most disturbingly, he saw flashes of his physical self in her: in the dark bend of her eyebrow or the length of her stride.

Frances was disrupting his life in Toronto. She bled into his thoughts as he lectured to a crowd of young people who had once been as young as Frances, reminding him that he had once been as young as Frances.

This split life, this split mind, would not do. It was unsustainable, depleting. The invitation from Humboldt-Universität zu Berlin was strong enough to free the idea festering for four years in the back of his mind, propelling him toward a plane ticket and a packed suitcase.

When Frances fell asleep, it was to the sounds of her mother yelling, a shrieking bark-yell that was scratchy in the air, sobbing, saying she had heard this story before, different words but she had heard this story before. The sounds faded as Frances faded, her mind pillowed with darkness, slumber.

‡‡

She remembered, in this collapse, her father hugging her, his forearms hard as steel rods against her back, saying in her ear, Frances, my little Frances. Picking her up and squeezing her harder, setting her down and kissing her on the head, hard, his lips hard like steel bolts in her hair.

She remembered, in this collapse, her mother staring for hours at the TV, her mother going to bed early, her mother waking up late, the house falling into disarray. Fruit flies like living black-and-orange clouds in the kitchen, clots of dust and hair in the corners of rooms, the smell of garbage as you entered through the front door, the smell of sedentary bodies, unwashed armpits, rank breath. Frances remembered learning to wash dishes, wash clothes, learning to call her grandmother, who would drive from Nilestown to scrub floors, prepare meals that she sealed in Tupperware containers, plastic wrap, and shiny tin foil.

Frances remembered, in this collapse, the winter after her father left—this deep winter during which her father did not return in December as he had promised. Another half course, another semester, only! His voice buzzing, electronic, through the phone. And Frances's mother, robotic, in the kitchen chair, looking out the window. A deep winter with deep snow piled up against the glass door at the back of the townhouse. Frances had trouble sleeping. She would often wake in the middle of the night and sit upright in bed, looking around her room or out the window, listening to the sounds of the townhouses in slumber. She would go downstairs and eat a snack or watch TV quietly. She would sit on the floor by her nightlight and read a book, not wanting her mother to see her lamplight.

━━

One night, when she had gone down to the kitchen to get some milk and maybe a slice of cheese, she looked out the sliding glass door at the back of the house and saw someone lying in the snow beyond the fence.

It was a man, it looked like a man, in a large winter coat. But as she kept looking, she saw that the legs sticking out of the coat on one end were short and skinny, that the head sticking out on the other was small and swallowed up by the collar. The hair on the head was mud-brown against the snow.

Frances grabbed her boots and coat and mittens and went outside. In the yard she looked up and saw the moon moving fast behind the clouds.

When she was past the fence, she said: Jasper.

He didn't seem to hear. His eyes were closed.

Jasper, she said, approaching him, you need a hat. You're starting to disappear. Aren't you cold?

She should have asked, *What are you doing out here? Why are you awake?* but was afraid he would ask the same thing of her.

I don't feel cold, said Jasper. His lips were pink against his skin. His ears were pink behind his hair.

But aren't you? she asked.

I guess so.

Here, you can have my mittens. She pulled them off and wagged them in front of his face. Just give them back tomorrow. I need them for school.

That's okay, he said.

Here, take them. I'm not as cold as you.

I'm leaving.

Me, too. Let's go inside. My mom will kill me—

No, I'm leaving.

What?

My mom said. After dinner, after we finished eating, she told me we're leaving. She got a job in Toronto. We're going in three weeks.

You're moving?

Yeah, we're moving. Jasper opened his eyes but didn't look at her. He looked up at the sky. The dark eyelashes ringing his eyes, she now saw, were wet. The whites of his eyes were laced with red squiggles like spiders' legs.

I've lived here my whole life, you know, he said.

Frances slipped her mittens back on. The moon seemed to be shooting faster behind the clouds. A cluster of shadows passed over Jasper's face.

I've moved before, said Frances. I used to live with my grandma and grandpa.

She thought of her grandfather in the living room with his arms spread wide as wings. This image, suddenly cutting into her mind: her grandfather in the living room with his arms spread. *Wouldn't you want to come right back?*

It's not so bad, said Frances. She swallowed. Toronto's not so far either.

And what about you? asked Jasper.

What about me? I've moved before, I told you.

No, not like that. What about you? I won't see you anymore.

His eyes, wide open, were dark in his face.

Frances followed his gaze and looked up at the night clouds stretching, pulled apart to near-wisps by the wind. She thought of something, an occasional joke between them.

You can take me with you, if you want, said Frances. I'm not real, remember? Remember I'm just pretend, your imaginary friend?

Oh, yeah. Jasper closed his eyes and smiled. I forgot.

Me, too. Frances giggled. I always forget I'm not real. She fidgeted in her boots, the cold cutting into her toes. She lifted her feet and stomped in the snow. Not real, over here! she called, not caring anymore about disrupting the silence or the stillness, not caring if she woke her mother or the whole row of townhouses. Not real! Here I am, not real, kicking the snow! She kicked the snow. Here's the not-real-girl doing a somersault! She somersaulted, nearly slamming Jasper with her boot heels. He flinched out of the way and laughed. Frances lay back, her boots by his head and her head by his boots, and breathed out, a great, heaving exhalation.

Jasper grabbed her mitten with his bare hand and said, I'm cold now. I can feel the cold now. I have to go inside.

She could feel his hand shaking in hers. She looked up to see his whole body shaking in the snow, his cheeks and the tip of his nose dark with blush.

I'm cold, too, she said.

No, he said, not like this. I'm so cold—and she could hear his teeth clatter in his skull between the words. I'm so cold, Frances. I'm so, so cold.

‐‐

When Frances's father left, he didn't take everything with him. Frances and her mother were surprised for years afterward by his stray belongings: a black sock flattened behind the couch, an embossed pen in the drawer, a political science textbook jammed stiffly into a pile of her mother's fiction.

Once, when Frances was walking past her mother's open bedroom door, she saw a book pressed between the bookshelf and the wall, presumably having fallen from above. Her mother was out running errands. Frances ducked into the room and out again, holding in her hands a dusty copy of one of her father's journals. It was black, leather-bound, and not much bigger than her open hand. She brought it to her room and closed the door.

卅

September 5, 2003

Was it a mistake to come here? Jeanette seems pleased, and things are running smoothly. But then there's Frances. I don't know what to do about Frances.

Take last night, for example: I had just come in from smoking, was just pulling off my jacket, when I noticed Frances standing at the top of the stairs. Her eyes were open, but I could see from the way she was swaying that she wasn't fully conscious.

"Frances," I said.

"Dad."

"Are you awake?"

"I heard something in my room."

"What did you hear?"

"Can I sleep in your bed tonight?"

"What did you hear?"

I led her back to her bedroom and put her under the blankets. Her hair was wild against the pillowcase, like a cluster of softened corkscrews.

"Now sleep," I said.

I went to the door and watched her until she closed her eyes, and then I left the room. I went to brush my teeth. Afterward, just as I opened the bathroom door, I saw Frances standing again at the top of the stairs. Her toes were curled over the lip of the top step.

I pressed my hands against her shoulders and told her once more to go to bed.

"I heard something in my room," she said.

"Okay," I said. "It's all right." And I put her under the blankets.
"Will you stay?" she asked.

I had only slept five hours the night before. I noticed on Frances's digital clock that it was already nearing midnight. I relented, thinking it wouldn't be good for Frances to get up again and wake Jeanette. I lay with her, her head tucked in the crook of my shoulder. Her skin smelled like milk and mint. She turned over and put an arm across my chest, pushing her toes under my legs. I couldn't see her face, only the point of her chin and her mountain of curls against my sweater, but I heard her breathing deepen, and I knew she was asleep. I counted her exhalations, and the next thing I knew, morning light was piling up behind the curtain. I could hear the birds starting up in the trees outside. I slipped my arm from under Frances's head and disentangled myself from the blankets. I left her alone in the bed. It was six o'clock and I didn't want to wake Jeanette, so I went downstairs to rest on the couch.

You can see why it might have been a mistake for me to come here.

A new semester starts in Toronto in a couple of days, and I've somehow got to dig my lecture notes out of the boxes in the basement that I haven't had time to unpack. My students will be expecting…

𝍤

Frances remembered that night, but she remembered it as if it were a dream. She thought it had been a dream. It was a dream, it must have been a dream, and all the colours in the dream were grey.

She remembered her head lying in the crook where her father's arm met his shoulder. He had worn a thick grey sweater. It smelled warm, like heated laundry detergent and skin. Below her chin was the blanket, under her body was the bed, along one side was her father's torso, and along the other was his arm. She could feel him breathing against her right shoulder, and to her left was the bedroom wall and the window, the curtains drawn across to block the street light outside. The carpet—which was, in reality, cream-coloured—looked grey under the layer of shadows covering the room. The ceiling was grey, the blankets were grey. Her father's socks sticking out at the end of the bed were grey.

Her father had come to her bed because she'd had a nightmare. She remembered now.

She'd had a nightmare that she was standing at the edge of a deep crack in the earth, and when she looked down she saw darkness, and something moving in the darkness. But she couldn't look away. Her neck was stiff and she couldn't look away. There was something else as well. She tried to remember—it was something crucial, central to the dream itself.

Yes, that's what it was. Of course.

Something was scratching the wall behind her.

FIFTEEN

Frances had no skin left over her bones. She had no lips left over her teeth. No eyelids left over her eyeballs. No hair left over her head. She was empty, she was air. She couldn't remember what the floor felt like under her feet. She couldn't feel the blankets wrapped around her legs. She looked at the little square of window, of light, up on the wall, and she felt it was touching her, kissing her. This was all she could feel. The pulse of moonlight on her toes. She was nothing, not anything, and she had no bones. Most of all she had no skull. Her thoughts streamed out. She watched them tangling with the light. She watched them come back up through her nose and settle with moonlight in her head. She couldn't remember if she was asleep or dying. She couldn't remember if she was already dead.

In the wall, she heard scratching.

Frances didn't dare scratch the wall in response, but she scratched her bedpost, the floor, her skin—scratched her shinbones, her thighs, the spongy hollows on the backs of her knees.

<del>卌</del>

Frances's father had been gone for fifteen months. It had been ten months since Jasper had moved away with his mom, and an elderly couple had moved into their townhouse down the street. Now it was November, and it had started to snow again.

Frances began playing with her old dolls, the ones from when she was a little girl.

She began ripping pages out of her journals. She began rocking in her seat.

She stopped eating dinner. She stopped eating lunch at school. She stopped eating breakfast. Her body, already small, shrank quickly. The vertebrae on the back of her neck poked out like round pebbles from her skin. Her stomach became pouched, swollen, and her cheeks and eye sockets were hollow. This happened over a period of months, so that people who saw her daily—her teachers and classmates, her mother—barely registered the transition. All they knew was there was something off-putting about her, something sickly and indecipherable.

Her mother, of course, noticed that Frances was hardly touching her meals. But this was something she herself had done routinely as a teenager in order to lose weight. Fasting was efficient, it was cleansing, it wasn't something to actively worry about, and in her warped pride and determination to support her daughter, she failed to remember that Frances was only twelve, wasn't yet a teenager, that she had no weight left to lose. She failed to notice that the way Frances pushed her food around at dinner—the way she placed it in her mouth and spit it out again, looking ill, even confused, upset—did not stem from a diet plan but from a lack of appetite, a steady listlessness, a fog drawn over her like a blanket over her head.

Near the beginning of December, Frances's mother sat with her at the table in the townhouse, and in her erratic, happy way—she was erratic and happy now, more than a year after Frances's father had left, able to clean the house with spurts of overzealous energy, able to work full shifts at the restaurant, drop Frances off at school and pick her up—she said, Maybe you should join a club. Maybe I can sign you up for gymnastics, for piano lessons, maybe you could play soccer.

And Frances said, No thank you.

Her mother said, Well, at least let's get outside together. Let's go to the playground, I'll push you on the tire swing.

And Frances said, No thank you.

Well, at least eat your dinner.

No thank you.

How about dessert? I've got ice cream in the—

No.

Frances said *No thank you* for two weeks, until her hair came out in clumps in the shower and she stuck it up on the wall and her mother saw it there. She said *No thank you* until she fell over during gym class at school. Her mother took her to the doctor, and the doctor asked to speak with Frances alone, and during a moment of admission, Frances told him the problem was that she wasn't real—Jasper had told her she wasn't real. So the doctor suggested Frances see a psychiatrist, and her mother spent the night crying in her bedroom with the door locked because she didn't want Frances to hear. But Frances heard through the wall.

The next morning, her mother sat with her at the table, less erratic, even focused, so focused that her expression was strained, that she looked as if her eyeballs were being pulled back into her head. She said, Your father's dead.

Frances didn't lift her eyes, she didn't flinch, no tic in her eyelids or lips, which hung limp at the bottom of her face. It doesn't matter, she mumbled.

Can't you hear me? Your father died. In Germany. He was in a car accident.

Frances stared down into her cereal bowl, which she hadn't touched and wouldn't touch. It doesn't matter.

He won't be coming back, said her mother. Do you hear me? He's gone. He's never coming back.

Frances shook her head. It doesn't matter.

But the next morning, she remembered what hungry felt like, and she ate a sandwich before school.

By Christmas she was fine, to all concerned, she was fine, eating, and hadn't said another a word about her father, or Jasper, and certainly hadn't mentioned not being real, and whether she still thought those things or not didn't matter because her mother had heard her laughing with her toys in her bedroom, had heard her singing in the shower, had seen her writing in her journal and doing her homework and watching TV.

On Christmas day Frances and her mother went to her grandparents' house for dinner. She opened her presents—a hand-crocheted doll, a pair of rain boots, a notebook and pen—and her grandfather said, We got you extra this year because your dad isn't around.

And Frances said, You can say he's dead, I know he's dead.

Her grandmother and grandfather looked at each other like they'd never seen each other before, and they looked at her mother, and later, while Frances was braiding the hair on her doll, she heard her grandmother say in the other room, How could you tell her something like that? Really, Jeanette, how could you?

But Frances was happy to know her father was dead. If she didn't know, then she would be living in make-believe, and that wasn't a place she wanted to be, and that wasn't something she wanted to experience. It was one thing to exist as a make-believe person, to be pretend like Jasper said she was. It was another to live in a whole world of unreality, to not see or touch or know anything for certain.

Her father was dead and she knew that. The doll in her hands was real and she knew that. Her hands holding the doll were made of bone and skin and nails, she knew that. What could be worse than not knowing? She didn't know what could be worse.

She ate her Christmas dinner, turkey and mashed potatoes, stuffing and corn, and thought it tasted good, and knew those thoughts were real, because the food was real, because it tasted good in her mouth.

Do you know how to tell a story? she asked the wall.

The wall listened quietly.

Do you know what a story is?

The wall was quiet.

I have a story inside me. She placed a hand over her stomach. It's called hunger. My story is called hunger. It has a beginning, middle, and end. I know the beginning, and here I am in the middle, but what's the end?

The wall listened.

Do you know how to tell a story? she said. The ending has to be good. It has to be what you need, and not what you want. That's what they taught us in school about stories. That's what they told us about stories. I haven't been to school in a while. I've been down here for a long time. But I remember what they said about stories. And I always wondered, do I know how to tell a story? If it's what you need and not what you want, do I know?

Do you know how to tell a story? She coughed, because now coughing came from hunger. And do you know how to make it good?

The wall was quiet. It listened.

Do you know how to tell a story?

Do you know what a story is?

I have eaten all the books from the bookshelf.

I have drunk all the vinegar from the cupboard.

I have pulled all the hair from my head.

I can't remember if I'm sleeping or dying.

I can't remember what I've already said.

Do you know how to tell a story?

The walls were wet. Like a mouth, they were wet. The basement rolled like a tongue out from her bedroom to the bathroom, and Frances moved back and forth along this tongue.

In between were the stairs, and the stairs, she thought, were the throat. Peristalsis moved her up and down, tugged her to the basement door and back to her bedroom. Then again, maybe the basement wasn't the mouth, but the gut. Maybe the house was digesting. Either way, the basement was hungry. She felt saliva on the walls.

+++

Blood on her hands: she could feel wetness between her fingers. Blood bubbling from under her nails, from scratching—what had she been scratching?—and grinding—what had she been grinding?—that noise, grinding, scratching, in the canals of her ears, vibrating in cartilage, the bones in her fingertips vibrating as she ground her fingernails into her bedposts, her kneecaps, the walls.

Had she been grinding, scratching the wall? She looked and saw marks there, deep trenches, black and brackish from dried blood.

Was she sleeping? Had she been dreaming?

+++

Was this dreaming?

SIXTEEN

Frances remembered high school. Those memories were plummeting now, rolling like a somersault, seen in vivid yet incoherent upside-down flashes, spasms.

In Grade 9, five years after her mother told her that her father was dead, Frances searched online and discovered that her father was still alive. He was still a political science professor, working at Humboldt-Universität zu Berlin, and had published six articles and contributed to one book—all written in German, all unreadable to her.

Of course, she already knew he was still alive, had known it maybe from the moment her mother told her he was dead, but this solidified that knowledge. It solidified something else, too, something as small and twisted as a walnut shell in the centre of her chest.

Frances bought a flat iron and straightened her hair every morning with long, rhythmic strokes in front of the mirror. She didn't own much makeup—sometimes she wore mascara. Her clothes were as close to what everyone else wore as she could manage: jeans, T-shirts, yoga pants, loose-knit sweaters, woollen socks. She didn't talk, generally, unless someone talked to her first. Not many people did. She had two friends, Stephanie and Christine, whom she sat with in the cafeteria at lunchtime and waved at between classes. She never saw them after school or on weekends, not unless they met up before a school dance or one of them decided to have a birthday party. That was how the majority of high school passed for Frances: quietly and uneventfully, with her voice stuffed so far down her throat that she forgot it was there.

Her mother still worked as a waitress, but only over the lunch shift. Any money lacking for bills and rent was mysteriously supplemented by an apparently limitless fund to which her mother had access. Frances eventually learned, when her mother announced that he would be paying Frances's university tuition, that this fund came from her father. Her mother never addressed the fact that he was supposed to be dead—perhaps the fib was just a foggy and distant memory to her, same as all small lies told to children, all things done for their own good.

During that same conversation, her mother said she didn't want Frances to live in residence for her first year of university, that it would be better if she stayed home. She could save money, her mother reasoned—and did Frances really want to leave her so lonely, the house so empty in the evenings, the rooms so hollow?

Frances swallowed guilt each morning at the breakfast table in the same way she swallowed her cereal or oatmeal or scrambled eggs. But she also wondered: Was it her mother's fear of loneliness that kept her nagging Frances to stay? Or rather her fear of losing the monthly payments from Frances's father, which, after all this time, might only be ensured by Frances's presence?

She had been lied to by her mother so often, been fooled and made to look foolish, that she had learned to question and to wonder—to doubt every word her mother said. And with this realization came another lesson: she too could lie, she too could exaggerate, manipulate, and disobey. Not just out loud in class with her teachers, her peers, her mother at home, but also on paper, alone, to herself.

Her father had taught her how to write before she even knew how to read, before she knew letters other than those that constituted her name, when her fingers were still too round and uncoordinated to hold a pencil in anything more delicate than a fist.

In her box of journals in the closet was a stack of small leather-bound notebooks. These were books that her father had bought and entrusted to her, books filled on every page with line after line of long wordless scribbles. He had praised her for this, she remembered. Incredible, he would say, genuinely startled that a child could work so meticulously at something she didn't yet know how to do. You have written so much!

That was what Frances came to know as writing: not putting words together, not grammar, not even emotion, but rather a blind, slow, thoughtless scribble, from one end of the page to the other.

Writing became habitual while her father was around, and she only stopped, briefly, when he left. She found the process soothing and necessary, like showering or brushing her teeth, a sort of wringing out of her mind. Her grades were good because of this. Not only because she could write, but because the act of sitting quiet and still—she imagined her father at his desk bent over his books, looking at her if she moved—was exactly what her education required. The long focus she brought to her writing was something the teachers adored in her. A brilliant student, they told her mother, meaning in most cases that Frances was the kind of student they could forget about while dealing with the others, the kind of student they could trust insofar as they knew she was afraid to break the rules. She made their jobs easier.

In high school, Frances's grades began to matter more. Suddenly her classmates were peering over her shoulder to see what mark she'd received on a test. Suddenly they were asking her to join their group projects.

In Grade 11 and 12 they began discussing universities and the courses required for each discipline. It was something Frances hadn't given much thought because, as she told her teachers and guidance counsellor, she had always just taken the classes she liked and assumed that would lead her into the right program. Besides, with her grades she would be able to attend any university she chose, so the decision felt less pressing.

If she had been honest with the guidance counsellor, Frances would have told him that her apathy actually stemmed from worry: worry that she might not be able to leave home at all, that her mother would do something terrible to herself if she left. The thought didn't sit well with Frances—she was, after all, as good a daughter as she was a student.

It was at this time that her nightly journal writing began morphing slowly into something she didn't recognize. What had always been a strict notation of daily events now began to turn toward fantasy.

Who would know? she asked herself, as she began recording things disingenuously. *Sideways*, she called it. Instead of writing about what was happening in homeroom, she wrote about the bird she imagined outside the window, or what the icicle felt clinging to the overhanging roof. She wrote that during gym class she spiked a volleyball so hard she made another girl bleed, and that on her way home from school she had enough change in her pocket to buy a slice of chocolate cake from the grocery store, which she devoured before her mother returned from work. These were juvenile fantasies, but she didn't care. *Who would know?* she asked herself. *Who would know the difference?* When reality stopped and her own writing began—who would know?

It was at this time also that Frances began to write stories. The images that came out of her in those moments of pure make-believe were too alarming to think about afterwards. The stories were violent and fragmented and bewildering. Yet she felt a certain kind of power build up in her fingers, a certain kind of thrill and control, and she tore each story into pieces the moment she finished it, disposing of it as an unidentifiable crumple in the kitchen garbage, the ink barely settled on the bottom of the page.

‡

Frances was doing her homework at the kitchen table. It was January, cold. Behind her, through the sliding glass door, were heaps of snow on the porch, the yard, and the playground beyond the fence. The snow was new enough that it hadn't been touched, old enough that it had begun to sink into itself, deflated and wet, like damp pillows in a pile.

What's it this time? asked her mother, who was chopping vegetables at the counter.

Psychology, said Frances. She didn't look up.

Psychology? That's a subject in high school?

Sort of, said Frances. It's called PAS: psychology, anthropology, and sociology. This is the psychology bit.

And what does the psychology bit entail?

Frances sighed, drummed her fingers on the tabletop. You really want to know?

Yes, Frances, said her mother, a tone close to sarcasm curling around her lips. She was cutting carrots now, in groups, the knife pounding, her arm pumping up and down. I really want to know.

Okay, said Frances. She put down her pen. Freud.

Freud? Oh, I remember Freud.

Do you?

From university. Something about mythology, wasn't there? Something about a prince, or a king—

Oedipus.

Yes! Oedipus.

And Electra.

Electra?

There's the Oedipus complex and there's the Electra complex. They're opposites.

Of what?

Each other.

Oh. Her mother frowned as she scooped the carrots into a bowl.

It doesn't matter anyway, said Frances, picking up her pen. It's stupid anyway.

####

Her mother set the table for two. Frances ate her salad and chicken breast in loud, chomping bites, her jaws striking as steadily as her mother's knife had done earlier against the cutting board. Her mother watched from across the table, her fork balanced between finger and thumb, her posture stone-like and her expression immobile.

Frances noticed her look and returned it, eyebrows raised. Their reflections sat dumbly in the glass back door, warped and discoloured in the yellow kitchen light.

The school called today, said her mother.

Frances chewed and chewed, the vegetables exploding between her teeth.

You missed class.

I was sick.

Were you?

Yes. I wasn't feeling well.

And now?

Now I'm fine.

Why the change?

Frances chewed and chewed and chewed.

Frances, said her mother. She put her fork down and raised her fingers to her temples. Stop that.

Stop what?

That noise.

I'm eating.

Well, stop it.

You want me to stop eating?

Stop it.

Frances chewed and chewed and chewed.

Stop it! Frances's mother shrieked. She slammed her hands down onto the table—*bang*—making the utensils clink against the plates and the picture frames snap against the wall.

Frances chewed.

Stop!

Bang

It!

Bang bang

Stop it!

Bang

Frances set her teeth together and swallowed. She pushed her chair back, as if to stand. In her eyes was something distant, something electric.

You liar, said her mother. Her voice was quiet now, her eyes closed. You liar. You aren't sick and you weren't sick. You skipped class for nothing, and now I have to call and what do you want me to say?

I was sick, said Frances. She stared at her mother across the table. I'm telling you I was sick.

You liar, her mother whispered.

I'm sick.

You liar.

Frances put her hands in her lap. She twisted her fingers together, perhaps too tightly, her knuckles knotted, her knuckles turning white.

I'm not the liar, she said. She shook her head. I'm not the liar.

What's that supposed to mean?

I'm not the liar. She shook her head.

What?

I'm not the liar.

Frances, her mother said, shut your mouth.

I'm not.

That's enough.

No.

Frances. Her mother stood and moved around the table in two steps. That's enough.

No. Frances shook her head. I'm not the liar.

Frances!

I'm not the liar.

Shut up! She put her mouth to Frances's ear. Shut up! I'm not.

Shut up. Shut up. Shut up or I'll rip out your hair.

Mom!

Shut up or I'll put you outside. I'll take off your clothes and I'll put you out there and I'll watch you freeze.

Mom.

Shut up.

##

Without confrontation, without confession or bickering or fights, without hardly any communication, Frances applied for a shared room in Western University's residence. She took out a student loan from the government, she made use of the money her father had begun to deposit into her bank account for tuition payments, and she packed two suitcases, nearly everything she owned, leaving only her journals in the closet—they were too heavy and bulky to bring, too sentimental to throw away. She took the bus across town to the university, where she shook hands with her new roommate and settled in, placing her clothes in the drawers and her books on the shelf and her posters and photographs on the walls. She turned on the lamp and lay down and thought about her mother alone in that house for the first time. Her mind moved strangely to the old man who had lived in the house before them, who had died on the toilet and smelled like vinegar, and she wondered vaguely how she remembered these details, where that memory had sprung from. Then she fell asleep, her mind turned black, and she didn't think of anything at all.

※

Mice was what she should have thought, but she didn't think *mice*. Mice were what lived in walls. Mice were what scratched in walls. Mice were what shuffled around behind walls, rubbed their little bodies against walls, sniffed their brown or black or pink noses at walls. But Frances didn't think *mice*. She thought bigger. She thought *creature*. She thought—although she wouldn't admit it consciously to herself—*monster*.

Frances was sitting in bed with a book open in front of her. It had been a week, maybe two, sometime in the *after*, since the tapping in the wall had begun. She couldn't remember getting into her bed or opening the book. She couldn't remember reading, she couldn't read now. It was dark (had she been reading in the dark?), and the words on the pages weren't really words but smudges, swirls, and scribbles, and behind these smudges, swirls, and scribbles was the sound. Perhaps the sound was what had woken her. (Had she been sleeping?) The sound was like grinding wood, like clay being put through a paper shredder.

Frances put the book aside, pulled her body from the bed, the blankets, and put out her hand. The sound from the wall, coming, as always, from the wall. From inside it, from behind it. She put her ear against it.

No, lower.

Lower.

She moved her face down the wall, the house cool, caressing her skin. Frances put her palm against the wall. Her cheek.

Here. Here.

She heard the scratching against her ear. She lifted her fingers and looked at her nails—longer than she remembered, stretching out half an inch past her fingertips. She lifted these fingers and curled them, pressed the heel of her hand into the wall, and scratched back.

The scratching on the other side stopped. Frances pulled her hand away, stared at the wall, and listened.

She waited. She imagined some furry thing tucked in the dirt just a few inches from her face. She clicked her fingernails against the floor, breathed. She had only just relaxed, just decided to scratch again, to see if the thing on the other side would respond, when

Bang

the sound of a sledgehammer filled the room, a slam, a brick, a punch, a kick.

Bang

Frances felt it in her skull, felt the echo knocking around inside her head. She skidded backward across the floor to the side of the bed, nearly to the closet, propelling herself with the heels of her feet, and held her hair. Her fingernails pulled against her scalp.

Bang

Bang

Bang

Frances held her ears, held her eyes, but still felt the sound beneath the floorboards, still heard the sound behind her eye sockets, in between her teeth. She watched as the wall buckled with each *bang* toward her, bending inward, displacing dust, the ceiling rattling, the lampshade on her bedside table shaking.

Let me tell you a story, she thought. She thought in her grandfather's voice.

Let me tell you a story. (She was back in Nilestown in her bed, waiting for her mother to come home.) It might scare you because it's true. (She was back in Nilestown on the back deck, sitting between her grandfather's knees.) Let me tell you about the Blue Man who lived in the cellar. He used the cupboard down there as his bed and the old toy bucket as his bathroom.

Bang—bang—bang

But why was he blue?

Let me tell you. That's part of the story. He was blue because

Bang

he used to be a very little boy, almost a baby. And when he was this little boy he lived in the house and he snuck down into the cellar, because his mother told him not to, and because this was where the toy bucket was.

Bang

And his mother couldn't find him. He hid for a long time and then got bored and tried to leave, but the cellar steps were too high for him to climb. So he looked around, and he found the metal bin that caught drips during storms, and it was full from the last rainfall, and as he was watching his reflection he lost his balance and fell in, fell *through his reflection*, and he was hardly more than a baby, remember, and he couldn't get out

Bang

and he turned blue.

Bang bang bang

And he turned blue, but here's the trick, here's the real point of everything: he still grew up down there, in the cellar, even though he had turned blue. He grew up into the Blue Man and lived there a long time. He used the cupboard as his bed and the old toy bucket as his bathroom. And he never came out of the cellar even though he was grown and could climb the stairs now, because he knew his mother wouldn't recognize him, and wouldn't that be worse than anything. So he lived there and pretended he was little, and if you go down at night maybe you'll hear him crying, because he grew up and no one saw him grow. Because he's old now and still blue, and nothing ever changed, not really, and isn't that worse than anything, isn't that bad enough to make you want to die.

Bang bang

And Frances, who was young now, who had imagined herself young and out on the back deck with her grandfather, said, Grandpa, I don't like that story, I don't

Bang—bang

like it, I don't

Bang

want to hear it again.

<hr/>

Frances didn't think *mice*, even though *mice* is maybe what she should have thought if she had been thinking clearly. Because if she had been thinking clearly, she would have excused the bangs from the other side of the wall as nighttime imaginings, as the stuff of nightmares, and she would have wished it all away. She would have remembered that these things couldn't happen, because without explanation they couldn't happen, and without explanation they disappeared, or took on the shape of mice, and squeaked and sniffed and died.

But Frances was not thinking clearly.

SEVENTEEN

Frances was still a virgin upon entering university. It was something she hadn't thought much about, but it became a continual concern after moving into residence and discovering that sex was a regularly occurring and fairly casual topic of conversation for everyone living on her floor.

Throughout high school, though she'd had shifting but consistent crushes on boys, and rather disorienting feelings for girls that grew to more than admiration, Frances had only been in two real relationships.

The first was with a boy named Ricky, whose self-proclaimed trademark was eating pizza folded in half like a sandwich. It didn't last long. They went to the movies, they kissed maybe three times. At about the same time that Frances began to resent their dates, his sticky breath and quick smile, Ricky told her he had feelings for someone else. This almost made Frances angry, almost for a moment, but in the end she was grateful she didn't have to break up with him herself.

Her second relationship was with Timothy, a boy to whom she was kind in math class and who followed her around during lunch break until the rest of the school decided they were dating. She had gone along with it for a while, even allowing him to kiss her in the hallway as other students glanced surreptitiously from where they stood at their lockers. (Timothy was much shorter than Frances, and to see them kiss was a strange spectacle: Timothy craning upward like a long-necked bird, eagerly, almost beseeching, and Frances sloping downward to touch his lips, briefly and gently, with her own.) Frances liked having someone who admired her so openly, who listened to her, and she believed she was doing something good, something almost sacrificial by letting Timothy into her life. Then she heard, from another boy, that Timothy had been telling his gym class about how he touched her, about the number of times and the ways in which they had had sex. Frances felt much angrier than she'd ever expected she could be—yet at the same time she felt numb, as if her limbs had disappeared from her torso. At the end of the school day, when Timothy met Frances at her locker to say goodbye, she didn't feel her fingers as she grabbed him by the collar and told him she had never liked him, that she felt sick when she kissed him. She didn't feel her hands as she released him, didn't wait around for the other students to drift away, embarrassed, as Timothy started to cry.

When Frances moved into residence, she was still more or less uninterested in the act of sex itself but felt it to be an obligation, a route of access into the social world. She downloaded Tinder, and one evening when her roommate was out with friends, she brought a stocky, lumbering boy with tattoos on his arms up to her room. He tried to talk to her, to kiss her, but Frances explained that she wasn't interested in getting to know him, that she wouldn't likely be seeing him again. The boy, hurt, proceeded to undress, and neither of them much enjoyed the next twenty minutes they spent together.

But Frances was satisfied with her decision. She felt she was now in a place—away from home, starting university, and no longer sexually ignorant—where her life could truly begin.

Her degree, she decided after her first year, would be in English literature with a minor in psychology. Job prospects with an English degree were slim, she knew, but she had always been good at writing, had always felt released and powerful with her pen on a page, and she frankly couldn't imagine doing anything else. She dove into her courses at a maddening pace, tearing through books voraciously, hungrily, and found herself, for the first time since childhood, hopeful. It was an emotion she had always known to be dangerous, a mindset she had always warned herself not to entertain. But this time she didn't listen. This time, she thought, might be different.

Surely it was hope that led her through her first three years of university, from a residence that was lonely and loud to her basement room in the house on Ford Crescent. Surely it was hope that made her go to class even after she stopped eating and felt dizzy walking up the stairs. Surely it was hope that made her text her mother to tell her everything was all right, hope that made her look out the living room window when she couldn't find the energy to go outside. Surely it was hope that existed in these small acts of resistance. Surely it was hope, though it was so minuscule and voiceless and deformed that even Frances, in those moments, could no longer recognize it.

EIGHTEEN

What do you do when you hear scratching in the wall and there's nothing but earth beside it?

Really, what do you do?

You tell someone. You tell someone and you get them to come and listen, and if they hear what you hear, you know it's real. Because that's how reality is qualified, by shared experience, by communal agreement. This is how you know that the scratching in the wall isn't just scratching in your head. This is how you know for sure.

But what if there's no one to tell? And what if it's dark—dark-dark like that blinding, black quality of your childhood nightmares? What if the walls are dark and the window is dark, the rooms are dark because it's always night? What if the window won't open and it only looks onto a square of snowy backyard, locked in by hedges—what if the door at the top of the stairs won't open either? What if nothing will open for you, and here you are with your brain and bones, and also the scratching? What do you do? When it's been days or weeks, what do you do? When it's been months? When it's not always just scratching but banging, when covering your ears doesn't help, and covering your mouth doesn't stop the retching, because the banging seems to flood up from your stomach? It's fear, an outsider watching would call it fear, but it feels like nausea, like acid under your tongue, like cold hands against your neck, like a hunching of your whole body, like your joints have disappeared, and everything—limbs and cartilage, blood and muscle—buckles together. Fear, after weeks of feeling it, is a fog between your eyes. It shows itself minutely, as a crease between the eyebrows. Here you are and here also is the scratching.

What, then, do you do?

This is what Frances did. She went out to the kitchenette in the dark. She opened the drawers and fumbled through the extra utensils until she found, as she knew she would because she had watched Ky put it there when they first moved in, a long, serrated breadknife. She brought it back to her bedroom.

In that shadowy light from the bedroom doorway, leaking in from the bedroom window, she was a drifting, amorphous shape, the lines of her body dripping off into the walls and floor, her hair like a floating haze around her face, like some ghostly mane. The only definable parts about her were those that caught and reflected the light. Her eyes sat glassy in her skin, as round as the tops of lollipops. If you looked closely you might see her nails extending out of her sweater sleeves like abnormally long fingers, stiff but somehow jointless as they spiralled toward her palm. And the knife in her hand, a wedge of silver, a slice out of the darkness, hovering as if suspended in front of her body.

Frances sat on the floor in front of the wall, and although she couldn't hear any scratching, she knew exactly where to place the knife, to press and turn and force the knife. She had placed her hand there many times before, had felt the many vibrations and bangs. She worked with the knife, back and forth, carving in circles, until she cut a small hole in the drywall. Into this hole she was able to grind and scrape, to plunge, and then she was able to saw with the serrated edge of the blade, moving in and out, her wrist burning with the effort, through the insulation and into what should have been cement but wasn't—into emptiness, into openness, an open nothingness beyond the drywall. She took the knife away and placed her eye against the hole, but it was black, black, black: as black as sleep against her eye. And cold. A stab of icy air hit her eyeball. She blinked and pulled away. She pressed two fingers into the hole and wiggled them, fiddled with the sticky insulation. She felt, on the inside, long divots gouged out of the drywall. These divots were deep and frayed up at the edges.

If you did that with your fingernails, you would bleed, thought Frances. *If you did that with your fingernails, you wouldn't have fingernails anymore.*

Frances pulled her hand away from the wall.

Frances surfaced to a shushing sound, a shifting. She looked up from her bed to the dull grey square of window, trying to distinguish through it the shape of something outside— anything—a tree, a lump of snow, a blade of brown-stained grass. Anything to confirm the outside world, to confirm a world outside herself. The window was nearly opaque, only dark and grey, only layers of shade, only curtains of smudge and fog pressing into the basement.

She heard it again: a soft shifting, like limbs moving against each other under blankets. Frances lifted herself on an elbow and turned toward the sound.

It was coming from the wall on the other side of the room.

She saw, as a moving shadow in the dark, a cluster of fingers poking through the hole she had made. The fingers were long and pale, much too long and pale. They waved like lazy antennae, feeling the air in a wide circle around the opening.

Frances rolled from the bed, the blankets trailing behind her onto the floor. She shuffled on her knees to the wall. She reached out, reaching without thinking, without wondering, and touched the fingers with her own.

They retracted, like snail eyes, back into the wall.

Frances waited, but the hole remained silent and motionless and dark.

NINETEEN

From a dark wood, Frances was emerging. Like a girl in a fairy tale, like Gretel following bread crumbs thrown long ago by someone she couldn't remember, a past self, wary, suspicious on entering these woods. Like a girl in a fairy tale, emerging from these woods.

Long ago, when she went to buy shoes before the start of school, she'd asked, *What will hurt me, Grandma?* Pine cones were the only things Frances could imagine hurting her feet.

Sharp and hard things, responded her grandmother vaguely, finding her granddaughter's question inconsequential, thinking it only natural that children should not know how they will be hurt.

What will hurt me? Frances had wondered when her mother came home late from work, shifting into their bed, the sound of her breathing filling the room, the texture of her breath in the room.

What will hurt me? with Jasper on the tire swing.

What could hurt me? when she leaned into the hardness of her father's arms.

From a dark wood, Frances was emerging. She felt light now in her hunger, feather-thin. She was soft now, every part of her soft and hollow. When her feet touched the floor, they didn't walk, they glided. Her skin, covered in soft tufts of hair. Her skin so thin, finally, finally no weight upon her. Finally no thoughts upon her, no worries, only air inside her head. And air inside her room, dark air that she could push her fingers through, cold air, air as cold as drifts of snow piling up around her bed, pouring out—almost palpably pouring out—from the hole in the wall.

What will hurt me? Frances asked.

All of this will hurt you, her grandmother should have said. She should have said, *There is nothing here that won't hurt you.*

So many things her parents, her grandparents had done to protect her, so many things they had said. But protection is not preparation, and Frances had not been prepared.

Frances was not prepared.

The moon, soft on her toes: this is what she remembered. Moonlight, soft, weaving between her toes. In Nilestown and the townhouse in London, in her bed and almost asleep, barely conscious, the moonlight a tickle, a tickle like a father's playful fingers, a mother's cupped hands, on her toes. How the snow looked with Jasper inside of it, disappearing in an oversized winter coat. She remembered the wrinkles of her grandfather's jaw against candlelight, jowls waggling.

Do you know how to tell a story?

She remembered the beginning, and here she was at the end.

She thought of her grandfather saying, *I hadn't even gotten to the best part. Not the scariest part, but the best.*

And her grandmother. *Ideas are different with Frances.*

Ideas are different with Frances.

They start as a seed in the centre of your brain. They find this weakness in your bone.

She had thought, consciously or not, *monster*. She was not prepared.

She woke from a dark wood, a dream in which she had been walking in a dark, dark wood.

The room was dark around her. She heard a sound of shuffling, of shifting, as of limbs being rearranged. Or maybe it was the sound of leaves shuffling, shifting at the tops of trees. Hadn't she just been walking?

Was she sleeping? Had she been dreaming?

Was this dreaming?

She could hear shuffling, shifting. She sat up and looked at the hole in the wall, the hole that she had made with the breadknife, the breadknife that was discarded to the side. The desk, the toppled books—all lumbering shapes in the dark room, indistinct, her own hand indistinct in front of her. And continually this shuffling, this shifting.

She looked at the hole in the wall, and in the dim light from the window she could see something moving there: the movement of some kind of body, pale and pushing at this hole in the wall, fingers much too long and pale, pale and worm-like, with fingernails like hardened shells, emerging.

Waving. Like snail eyes waving.

(She had thought this was a dream, fingers waving like snail eyes and then retracting as she touched them.)

Not a dream, and here it was, the not-dream, the real. Here *she* was. More awake than she had been in the last four months, since coming down into the basement, snapped awake by a rise of bile in her throat.

She watched the fingers turn and grab drywall, chunks of drywall snapping off, a puff of dust, and disappearing into the dark vacuum behind the wall. A black space, that hole expanding as another hand pushed out to help the first, pulling back, breaking down this barrier.

The hole like a mouth widening.

The hole like an eye opening.

Arms, up to their elbows reaching out, grappling with the drywall. Faster, grasping, desperate, as desperate as hunger, starvation. Frances noticed something wrong with these arms: not only were the fingers long but the limbs also, joints bulging, the muscles beneath the skin bulging, and the skin itself white, white as untouched snow, albino-white, skin never touched by sunlight. And the skin was also sore-looking, flayed, thin papery patches peeling off and revealing pinkish-red beneath.

Like the decayed siding of a house, Frances thought, in what little space her brain had left to think.

Like the paint stripping off a house, skin stripping off a house.

This hole in the wall had widened, a lidless eye opening, a toothless mouth gaping. The white arms slid back into the wall, and from the depths of the hole came a nearly imperceptible movement, a shuffling, a shifting. An adjustment.

Then a head began to emerge, bald and white, spotted with red sores.

Frances held back vomit, watching the head emerge like a bulge of pus and blood erupting from skin. Like a thing that has ripped open its own birth canal, the head slumped to the bedroom floor, followed by its body, a pile of bent joints, similarly white and flayed—hairless, naked.

The thing lay still. Frances thought of screaming, but she had screamed before and no one had heard. She had banged before, bellowed and scratched before, and no one had heard. For years no one had heard her. From the beginning of everything, from the starting point of her very self, no one had heard. Where could she go? The basement door, that outside world, was locked to her. Where could she run?

Her body knew it before her brain did. *There is nowhere left to run.*

Frances sat in her bed, unmoving. Silent as in a game of hide-and-seek. Her jaws open, breath moving in and out. Frances, with nowhere left to run, was motionless.

The thing on the floor was motionless, the body motionless—or Frances had thought it was motionless, but now she noticed movement. The skin on its scalp was *flexing, wrinkling, stretching*, like when ears are pulled back, like when eyebrows are raised. She saw now the movement came from the thing's face, its face pressed to the floor, something moving in its face: jaws working, up and down, a muffled wet sound of saliva, of chewing, as if trying to—

Eat. But as the thing raised its head, Frances saw that it had no mouth. No face at all, no eyes, no ears, no nostrils, only a lump for a nose, only a long plane of white skin splotched with raw pink patches like splashes of paint, these patches ringed with more raw skin, dry skin sticking up like flaps of torn paper. Frances watched the jaws moving under the skin, up and down, a muffled wet sound of saliva, a grinding, a moan reaching up from the throat, as if trying to—

Speak. As if trying to speak. Frances, frozen in her bed, watched the creature hunch, elbows bent like an insect, drag itself across the floor. It stumbled, fell to its side, and righted itself, limbs twisting, buckling, like a newborn foal swaying, joints giving way. The thing searched along the floor with its long fingers, wrapped its hand momentarily around the bedpost—Frances, in the bed, shuddered, completely silent, as in a game of hide-and-seek, watching the monster searching, probing, feeling cold relief roll over her, seeing that it couldn't see. It had no eyes, it couldn't see her, it couldn't look and see her.

Could it hear her? It had no ears.

Could it smell her? Like an animal, smell her? It had no nose.

It could touch her, this much was certain. She listened to the sticky sound of its fingertips searching lightly, dappling along the floor, a sound like pebbles being dropped in still water, and imagined the pale, frog-like fingers touching her. If she stayed very still, if it touched her, would it distinguish her from the rest of the furniture? If she imagined herself invisible—

Frances's thoughts, buzzing almost loud enough for the creature's non-ears to hear, were cut off by something metal, something hard skidding across the floor. In terror, she remembered the breadknife. In terror, the knife she had left by the desk, the toppled books.

Don't touch me or I'll kill you, I'll take off all your skin—

This voice, this child's voice, building up into her throat, piling up on the back of her tongue. This voice shrieking from deep inside of her, like a gag, a reflex—*Don't touch me or I'll stuff your mouth with dirt—*

The thing—with the knife now in its hand—stood. It was monstrously tall in the middle of the room. It swayed, hairless, faceless, naked. Closer now, Frances saw that it had no genitals, nothing definable, only a white plane of skin wrapping between its legs. Like a non-human, it swayed. An almost-human, the idea of a human. It raised the knife—

Do you know how to tell a story? the child voice inside her shrieked. *Do you know how to make it good? I have eaten all the books from the bookshelf, I have pulled out the hair from my head.*

Raised the knife—

I can't remember if I'm already dead.

(Was this dreaming?)

Raised the knife and plunged it between its own jaws, breaking apart the white plane of skin there. A harsh ripping noise, a wet snapping noise. The breadknife in its face, the creature began to saw with the serrated edge.

*Don't touch me or I'll take off all your skin—*this voice bucked up inside of her, like vomit, vinegar vomit bucking up to her mouth—*Don't touch me or I'll kill you—*and her grandfather's voice, *This woman, she cut off her hands.*

The monster's hands were around the knife handle, sawing with the serrated edge.

This woman, she cut out her tongue.

The monster had made a cut, but there was no blood. Only its skin, split and flayed, ragged lips around—yes, Frances could see now—teeth.

The creature tried its jaws, the hinges rough, slow as if rusted, but functional. A hot gurgle rose from its mouth, a moan, a gasp and almost-laugh, a flash of red tongue, saliva.

The creature brought the knife to its nose.

The creature brought the knife to its ears, to its eyes.

Don't touch me or I'll pull out your eyes and I'll cut off your feet, don't you dare— This woman, she cut off her feet, she cut off her hands and her tongue. She cut out her eyes.

But how could she cut off her tongue if her hands were gone? Frances asked. *How could she cut out her eyes?*

The monster had started with its mouth. That's where it had stuck the knife: into its mouth, or what soon became its mouth. Because that's where the knife should be stuck, without hesitation and deeply, right up against our teeth, if we are advanced enough to have teeth. It had cut into that skin and opened a gash, and from this gash came a moan, a black shriek, a laugh, all at once and garbled. Frances heard earthworms in that laugh. She heard a buildup of saliva that fell from the lips into the throat and gurgled, if you could call the skin on either side of the tear lips, if you could call that tunnel a throat.

Next it punctured nostrils, two quick jabs into the centre of its face. And Frances heard it breathing, heard it inhale into the back of its head. Next the ears, two crescent cuts, then the eyes, and with these it was more delicate, its long fingers wrapped full, firm, around the knife, slitting in the skin, eyelids, minutely too far apart. The creature dropped the knife. With its fingers it split the slits open and looked with what couldn't be called eyeballs, with what were red jelly with black circles in the middle. The creature looked around the room with its fingers spread apart to keep the eye slits from closing.

It's right, Frances thought, in that one mad moment before it spotted her, *the creature is right, it did it right.* You start with your mouth and finish with your eyes, and with the eyes you are careful, and with the eyes you hold them open, and look around and see and keep looking. You finish here and you put the knife down and you hope that you have cut deep enough. And you hope that it will be enough, this cutting. And you hold your eyes open. Keep looking.

Frances shifted to the end of the bed and stood on the floor. Frances, who knew in both her mind and body that there was nowhere left to run, shifted to the end of the bed and stood on the bedroom floor, this basement floor.

Despite this knowledge, *there is nowhere left to run*, Frances stood. Despite this hopelessness, Frances stood.

There is nowhere left to run, said the adult inside of her. Frances the child, the little girl, all that was left, stood. She stood, and she ran.

Outside the house, it had started to snow.

PART TWO

WAKING

ONE

It was the last snowfall of winter—a thick snowfall, a numbing snowfall, tapping wetly on the windows—when Ky decided to go into the basement.

It had been a long winter. It had been a dark winter. To Ky, each winter felt longer and darker than the last. She couldn't remember feeling this length, this darkness, as a child. Never this period of waiting. When had it begun? As if waking from a dream, she had noticed the shortened days, the nearly six months of cloud-covered sky. The snow was a facade of brightness, a fake opposite to darkness, swallowing colour, swallowing sound—cold, numb, and quiet.

She had lived in London all her life. When had the city changed for her? Inside buildings and cars, she felt stifled, overheated. The early sunset, imperceptible behind the cloud cover, gnawed at her brain. The roads thick with slush, her body wrapped in damp winter clothing, wind like razor blades scratching at the skin of her neck, her face. The long and pillowed expanse of sky.

Now—suddenly, it seemed—it was the last week of March. Soon classes would end, soon springtime, soon exams. Soon graduation, and then—?

Jobs at research facilities, universities, in London or Toronto, as her parents had expected. Entry-level positions for which she was qualified but for which her competitors, she suspected, were overqualified: people who had completed master's programs, maybe PhDs.

The last couple of months had been harrowing. Along with finishing schoolwork and maintaining her grades, Ky had written resumés and cover letters, done company research, kept track of application deadlines, and attended scattered interviews, mostly over video chat online, mostly formal, dry, and discouraging. *We are sorry for the inconvenience, but we can only notify successful candidates.* She felt sick during the indefinite period of waiting after each interview, falling into what was, she admitted to her closest friends—namely Katie and Reese, her roommates—a depressive episode.

She didn't receive a single job offer. She didn't tell her parents. And with this failure came a feeling unfamiliar to her. A taste of bitterness, disappointment, at the back of her throat. Her first real bitterness, her first real disappointment, compounding somehow—although these disappointments had only recently arisen—with the length and darkness of winter.

When had the city changed for her? Its alteration was insidious, creeping, and then abrupt, all at once. Abrupt darkness, like a blanket thrown over a lamp.

As a child, she had experienced winter as a sprinkling of Christmas lights around the Old North neighbourhood where her parents lived. Winter was tobogganing in Doidge Park, building snowmen with her friends, and occasionally—those jumping, electric moments!—listening to the radio in the early morning to hear if school was cancelled for the day, the snow too high to pull the car out of the driveway. She remembered the hard grip of her father's hand on her own as he taught her how to shovel. She remembered skating in Victoria Park, the delicate cream colour of the skates on her feet, the icy air seeping into mittens, then the thawing warmth of the bathwater when she got home. She remembered the long drive to her family's cottage on March break, trundling down a pitch-black path at nighttime to listen to the ice crack on the frozen lake.

Ky searched for dissatisfaction in those memories, a hint of trauma, some gloom settling over the scene like twilight insistent on the horizon. Her childhood might have been too perfect, she thought; everything came too easily. Perhaps she would have done better with a proper education on suffering. She felt herself circling an important truth, the heart of the issue, something raw that made her brain skirt away. *No*, she thought. *No, the trauma must be deep.*

Or perhaps, she thought, this change in her, this depressive episode, had no foreshadowing. Maybe it was only her recent disappointments that made the house and city dismal, her depression palpable on the winter streets. She felt stunted, strangled by lethargy to near-immobility. As she forced herself through final assignments, research papers, and presentations, she routinely chided then forgave herself for this lack of energy.

At the same time, behind all of this sluggishness, this inertia, was a dull buzz of anticipation, like a live wire sputtering. School was ending, a new life beginning. The idea burst like a sunspot in her brain. A new life. A real life! She felt alternately suffocated by this idea and exhilarated by it. The idea of a career, a title. Eventually a house, a dog, maybe—a husband? What would come with this official establishment of herself? An establishment that, despite her recent disappointments, was inevitable. What would come with the concreting of herself as a person? What opportunities would open to her? She didn't know. She couldn't imagine.

But first, this period of waiting. This depressive episode she must endure.

Outside was the last snowfall of winter, a thick snowfall, tapping wetly on the living room window. Ky sat on the couch, looking out the window at the grey yard, the grey, slushy road. Ford Crescent. Three years in this house, and it would all be over soon. In her lap was a basket of dirty laundry, two weeks' worth at least. Chores had fallen to the wayside in the wake of assignments and job applications. She huffed at the prospect of going down into the basement to do her laundry. Laundry was the only reason she ever went into the basement. She hated it down there, hated the low ceilings and lack of windows, hated the yellow light and strange, musty smell that seemed to emanate from everywhere, from the sinks and walls, the rugs and bookshelf, and the rarely changed garbage in the bathroom. Most of all she hated—

Seeing Frances.

She had almost thought, *encountering Frances*, in the way you encounter a bear in the woods or the way women in old Victorian novels encounter shrouds in Gothic hallways, ghosts.

Ky nearly laughed at herself.

Frances was no wild animal, no ghost. She was merely uncanny, Ky decided, in the same way that ghosts are: Frances was someone familiar, someone Ky had lived with for three years. And yet she knew nothing about Frances or her history, she had spent no significant time with her. She still felt uncomfortable saying hello to Frances when they crossed paths in the kitchen. Whenever she saw Frances, she still felt her own face contort into the tight, disingenuous smile she tended to throw at people she didn't want to speak to. Although she tried to dissuade herself and use more sensitive language—Ky tried, even in her thoughts, to use more sensitive language—her rare meetings with Frances were still, very much, *encounters*.

Ky turned her face from the window, the wet snow tapping, and looked toward the kitchen and the basement staircase beyond. She toyed with her laundry, pulling fabric through her fingers, and listened to the silence of the house.

TWO

Ky had last seen Frances more than a week ago.

Ky was in the kitchen scooping almond-milk ice cream into a bowl, a late-night snack to accompany an episode of *The Office* before bed. It was a reward, really, after a long day of classes and studying—she had even gone for a run in the late afternoon.

Mid-scoop, she heard a noise behind her—the basement door opening—and she turned to see Frances in the doorway, her eyes squinting, almost closed against the kitchen light.

Ky's first thought had been, *Was she waiting there for me?* She hadn't heard Frances come up the stairs. Frances must have been standing just behind the door the whole time, listening.

"You alright?" asked Ky.

Frances looked haggard, but this wasn't particularly unusual. Since Ky had known her, she had always been uncoordinated, careless with her hair and makeup, dressed sloppily—inattentively, Ky corrected herself, amateurishly. Throughout the last couple of months, those habits had worsened. Ky had noticed body odour lingering in rooms where Frances had recently been, in the basement especially. She had also noticed grease nearly as thick as paint in Frances's hair, and dark stains on Frances's clothing—once, what she had suspected was vomit.

But it was the end of the school year and everyone was having a hard time—chores had fallen to the wayside in the wake of assignments and job applications, after all. And considering Frances's occasional rough patches, as she and Katie and Reese liked to call them, none of this was particularly unusual.

Wasn't it so much easier, said a voice at the back of Ky's mind, *wasn't it so very convenient, that none of this was particularly unusual?*

Frances stood in the basement doorway, her skin shining with grease, her lips chapped, and her eyes sunken darkly into her skull. She wore a long-sleeved T-shirt and pyjama pants—baggy clothing that made her wrists and neck look minuscule, breakable, where they poked out of the sleeves and collar. A smell drifted toward Ky, not just the smell of body odour but the damp, unmistakable smell of the basement, which must have woven itself into Frances's pores, into the fabric of her clothes.

"You alright?" asked Ky again.

Frances shuffled past her into the kitchen and began opening cupboards, drawers, the fridge door. She touched the peanut butter, a loaf of bread in a plastic bag, a carton of milk, touched them and then pulled her hand away, rummaging, pushing things aside. As she bent over, Ky saw the lumps of her vertebrae beneath her shirt.

"Frances?" said Ky. "Hello? Looking for something?"

"What?" said Frances, turning around. She stared at Ky, blinking like a bug with magnified eyeballs, her pupils shrinking rapidly as she faced the light.

Ky felt a chill run through her body. Frances's skin was pale, nearly grey.

"What?" said Frances again.

"Nothing," said Ky. "Sorry."

"What?" said Frances. She turned back and continued pushing through the shelves of the open fridge. Then, without looking at Ky or pausing in her rigid, rapid movements—opening a drawer and closing it, unscrewing the lid off a pickle jar and twisting it back on—she began speaking, saying, "What? Who, me? I'm fine. I'm fine. Just tired. Just hungry. Just need some sleep. I've been awake for ages."

There was a slow, slurred, dream-like quality to her words. Ky realized that Frances must be sleepwalking. Frances must not know what she was saying, what she was doing. Frances must be dreaming.

"Who, me?" Frances continued, as if hearing Ky's thoughts, as if responding to them. "I've been awake for ages."

"Frances," said Ky, reaching forward to touch her shoulder. "I think you're sleeping. I think you should go back to bed."

Frances straightened up to look at her. "What?" she said.

"You're sleeping," blustered Ky. "You're sleepwalking. Go back to bed."

Frances swayed for a moment in the middle of the kitchen.

On an impulse, Ky slung her arm across Frances's back and pushed her toward the basement doorway. "It's okay," she said. "Just go to bed. Just go back to sleep."

Frances nodded groggily, a word—"What?"—sliding from her lips. Her breath, up close, was rank, sour.

Ky helped her through the doorway and down onto the first step. She guided her hand to the bannister. "Go back to sleep," she said. "It's okay."

The basement was dark. Down below, at the bottom of the stairs, Ky could see no hint of light, just the final step leading into blackness. The smell of must, possibly mould, rose up into her nose and mixed with the smell of Frances's breath, making Ky think of vomit, of rotting acid, of stomachs churning, digesting.

She let go of Frances's shoulder and stepped away from the staircase. Frances looked back at her, her grey skin blending now with shadows, making sense in the context of darkness. She looked back at Ky and a flicker passed over her face, a flicker almost of recognition, of waking, consciousness rising into her eyes, her lips tensing, nostrils flaring, a look of alarm, confusion, surprise.

"Go to bed," said Ky quickly. She shut the basement door. Then she stepped back and leaned against the refrigerator, staring at the closed door, listening. It was a long moment, almost a minute, before she heard the sound of Frances descending the stairs.

Ky exhaled. *Fucking psycho*, she thought, and then corrected herself. Or tried to. She stopped her thought and tried to think of an alternative phrase, words to better express—more appropriately express—what she was feeling. What was she feeling? Disgust. The rise of revulsion from her gut. She wished briefly, spasmodically, that there was a lock on the basement door, that she could be sure Frances wouldn't come back up the stairs.

Stop it, she thought.

She stopped thinking, she stopped her thoughts. She took her ice cream, half-melted, and went into her bedroom.

THREE

That was more than a week ago.

Ky sat by the living room window with her laundry in her lap and thought again of going into the basement. Most likely she wouldn't encounter Frances, most likely Frances was sleeping. Frances was often asleep during the daytime.

Ky stood and went into the kitchen. Then she opened the basement door and turned on the light.

Frances was lying at the bottom of the basement stairs.

When Ky saw her, she lost control of the muscles in her hands, her arms. Her laundry basket hit the top step and bounced, flew up into the air, and flung her clothing out in a mad spiral as it descended, hitting step after step and rolling, vomiting up a cardigan here, a pair of ripped jeans there, until it reached the bottom, teetered for a moment, and lay still. On top of Frances. The laundry basket lay still on top of Frances. Halfway down the stairs were a pair of mismatched socks, lying quietly like dead mice. One of Ky's bras was twisted, the cups dented, by her right foot. A striped T-shirt hung off the bannister. Even with the light turned on, the basement was dim, dull, and Frances in her loose-fitting sweater and pyjama pants looked just as inanimate, as limp, deflated, as the clothes scattered down the stairs.

"Frances?" called Ky. Her voice cracked. She couldn't move her arms, but her legs brought her halfway down, stiff beneath her, numb. Coldness, a feeling of freezing, spread in her joints as she approached the place where Frances lay, and with this coldness came a memory flipping through her mind, a memory from the day they first went through the house together: Frances standing at the bottom of the stairs, her arm held out in front of her, feeling the air.

Can you feel that? asked Frances. Right here.

It's cold, said Frances. Right here.

Reese had laughed. Ky could remember her laughing. And Katie had said—what had Katie said?

Maybe it's haunted. With her black humour.

Ky remembered that moment, the stiffness of that moment, as if the air itself had solidified. She usually would have assumed Frances was exaggerating, perhaps looking for attention. Or feeling unwell, as the man showing them the house—the landlord—had suggested. But something in the way Frances trembled, the way her fingers shook at the ends of her hands, the way she gritted her teeth and breathed in shallow gulps, made Ky believe her, made Ky wonder.

Maybe it's haunted, Katie had said.

Haunted only for Frances? Ky had wondered.

Haunted only for Frances?

Now, looking at Frances lying at the base of the stairs, Ky's hands were like chunks of ice hanging off her arms. She felt suddenly frantic, kicking aside her laundry as she went down the remaining steps.

One of her T-shirts had fallen over Frances's face, and she reached down to pick it up, terrified that Frances—lying so still that she must be pretending, that she must be playing some trick—would reach up and grab Ky by the ankle, by the elbow, by the tangled clump of her ponytail. It was in this moment, as Ky pinched the T-shirt and pulled it upward, that she noticed simultaneously Frances's finger-nails—which were long and curled into her palms, which were bent back, broken in places, and crusted with what looked like, what had to be, blood—and an unfamiliar smell rising from Frances's body, a smell of rot and sweat, a smell of urine and feces, that Ky had never smelled on a living thing before. She shrank away, holding her nose, holding the T-shirt in her hand, and looked down at Frances's face.

"Frances?" said Ky, whispered Ky.

Frances's eyes were open. They were dull and opaque, like cloudy marbles in her face. The shadows around her eyes were so deep they looked as if they had been smudged with charcoal. Her skin—pale, near-translucent, the colours of cold, blue, grey—seemed to have stiffened like cement, seemed to have retracted, her lips pulled away from her yellow teeth in what almost looked like a smile, showing gums. Her chin looked pointed—a witch's chin. Her nose looked long—a witch's nose. And maybe this was some magic, some witch's magic, some trick that Ky couldn't understand. It certainly wasn't real.

Ky had never seen anything so absurd.

She started laughing. It bubbled up from her stomach and poured out of her mouth, laughing and laughing, hiccupping and choking, coughing, her abdominal muscles seizing, aching, all while Frances lay on the floor staring blankly, smiling back at her.

Ky noticed now that Frances had raw patches under her chin and on her neck, purple patches of skin stippled with capillaries. She looked again at Frances's fingernails, crusted with dried blood. *She's done this to herself*, she thought, and then the smell hit her again, plunging up into her nostrils, and she leaned over and vomited on the stairs, bile spurting up through her nose. When she recovered, she found that she was crying, sobbing, a scratch-heaving raking up her throat.

She stood, stumbled to the stairs, and pulled herself up by the bannister. She found her cellphone on the kitchen counter. She would never remember what she said to the woman who answered her 911 dial. She would never remember her words: *There is a dead girl in my basement*. She would never admit these words to anyone, never say that in that moment she had forgotten Frances's name.

There is a dead girl in my basement.

She had almost said *thing*. She had almost said, *There is something, there is a dead thing in my basement.*

48 Ford Crescent.

When the woman asked her name, she said, "Ky Johnson. Kaya Johnson." When the woman asked how the girl had died, she said, "What girl?" and the woman on the phone had to remind Ky why she had called 911 in the first place.

"Oh," said Ky, "I'm so sorry. I'm so, so sorry."

"That's alright," said the woman. "Can you tell me how the girl died?"

"I don't know," said Ky. *She's done this to herself.*

"How long has she been dead?" asked the woman.

"I don't know," said Ky. "Oh god, oh god oh god. I don't know."

"Can you find a place to sit down?" asked the woman. "Please find a place to sit down. The paramedics will be there soon."

Ky went into the living room and sat on the couch. She looked out the living room window. It was after three o'clock in the afternoon and four children were trundling down the road, their backpacks huge on their shoulders and their snow pants heavy, sagging on their legs. One balanced on the curb, his arms pointing out like airplane wings from his shoulders. Another scooped up clumps of new snow and sucked it off her mittens. Ky stood and went around to the front door. She went outside in her slippers and onto the road and watched the children until they turned the corner and disappeared. Snow fell on her face and melted on her skin. She didn't feel cold. She didn't hear the sirens until the ambulance and police car turned carefully onto Ford Crescent. They parked on the side of the road.

"Are you Kaya?" asked the man who got out of the police car.

Her hair was wet, it dripped down onto her forehead. There were snowflakes in her clothes. "Yes," she said.

"Can we enter your house?" asked the man. "Can you show us the basement?" A group of paramedics dressed in green-and-white jackets, two men and a woman, came to stand beside the police officer.

"Yes," said Ky. Her voice was far away. Her legs that led her back up the driveway and through the front door were far, far away.

The police officer and paramedics followed her into the house. They followed her into the basement.

FOUR

After Frances was carried out of the house on a stretcher, placed in an ambulance, and driven away, the house was silent. The snow clumped in wet layers on its roof like a misshapen, lumpy hat. The blinds in its windows drooped.

It could have been sleeping—so thought the children walking by the next morning. Those children always envisioned faces in the houses they passed on their way to and from school. They made up stories about these faces, a game they played effortlessly, intuitively: happy faces and grumpy faces, dumb-brick faces. This house, 48 Ford Crescent, was always a closed-up face, folded in, always sleeping.

Maybe the children were right. Maybe the house, sunken snugly into the earth, had been sleeping for years. But now something had changed, something indecipherable. The house now watched from behind half-closed eyelids. The house was conscious. Finally. The house had woken up.

The children didn't notice any change in the house's expression. They walked by, singing songs and watching their boots make indents in the muddy slush on the side of the road. They chased each other, squeezed snowballs in the shallow scoop of their mittens. Back and forth, to school and home again, twice, before the silence of the house was broken.

Two cars pulled into the driveway, another on the side of the road. Three women emerged, and three girls beside them. Ky and Katie and Reese, back for the first time in days. Their mothers huffed, hauling suitcases and large handbags out of the vehicles, stacks of empty boxes. They had come to purge, to pack up their daughters' lives—the U-Haul would pick up the remainder of the furniture later—and bring them home, away from this place that had grown rotten. It had grown, they believed, invisible spores, airborne contagions, like a house filthy with disturbed black mould.

A girl had died here. A girl their daughters' age, in the same stage of life as their daughters, had died here. Not only had she died, but she had lain dead here, undisturbed, undiscovered, for longer than any of them cared to say out loud. Five days at least. Five days in darkness at the bottom of the basement stairs, the shape of bones showing through her skin, starved, shrinking smaller, ever smaller, with death.

The preliminary autopsy report suggested Frances had died of heart failure, weakened from lack of nourishment. The police had found the plastic scraps of a torn-apart vinegar jug in the basement garbage, books ripped from the shelves with shreds of pages, stiff with dried saliva, sprinkled across the couch and rug. They had found clumps of hair on the bathroom floor, streaks of brown blood and missing paint from the back of the basement door. Frances hadn't eaten. She had starved herself, probably started to hallucinate. There were sores on Frances's body, raw purple patches of skin where she had scratched herself until she bled. Frances's fingernails and toenails were untrimmed, long and beginning to curl. Her teeth were fuzzy with plaque. Her mouth was dry, tongue withdrawn, grey, and foul-smelling when the coroner shone his flashlight between her jaws.

Like priests with holy water, the mothers of Ky, Katie, and Reese had come to exorcise, to purge, and then depart. The knowledge of Frances's death had plagued them the last three nights, a haunting that kept them from sleep. And here they hoped to dispel this haunting, rid themselves of this disturbance, this knowledge of Frances's death. Especially this knowledge that Frances had lain dead for five days at least while their daughters lived above her, walked on the floor above her, used the bathroom and slept in their beds, did their homework, ate their food while Frances's rot—dared they think it?—while Frances's rot seeped up through the floorboards and under the basement door.

A silent contaminant, this death.

The mothers hoisted the empty boxes, the handbags, up onto their hips. Behind them they dragged the suitcases. They moved steadily, laboriously, toward the front door.

The house, now conscious, watched them.

Ky and Katie and Reese lagged behind their mothers. Their boots were heavy like stones beneath them. They hadn't slept much either.

Since the news of Frances's death, the girls had been barraged by police officers, local news reporters, and academic counsellors from the university.

The academic counsellors asked, "What will your next steps be? How would you like to proceed?"

And the police officers, stoic but betraying incredulity, asked, "You never once went into the basement this last week, never even looked down the stairs?" Asked, but were careful not to accuse, "What did you think Frances was doing down there? Didn't you wonder why she never came up, never left the house?"

The girls could only give the most blunt, the most dumbfounded, replies. "I don't know. I didn't think." They didn't say, *I didn't care*.

And the news reporters asked, "Were you aware of Frances's history of mental illness? You lived with her for nearly three years. Did you notice any unconventional behaviour prior to this incident? Any cries for help?"

"I don't know. I didn't think." *I didn't care*.

FIVE

They tried to go to class the day after Frances was found dead.

Ky and Reese didn't think that, by midday, nearly every person on campus would have heard the news—that people would be looking at them when they entered the room, inspecting them while their backs were turned. They didn't realize their professors would pull them aside to offer condolences after class.

But Katie had expected this. Katie stared back at her classmates until they looked away. Katie brushed off her professors' advances. Katie had read the word *trauma* in the emails from academic counsellors, she'd read the word *shock*, and she'd thought, *Fuck your trauma. Fuck your shock.*

She didn't get upset, didn't experience shock from accidents she saw on the news, from people dying a city away or across the world, from children kidnapped by perverts, pedophiles, from schools and churches shot up in the US, bombs going off in the Middle East. Katie hardly flinched when other students from the university died—when, for example, a girl in first year had been struck by a drunk driver while walking to the gym in the evening. Katie certainly hadn't been offered aid from academic counselling then. How was this different?

She hadn't known Frances at all, had hardly spoken more than ten words to her since they moved into the house on Ford Crescent, hadn't invited her to parties or study groups at the library. And Frances hadn't been the most sociable either. She had kept to herself, to the basement. She only came upstairs to grab food from the fridge or rush off to class. So what if Katie didn't know what was going on in Frances's life?

All of these emails, messages, phone calls from family and friends, all of the inquiries and condolences felt like insults to Katie's logic and stability, her resolve. *Fuck your trauma*, she thought. *Fuck your shock*. She even said it aloud—"Fuck's sake!"—when a group of students inadvertently blocked the aisle on her way out of class.

She knew what her next steps would be. She was three weeks from finishing her schoolwork, less than three months from receiving her diploma. Soon she would be out of this place, this city. She had already arranged to room with one of her brothers until she found a job in Toronto after graduation. She would miss Ky and Reese, sure, but it was time to get out. Like a caged animal, a part of her had turned rampant, feral.

In her reply emails, she told the counsellors to proceed as normal, that there was no need to meet with her, to check back with her in a week. *Get out of my way*, she wanted to say. She supposed she could say anything now that she was the roommate of a dead girl. *Fuck your trauma. Get out of my way.*

‡‡‡

Ky and Reese left campus after their first lecture.

Reese went to stay with a cousin who also attended Western. She sat on the back step until her cousin came home later that afternoon. It was cold—her hands and feet ached, the wind was sharp against her nose and cheeks, her ears, too, when she pushed aside her hair—but she felt she deserved the cold, the punishment. There had to be some punishment.

She thought about Frances, everything she knew about Frances. Frances with a book in her room in residence, Frances quiet at a cubicle in the library. Hooking arms with Frances as they crossed Western Road, heading to

University Heights to see, for the first time, the house on Ford Crescent. Frances quiet, looking through the rooms. Frances at the bottom of the basement stairs, holding her arm up, saying, *It's cold. Right here.*

Reese swallowed, shivered. She couldn't think of Frances at the bottom of the basement stairs, couldn't think—

She thought of Frances, quiet, unpacking her things. Frances making food in the kitchen. Frances putting her shoes on at the front door. Frances sitting on the couch in the living room, looking out the living room window. Reese reached for these memories, fumbling for some crumb of significance. The images were smudged, foggy, she had trouble remembering Frances's face. *Did she have freckles?* thought Reese. *What colour were her eyes?*

God, she wondered, was this all she knew of Frances? Frances: quiet, sitting here, there, studying, reading a novel, looking out the window. They had talked, hadn't they? Shared a moment, a conversation, surely. Reese searched her memories. She gripped the cold stone of her cousin's back step, felt sobs tumbling up out of her chest.

It could have been her. That was what upset her most. Hadn't Reese struggled with anxiety, depression, too? She remembered the week she had pressed cubes of ice to the insides of her elbows and knees in order to hurt herself, to feel that deep, thumping ache inside her joints and muscles. She wanted to feel pain but not let anyone see—no cuts, no scars for evidence. Her friends, her roommates, would never know. The people closest to her had never suspected.

She had thought about dying. Once a month at least. Thought about soaking in the bathtub and slicing up her arms with razor blades, the loose parting of the skin, the hungry rush of blood. Or overdosing on pills—she hadn't thought long enough, deliberately enough, to know what pill she would use—but she'd thought about foaming like a rabid animal at the mouth, eyes rolling. That's what happened, wasn't it? That's what happened to people who overdosed on pills. She had thought about taking a walk on Blackfriars Bridge, not so far, not really, from where she lived, and scrambling over the safety railing and slipping over the edge, wondering if the fall would be long enough, hard enough, to kill her. She hadn't thought long enough, hard enough, to know if it would kill her.

Reese hiccupped, her face growing hot. Her eyes itched.

It could have been her. If she had let herself go, if she hadn't stayed so focused, resilient, pushing the thoughts away like she had taught herself to do, like she had learned, through brute mental strength, to do. It could have been her. So easily, it could have been her.

Didn't she know something about Frances, after all?

Without one memory to hold and rotate, to turn over and inspect like a stone in her hands, she knew more about Frances than she had ever suspected. She wished she could have hugged her, held her, rocked her, said, *I know how you feel*. Would this have made a difference? Would it have made a difference for Frances to know there was no difference between them?

Reese bit her lip to stop herself from crying. This was her punishment, then: to know that she should have known. That she should have acted differently.

It was a long time before her cousin came home and let her in the door, scolding her for not texting sooner. Reese made herself a cup of hot chocolate to ease the aching in her fingertips, in her heart, and behind her eyes. Soon she felt better, warmer, less empty, less alone. Her cousin started dinner in the kitchen, and a new show, some fantasy series she hadn't seen before, started on the TV.

###

Ky left campus after one of her classmates, a girl she liked to exchange notes with when one of them missed a lecture, hugged her and said, "I'm so sorry, Ky. So, so sorry. If there's anything I can do..." And then, cautiously, like a child asking for more dessert: "Were you really the one who found her?"

Ky left without answering. How could she answer this question? Yes, she was the one who had found Frances. But the details of the event were now obscure to her, corroded and warped like a piece of metal dropped in acid.

She remembered going into the basement with her laundry. She remembered a foul smell, like roadkill putrefying on concrete. She remembered, vaguely, calling 911. And then she was in the back of a police car, following an ambulance to the hospital, where the nurses treated her for shock and the police officer asked her questions. What was the name of the girl who had died? How had she known the girl who had died? When had she last seen her living? Ky managed to answer these questions in the moment, answered them with a cold sweat under her arms and a numbness around her lips.

Now she would not be able to.

Ky had learned the results of the autopsy report from her mother, who in turn had heard them from Frances's grandparents, who'd driven in from Nilestown to arrange treatment of the body and make funeral preparations. They'd met Ky's mother at the hospital.

Ky already knew, from her few conversations with Frances, about the grandparents. Curiously, at the hospital, without excuse, the grandparents apparently hadn't mentioned Frances's mother. But Ky knew that Frances's father lived in Germany and rarely visited home, which explained his absence. "What's home to him anyway?" Frances had once said, laughing and grimacing during a rare moment of disclosure after they first moved into the house on Ford Crescent. Ky remembered the strained bend at the corners of Frances's mouth.

But Ky could remember close to nothing about yesterday afternoon, except that it had been snowing, except that she had laundry to do. What she did remember, she didn't tell anyone. Not even the police, who asked, "When did you last see her living?"

She would never tell anyone about seeing Frances sleep-walking the week before, Frances coming upstairs to rummage through cupboards and open the fridge. She would never say that she had turned Frances around and sent her back downstairs—would never even allow herself to think about it.

In her mind, Ky was already rewriting events, re-envisioning her final living encounter with Frances. She had offered her food, hadn't she? She had asked Frances what she was looking for—this she remembered clearly—and then she had offered her food, something to eat or drink. She had asked what the matter was, what was going on, and if Frances was okay. She had been inquisitive to near frustration. Hadn't she?

These were the events Ky focused on and remembered. These were the things she thought. She didn't think of fingernails, brittle and coated on the underside with dried blood. She didn't think of purple sores descending into the collar of Frances's sweater. Or the dimness of Frances's eyes, a dead person's eyes, which she had only seen before in movies, and which was too absurd and grotesque to imagine in real life.

The evening after she found Frances in the basement, after she had settled back into her childhood room at her parents' house, Ky's father sat beside her on the bed and told her to guard herself against absurdities.

Her father, who had finished university and tried his hand at freelance writing, and who had failed, year after year, tucking himself further into debt like tucking himself into bed, who had—as he explained it—finally cleared his head and gone to law school, who became a lawyer and found success, found respect.

"Guard against absurdities," he said. After this kind of shock—she had heard that word over and over, again and again, like a drumbeat in her ears, *shock, shock, shock*—after this kind of shock, her father said, her mind would be apt to wander, to imagine certain things and exaggerate others. She must keep reality close, she must guard against absurdities. She must keep busy, must keep working—give her brain something to feed on besides itself. This was just one challenge of many that Ky would face during her lifetime. People died, death was inevitable. The imminent long-term grief of losing her roommate, her father said, was a hurdle—Ky thought of storm clouds bundling up like hard boulders in the distance—a hurdle she must overcome.

So Ky went to class the next day, to show her father that she would not only pass over this hurdle, but do it effortlessly, or at least in a manner that appeared effortless. Which she did—until the end of class, when the girl who she thought was her friend looked at her hungrily, almost excitedly, and said, "Were you really the one who found her?" And then a sickness rolled over Ky, as her mind retreated back down the basement stairs to where Frances lay, very still and quiet, where she could have been sleeping, a limp T-shirt tented across her nose, covering her face.

Ky left campus and went to North London, to the mall, avoiding downtown, where she might run into her father venturing out of the law firm. She went home around dinnertime, spoke easily about classes she hadn't attended, watched TV with her parents, and then went upstairs to her bedroom, where she didn't sleep, not really—where she lay and experienced fits of unconsciousness and scattered dreams.

The next day she spent with Reese at Reese's cousin's house, and the day after that was Saturday: a day without classes and the day Reese's mother was coming to London.

They had all planned—Ky, Katie, and Reese, as well as their mothers—to face the inevitable together, one more hurdle to overcome. They would drive to the house, 48 Ford Crescent, one vehicle pulling into the driveway and the others parking on the road. They would hoist boxes and handbags onto their hips, drag suitcases behind them. They would ascend the steps leading to the porch, stamp their boots to knock off the snow, straighten their shoulders, and open the front door.

SIX

In the hallway, the women took off their coats and hung them on the hooks in the closet. They took off their boots and placed them in a row along the wall. They rubbed their hands together, trying to grind away the creep of chill and anticipation from beneath their skin.

Ky, Katie, and Reese found that the main floor of the house was exactly as they had left it. Their toothbrushes still leaned inside cups in the bathroom, and their half-empty bottle of body wash still sat in the shower caddy. Ky's mug, stained brown on the inside from the coffee she had been drinking the afternoon she found Frances, was still on the side table in the living room. It seemed peculiar, made them uneasy, that nothing was amiss—that the furniture was positioned in precisely the same way as they remembered, that the blinds on the windows hung at the same drooping angles. It was uncanny, their possessions suddenly strange, as if switched out for identical copies.

Ky, Katie, and Reese—moving as if through a museum of their own lives—peered into drawers and studied posters. It took them longer than was necessary to start packing, dragging boxes into rooms and labelling them with black marker, deciding what should be placed in suitcases and what should be left for the handbags, the thick plastic garbage bags, and what should be left on the side of the road.

Each mother tackled her daughter's bedroom. This task was obvious, mindless, with no question of what was whose. The girls went into the kitchen and began sorting through cutlery and dishes, discussing who had brought what three years earlier, who had bought what along the way.

Behind their words were spaces of silence, pockets of air into which Ky found herself eavesdropping, listening for something, she didn't know what. Something disguised by the sound of their voices. She didn't hear anything. There was nothing to hear, only the void of the house, only the rummaging of their mothers working down the hall in their bedrooms.

"It's quiet in here," said Reese, as if reading Ky's thoughts. "Definitely quieter than usual. And cold. Is it just me? I'm freezing."

"Don't work yourself up," said Katie, smirking. "The heat's been turned down. No use warming a house with no one inside it."

"Right," said Reese, gathering her sweater around her shoulders. She tried to smile, even brought up half a laugh from her stomach before it transformed into a cough. She didn't know why she found it necessary to smile, to laugh. Was it to show Ky and Katie that she was okay with coming back here and packing her things up? Was it to make herself seem stronger, nonchalant, less affected? Or was the laugh directed at herself—you silly girl, it seemed to say, taking meaning from tiny details, like the temperature of a room. If she had been alone, she probably still would have choked up her half-laugh. You silly girl, don't you know this isn't make-believe? Nothing here is inexplicable. Don't you know that every thought you have, every sensation, can be explained?

Ky lifted a stack of bowls from the cupboard and placed them in a box. "It smells different, too," she said. "Must be the disinfectant they used to clean the place." Ky didn't say *the basement*, although that was the only part of the house that the cleaners had touched. Hired by Frances's grandparents, the cleaners—whose number had been supplied by the police—came in to erase the damage left by Frances's final weeks and eventual death. To mop up Ky's day-old vomit from the stairs and scrub blood from the walls. To eradicate the smell of vinegar and, beneath it, a deeper, damper smell, more sour than acid, furry in their noses and behind their eyes. The smell of the basement itself. They had found mould in the storage closet, the bathroom, and under the rug by the bookshelf. They had found collections of dust as thick as snowdrifts in the vents and beneath the furniture. Knots of human hair blocked the shower drain. The place hadn't been properly cleaned in years, and, with its odour lifted, the house felt lighter, the air sharper, somehow clearer, like when windows are left open by the sea.

"Do you think they did a good job?" asked Reese. "The cleaners, I mean." She also meant and didn't have to say—they all understood—Do you think there is anything left of Frances down there, in the basement? Do you think every part of her is gone?

"Only one way to find out," said Katie, who had known, even as she was walking up the porch steps, her boots still heavy with snow, that she would go into the basement. She went across the kitchen to the basement door and placed her hand on the doorknob. Looking back at Ky and Reese, seeing their expressions, shock forming in the O's of their open mouths, she laughed.

"What?" she said. "I've got a rice cooker down there. I'm not leaving it behind."

"Come on, Katie," said Reese, "don't you think—"

"Think what?" asked Katie, her hand tightening on the doorknob. She didn't open the door, not yet. "That it's disrespectful to the dead? She's not here anymore, you're being insane. Besides, I think Frances would want the best for us now that she's gone, and that includes getting my rice cooker."

Katie turned from their blunt, stricken faces and twisted the knob. The leftover fumes from the cleaning supplies drifted up past her nose and into the kitchen. The basement staircase was dark; even with light pooling over her shoulders, Katie couldn't see the bottom. She thought she saw a shift in the darkness, a shadow of movement. She muttered once more, to herself this time, "You're being insane," and flicked on the light.

The space at the bottom of the basement stairs was empty. The floor was clean and polished, reflecting the yellow light fixture hanging from the ceiling. The walls were smooth and bare, all the way down. Katie tried not to imagine dried blood, a pool of bile on the bottom step. She blinked. The basement was empty. The basement was empty.

"All clear!" she called with a breathy laugh, but Ky and Reese were already behind her, looking over her shoulders. She walked down quickly, keeping her hands away from the bannister, the walls, and marched across the basement toward the kitchenette. She flung open drawers and cupboards, hearing the soft, tentative sounds of Ky and Reese descending behind her.

Soon they were engulfed in the monotony of sorting, the rhythm of separating appliances and utensils into three piles, leaving—not touching, not even shifting for greater convenience—the things that clearly belonged to Frances. Katie found her rice cooker and Reese a blender she had forgotten about. Ky discovered a collection of wooden spoons and held them in her hand like a bouquet of stiff flowers.

"I was sure I left a breadknife down here," she said. "Wonder where it could have gone?"

"Forget about your breadknife," Katie said, "we've got the main things, we've got what's important."

Reese moved across the basement toward the bookshelf and couch, holding a cutting board like a shield in front of her. "I wonder if they cleaned her bedroom, too," she said, biting her lip and realizing that she had known, even as her mother was parking the car in the driveway, that she would go into Frances's bedroom.

Following the instructions from Frances's grandparents, the cleaners hadn't touched the bedroom. It had been maintained better than the rest of the basement and didn't need the same deep scrub. Besides the sour smell of sheets in need of washing and small pillows of dust in the corners, the room was almost clean.

Of course, it was by no means neat or tidy. A lump of clothes lay on the floor. The blankets on the bed were jammed between the mattress and wall as though thrown off, pushed off, in a hurry. The pillow, once white, had turned yellow. The desk had been shoved up against the dresser, a stack of books was spread across the floor like fallen domino pieces, and there was a hole—the first thing the girls saw when they looked into the room—there was a hole the size of a human head in the wall. The hole was rough-edged, as if cut into with a saw, and chunks of drywall, as well as the pink fuzz of insulation, lay quietly like confetti on the floor.

The girls stared for a long moment at the dark interior of the hole. Katie scratched her head. "Where do you think she was going?" she asked, pushing past Ky and Reese to step into the room. She knelt by the hole, squinting to see inside.

"What do you mean?" asked Reese.

Katie dragged her finger along the chalky edge of the drywall. "She must have been digging, right? Making a tunnel?"

"Like an escape route?" said Reese. "That doesn't make any sense. She could have just opened her window."

Wherever Frances had been going, she hadn't gotten far. Even from the doorway, Ky could see the concrete behind the tufts of insulation, the stiff, flat surface, the hard, mottled grey. She looked once more around the room. The space gave the impression, with its jumble of furniture, unmade bed, and heaps of clothing, of still being in use. Katie and Reese began to argue—inconsequential chatter, more to fill the silence than anything—and she felt the urge to look over her shoulder, to keep watch so they wouldn't be caught in the act of intrusion.

Here were Frances's books and blankets. Here was her sweat dried onto the pillow, her own particular dust clustered along the bottom of the walls. Her clothing, Ky was sure, still hung like shed skins in the closet. In the disarray of the room was a sense of waiting: waiting for the clothes to be folded and put away, the bed made, the books re-stacked, and the wall repaired. The room was waiting either for this or for its inhabitant to return, put on the clothes, and lie in the bed. Start digging, perhaps, as Katie and Reese suggested, into the concrete of the wall. The room couldn't remain the way it was; the moment of transition in which it existed was already passing. If no one touched this room, surely it would reorient itself, the desk sliding across the floor of its own accord and the clothes snaking up into the dresser drawers.

"My breadknife," said Ky, finally entering the room. She dodged the pieces of drywall, the insulation and books, and came to stand by the dresser. Beside it lay her breadknife, dull, unreflective, on the floor. She picked it up. The blade was spotted with white, chalky in places.

Katie said, in the same moment that Ky realized it herself, "Is that what she used? Is that what she used to cut into the wall?"

Ky didn't answer. On the serrated edge of the blade was something besides drywall, something pale, almost translucent, like a shred of paper. It flapped in an air current, as soft as a butterfly wing. Ky pinched it between her fingers and pulled it off, stripped it from the metal edge of the knife.

As she did so she thought of human flesh after a sunburn, the long fragile curls of peeling skin.

"Fuck!" she said. "There's something on it!"

She threw the knife away, and it ricocheted off the dresser and hit the floor, skidding toward the row of sprawled books. Katie and Reese jumped up, yelping, and backed toward the bedroom door. Ky began to shake her hand wildly, maniacally, bouncing from side to side: the strip of skin had stuck to her fingertips, and it hung there, twisting and jiggling, stretching and retracting like a white worm, until she reached up and brushed it off, raked it off, gagging, with her other hand.

The shred of skin turned once in the air and then floated, feather-like, to the floor.

"What is that?" Reese was saying. "What is that?"

Before Ky could answer, she heard the sound of a door opening from the hallway, a foot stepping onto the basement stairs.

"Ky?" a woman called. It was her mother. Ky imagined her leaning over the top step, listening, her hand placed for balance, perhaps, on the staircase bannister. "Katie? Reese? Are you down there?"

"Coming!" said Katie. She turned to Ky, who still stood in the middle of the bedroom. "Let's get out of here. For good. And leave that goddamn knife."

Ky left the knife. She didn't look at it, didn't look at the strip of skin lying amid the drywall and insulation on the floor. Didn't look at the bed, the wrinkles in the bedsheets, the subtle indents of limbs in the mattress. She didn't look out the window at the hedge-lined backyard, didn't study the lamp on the nightstand or the titles of the books beside the desk. She certainly didn't see—none of them saw—the faint outline of footprints where bare feet had walked, sticky, through the dust.

She saw none of this, didn't look, was done looking, done thinking about Frances and how she had lived in that basement, how she had died. *Some things should be left alone*, she thought, some things left unquestioned, unexplained, and if she couldn't remember the precise angle of Frances's jawline as she lay at the bottom of the basement stairs, if she couldn't remember the exact colour floating behind the opaque fog in Frances's eyes, that was fine, all of that was fine. She'd had enough of it, wouldn't think about it anymore.

And she was successful. She thought of nothing as she finished packing up the car and drove away from the house.

Nothing as she ate dinner and went to sleep. Nothing, nothing, nothing in the deep corners of dream.

Nothing—until she awoke in the middle of the night, rising from the blackness of sleep into the greater blackness of her bedroom, sweating and cold, panting. In this moment she remembered that when she had dropped the knife, and Katie and Reese had leapt away, there had been another noise: a quiet noise from the closet behind her. A thump and shifting, muffled by the closed door.

SEVEN

On Sunday evening, Ky pushed through the doors of Harris Funeral Home, where the visitation was being held. Reese and Katie came in behind her as she hung up her coat and moved into the room on the left, holding her breath in anticipation of seeing the body.

The body was not there.

There was no coffin, not even a closed lid. Instead, propped in black frames at the front of the room were two photographs. The first: Frances in grade school with frizzy hair and a gap between her teeth. The second: Frances in university robes, half-smiling—the photograph that would have been used for her graduation, taken in early winter of the previous year.

But the body itself was absent, a void vacuuming the air out of the room, a gap like migraine aura in her eye. For a moment, Ky took this as bizarre proof that it might not have been Frances's body at the bottom of the stairs—perhaps it had been someone else's body, or perhaps Frances had been faking, sleeping. Perhaps there had been no body at all.

Guard against absurdities, her father had said. But what was more absurd: finding her roommate five days after her death, starved, blood beneath her fingernails and scratches on the wall? Or imagining the whole thing, losing herself to fantasy, wrapping herself in the dark folds of hallucination? What was more absurd?

She asked Frances's grandmother, the first person in the lineup of mourners, bluntly, while squeezing her hand, "Where's the body?"

The old woman raised her eyebrows. Her hair was short, a grey bob around her ears. Her skin looked simultaneously tough and sagging, like stretched rubber, and her lipstick was a shade too dark on her mouth.

"My dear," she said, holding Ky's hand, "Frances has been cremated. She's gone."

Ky wondered if the funeral director had suggested this, so as to not present the body. Maybe he had explained that with the starvation—and with Frances not being found until five days or so after her death—she really didn't look like herself, would never look like herself, even with embalming, makeup, and decent clothes.

Frances's grandfather, who was standing next in line, leaned in to listen. The skin on his face was red and swollen from consistent crying; even now tears were heaping up in his eyes. Ky had trouble looking at him. His lips were squished together like pinched worms, and the flesh under his chin jiggled. The puffy, drooping bags beneath his eyes reminded Ky of a bulldog. He was breathing roughly, almost wheezing. Ky focused on his hands, his long fingers fumbling for her own, the skin pulled like thin, wrinkled fabric across his knuckles. His pant legs trembled, and Ky wondered if he was on the verge of falling over, if she would be able to catch him, support his weight in her arms.

"You're one of Frances's friends?" he asked.

Numbness began to flood Ky's mouth and throat. She couldn't feel herself swallow.

Behind her, Reese had begun speaking to Frances's grandmother, saying sorry five times, six times, seven, saying that she had no idea Frances was so sick, that she wished she could have done something more. And Frances's grandmother replied, "No, no, I understand. Don't ruin yourself with guilt, you poor thing. There's nothing more you could have done."

Ky felt sick. She wanted Reese to stop talking. How could Frances's grandmother stand it? But she could, and Ky realized this was why she had been placed at the front of the line: to brace herself like stone against the initial crash of emotion from each person passing through. Absorb it, take it in—the shame and guilt, the confusion, shock, or even, as in Katie's case, the stifled indifference—take it all in so there would be less for the rest of the family, less and less as a person moved down the line.

"I'm so sorry," Reese said again, and Ky wanted to slap her, pull the words in fistfuls from her mouth.

Frances's grandfather blinked at her. "You're one of Frances's friends?" he repeated.

Ky cleared her throat. "Sorry," she said, and then flinched at the sound of that word coming from her own mouth. *It's all reflex*, she thought. All of this, custom and reflex. She felt smothered by the framework of language itself, the thick, suffocating consistency of sentences against her tongue.

She nodded. "Frances's roommate," she said. "I was one of Frances's roommates."

"Oh?" he said. "I see." A gleam came into his eyes, a rise of excitement showing through his tears. "Well then," he said, "I have to ask, were you the one who—"

Frances's grandmother, without breaking eye contact with Reese, who was now blubbering, nudged her husband in the ribs with her elbow, making him cough and buckle. Ky stepped back, taking her hand away, and watched him recover.

"I'm sorry," he said, and now he was smiling, embarrassed, a blush spreading up into his cheeks like a child caught in the act of stealing. "I can't remember what I was saying. But thank you for coming. Frances would've been so happy to see that you came."

Ky nodded, whispered a jumble of affirmations, and side-stepped into the surprisingly small, pale hand of a man she assumed must be Frances's father. He was tall, slender, his hair thinning and brushed back from his face. He must have flown back to Canada in the last couple of days. Besides a strain around his eyes, reaching out to his temples, betraying exhaustion, his expression was immobile. His eyes gazed down the length of his nose, watching her steadily. He took her hand, his grip purposeful and almost painful, stiff with muscle, shook it once, and then released it.

"Thank you for coming," he said.

Ky said nothing. There was something tight and explosive in the low tremor of his voice. She moved on.

Last in line was Frances's mother, a woman Ky had seen in passing two or three times over the years. She was a woman of average height and average build, thick arms and sturdy hips. Dark hair, dark lips. A slant to her almond-coloured eyes. Ky could see Frances in the deepening lines of her face, the tilt and worry behind her eyebrows. She was dressed in a black turtleneck sweater and dark jeans, a decidedly casual outfit for such an event. Her hair was drawn back in a frizzy ponytail. She smelled overly sweet, like vanilla.

Ky lunged toward the familiarity of Frances's mother and tried to hug her. Perhaps she was feeling relief from reaching the end of the line and also overwhelmed from meeting and being surrounded by so many people she didn't know—strangers, the room bustling like a beehive with strangers. In any case, it was an unsurprising, ordinary gesture of affection—even now Frances's grandfather was hugging Reese, rocking her back and forth. But Frances's mother stepped back in response, putting up her hands.

Jeanette—Ky now remembered that her name was Jeanette. She had introduced herself at the front door of 48 Ford Crescent while Frances was unpacking her things. *Such a nice neighbourhood*, she had said. *Such a nice house on such a nice little street.*

Jeanette reared away from Ky's open arms. She was shaking her head.

"Not you," she said. "Not you. I don't want to touch you."

Ky, frozen, dropped her arms. She almost smiled, thinking that she must have heard incorrectly or that Jeanette was kidding, making some bad joke to cut through the tension.

Frances's father stepped between them. He seemed over-large, doubled in height, as he leaned over Jeanette.

"That's enough," he said. "That's enough. You don't need to make a scene."

Jeanette blinked up at him, cowering back against the wall. "You shut up," she whispered. "Just shut up. You have no right to say a single word."

"I'm sorry," said Ky, who had begun to move away.

Jeanette looked at her, narrowing her eyes to focus, and Ky wondered if she was entirely sober, if she had taken something or had been given something, pills maybe, to blur the sharp edges of thought. Jeanette's hands were shaking. Her lips were cracked and flaking, Ky now saw, and her tongue dashed out to lick them.

"Shut up," Jeanette said. "Everyone just shut up. If she thinks she can just—if they think they can—" Her eyes flew to Katie and Reese, who had come to stand nearby.

Frances's grandmother moved forward and touched Jeanette on the shoulder. Jeanette flung her off, swinging her arms. The bustle of people in the room had quieted, turning to look at Jeanette, who panted, still pinned against the wall.

"Five days," said Jeanette. "They told me it was five days before you found her." Her face was white, her eyes huge. "And then you come in here and pretend you care. How dare you show your faces. Get out. Get out of here."

Ky didn't move. Reese shuffled beside her, and Katie, on the other side, crossed her arms.

"Maybe we'd better go," said Reese, tugging on the sleeve of Ky's dress.

"I'm so sorry," said Frances's grandmother, coming up and touching Ky's shoulder, gently, in the same way she had touched Jeanette. "She's had a rough time with—everything. It might be best for you to head out now."

Ky felt cold. She was stiff with something close to anger, a ball of acid building up inside her stomach. She couldn't take her eyes from Jeanette, who was crying now, holding on to Frances's father's arm, pieces of hair falling out of her ponytail, which bobbed against the wall. *Psychotic bitch*, thought Ky. She didn't try to alter the expression, the words bubbling up and exploding in her head. *Pathetic, psychotic bitch*.

Katie grabbed her hand and pulled her toward the door, manoeuvring through a crowd of open-mouthed observers.

"Fuck her," Katie mumbled against her ear. Reese stumbled behind them, wiping her eyes. "She can go fuck herself right to hell."

EIGHT

Ky didn't sleep that night. She spent the time pacing back and forth across her bedroom, transitioning between fits of vivid imagination—muttering aloud all the things she could have said, should have said, to Frances's mother—and fits of blankness during which her mind emptied and hours slipped by. She wore down a track in the carpet until the sun came up and sucked the night out of the curtains and the corners of the room.

Katie and Reese didn't go to the funeral. Ky went alone. She sat in the back, her pew empty except for a boy Ky's age, who sat by himself with his shoes kicked off and his legs crossed, his mud-coloured hair falling over his mud-coloured eyes. She listened to the eulogy read by Frances's grandmother, the funeral service given by the white-haired minister, the music played by the organ player as the family walked single file out of the church.

Jeanette saw Ky as she passed, saw her and the boy, and she drifted on, unconcerned, as if she didn't recognize either of them.

The whole time, Ky stared at the front of the room, stared at the table with the two photographs of Frances and wondered, *Where is the body? Where is the goddamn body?* Forgetting, momentarily, that she had already been told: Frances had been cremated. Frances was gone.

Where was the body? This absence disturbed Ky, made her uncomfortable, because she had seen the body and knew it existed—knew that it *had* existed, she reminded herself. She had assumed, from her limited experience with funerals—she had only been to one before, her grandfather's, who had died when she was five years old, and that had been a Japanese funeral, much different than this—that everyone would see the body, that everyone would look at Frances just as she had looked at Frances.

Besides Frances's grandparents and mother, who had identified the body, she was the only one who had seen. Alone, her mind drifted, images warped and bloomed. Alone. She was alone with her beliefs, convictions, her loosening sense of conviction.

Where is the body? she thought on the walk home. She remembered now, vaguely, the body at the bottom of the basement stairs, the face hidden by a fallen T-shirt. She had dreamt of it two nights ago, and the dream was coming back to her, of lifting the T-shirt and finding—not Frances's face, no, nothing but a smooth plane of skin, thick and rubbery when she touched it, thick like a car tire. And moving. It had started moving, the jaw beneath the skin jumping up and down as if trying to scream, as if trying to speak.

Where is the goddamn body? She opened the front door of her parents' house and grabbed her parents' car keys. In her memory, where was the body? She couldn't see it clearly. Driving down Richmond Street and through the university, pulling into the driveway on Ford Crescent, stepping out, still in her funeral clothes, she thought, *Where could it be?*

The wind was gentle in Ky's hair and against the back of her neck as she approached the house. Her key fit easily into the slot above the door handle. She opened the door. The house was quiet, perfectly quiet, as she had expected it to be. The house was cold. She slipped off her boots and felt the floor with her toes. She went into the living room and sat on the couch. She had been alone when she found Frances. The house had been empty, just like this. She had been alone.

She had been alone, yes—she had been alone. She had told the story to police officers, doctors, her parents, Katie, and Reese, repeating the words until they became artificial in her mouth. Remembering the series of events, trying to remember, until the images in her mind became entirely her own construction, shapes and colours concocted for better recollection. But still she couldn't recall much.

What she did recall came back to her in flashes, the helter-skelter of dreams. Always pieces of Frances's body. Disembodied pieces she tried to sew back together in her mind. A long fingernail, a foot, the bend of an elbow.

Why it mattered so much, she didn't know. Why this lurid fascination with Frances's emaciated flesh, the opaque fog in her eyes, a fascination so deep that Ky wanted to touch her, carry her, roll her over, and brush back her hair—she didn't know.

She had told so many people about finding Frances, but still she had been alone. She couldn't shake it off, couldn't rid herself of the loneliness cemented into that moment of discovery.

Now, she thought, if she came back to the house one last time, alone as she had been before, she might remember the body. She might be able to roll it over, at least, in her mind.

She stood up from the couch. This was how she had walked, through the living room and into the kitchen with her laundry, this was how she had opened the basement door.

This was where she had smelled a smell of dampness, of must and mould. This was where she had turned on the light.

But the space at the bottom of the stairs was empty, and Ky couldn't remember.

She went down the stairs slowly, careful as she stepped. The space at the bottom was empty; she stood where Frances's body had been and thought, *This was the last place Frances was alive in this house*. This staircase, the kitchenette, these ceilings and floors, were the last things she saw. The last thing she smelled was the sick, dusty scent of mould gathering in the back of her throat. The last thing she heard— What would have been the last thing Frances heard?

Ky listened.

And as she listened, she realized the house wasn't as silent as she had thought. There was a soft sound, like wind pushing back and forth down the hall. Like breathing.

Hello? Ky wanted to say, but she didn't say anything. She followed the noise down the hall, floated behind the noise, was dragged by it, to Frances's bedroom. The bedroom door was open. She remembered that, two days ago, they had closed it on their way out, but now it was open. The lights inside were off.

Shadows retracted in the doorway. She saw the hole, wide like an open eye, in the wall. She saw the end of the bed. Back in the darkness under the window were amorphous shapes, the desk and dresser, the stack of books. The thin light from the window painted everything grey, as if the colour had been peeled like a layer of skin from the furniture and walls. She saw the glint of something—a metal blade, the breadknife—on the floor. She remembered the cold sweat she had woken to nights previous, that damp prickling, like the padding of fingertips, on her skin. The soft shuffling in the closet behind her.

Ky stepped into the bedroom and turned to look at the bed. Frances's body was propped against the headboard.

She knew it was Frances's body because it was dressed in Frances's clothes, a brown plaid sundress that Ky hadn't seen since last summer. It had Frances's long limbs, the legs pointing out like rods from its hips and the arms draped across the pillows, elbows relaxed, palms facing upward. It had Frances's hair, the wild, twisting curls—or, rather, it had pieces of it. Patches of its head were bald, bare, red and sore-looking, as if the skin had been scratched off. All over its body, Ky now saw, were patches of raw-looking skin, as if rubbed with sandpaper. Between these patches, the skin had turned bluish-grey.

At first, because Ky knew this was a body, a dead body, she thought it was unmoving. Its skin was like concrete, it was stiff and quiet as stone. But as she looked closer, she saw that its chest was expanding and collapsing, laboriously heaving, synced perfectly with the sound of shallow, coarse wheezing. The body was breathing.

Its chin sank inward, the wrinkles of its neck piled up around its jawline. This was a body in the process of decay. Could it even be called Frances, could it even be called something that belonged to Frances, anymore? Its mouth wasn't a mouth. The lips had disappeared, the mouth was only skin, a gash pulled back around the gums, showing long yellow rows of teeth. Its nose wasn't a nose, only a lump under the flesh with two drooping, ragged holes where air entered and breath escaped. Its ears weren't ears—between the sparse chunks of hair, Ky could see the ears were only open cavities, like the nose. She wondered how this could be, where they had gone. Fallen off, torn away, disintegrated?

She thought of the strip of skin hanging from the bread-knife and shivered, thinking she might vomit like she had when she saw Frances's body the first time at the bottom of the basement stairs.

And now she remembered: the purple patch on Frances's neck stippled with capillaries, the sweat-stained pyjama pants and sweater, the texture of grease in her hair, the smell, her feet, her fingers, the bones swelling against the skin of her wrists. Every detail, Ky remembered. The point of her chin, her nose. Most prominently, the dark fan of lashes lining her eyeballs, the cloudy orbs of her eyes.

But the face on the bed had no lashes, no eyebrows. Its eyelids were slits in its skin; its eyes beneath them were red, almost maroon-coloured, the pupils angled upward, looking at Ky.

The thing on the bed, which couldn't be called Frances, breathed in short, shallow gasps, and looked at Ky.

Then it opened its mouth, the jaw moving up and down against its neck, the head bobbing. A low gurgle erupted from its throat, and drool spilled out onto its chin.

My god, thought Ky for the first time, *it's alive. I've made it living.*

Because, surely, this was something she had put together in her mind. A moving picture of her memory, an enlargement, an exaggeration. Her mind would be apt to wander, her father had said, to imagine certain things and exaggerate others. She must keep reality close. And this reality wasn't one she wanted to exist in, this body wasn't one she wanted to touch. She wondered, briefly, what it would feel like to touch something she had made up in her mind, what texture the skin would have, if the limbs would fall apart on contact.

Ky stepped back and slammed into the wall, smacking her head, and still the thing's jaw moved up and down, still it breathed, a harsh, liquid sound, still it gurgled and retched, a sound like paper tearing, still it stared at her without blinking.

Could it blink? she asked herself. Could it stand, could it sleep, could it move its limbs? As she thought this, the thing began to twitch, elbows and knees jerking, fingers jittering, as if it were a machine warming up, as if electricity jumped through its veins. Ky tried to leave the room and tripped, found herself on the floor and screaming. She could hear Frances, the thing on the bed, breathing. Ky picked herself up and lurched into the hallway. There was a ringing in her ears as she ran toward the stairs—her mouth was closed, but she thought she must still be screaming, she could hear screaming inside her head. But no, it was the thing behind her shrieking. Ky looked back and saw it tumbling after her out of the bedroom, limping, crashing against the wall, its hair and dress swinging, its bare feet thick, uncoordinated, on the floor.

"Frances," Ky yelped. She had begun to sob. She grabbed the staircase bannister and pulled herself upward. "Frances, stop."

On the stairs, Ky stumbled again. She felt her heart, rocketing, stumble and throw itself into her throat. The thing—Frances—mewled behind her. Like an animal.

The basement door was open above her.

"Frances, stop," she said. Almost mewled herself as her knees caught on the edge of a stair, but she stopped the sound before it reached her mouth.

As she scrambled up the stairs and struggled to get to her feet, her hair fell out of its prim funeral bun. Her hand made contact with the bannister, and she pulled. The garbled wailing climbed behind her—

Why had she come? Her brain hooked into this thought as her fingernails hooked into the wood of the bannister. She couldn't remember what she had wanted to discover.

The kitchen light, coming through the open basement door, slipped across her shoulder. Why had she come?

Her foot made contact with the landing, and she launched herself toward the kitchen. Why had she come? From the side of her eye she saw movement. What had she wanted to discover? The thing on the stairs lunged at the same moment that she lunged.

What had she created, by coming here?

The thing on the stairs—Frances, Frances, Frances (the name bloomed like a headache behind her eyes)—caught her ankle and pulled. Ky fell, hands slapping the tile floor of the kitchen and knees striking the staircase landing, the grip of long fingers on her leg papery and dry. A shock rolled up her body from that spot to the top of her head. Her scalp danced in pinpricks beneath her hair, a shock from the reality that this thing that was Frances could touch her, that she could be touched by it.

Had she created something in this coming? What was it? What had it become?

Far beyond her. This mirage, this memory-ripple of Frances in the basement, had moved far beyond her. It was something that had never been hers, had never been her.

Ky rolled over on her hip, hair hanging around her face, and saw the thing that she thought was Frances hanging off her foot, head bent down, hair in strips around its shoulders, dress hiked up around its knees. In the light of the basement stairwell, its features were stark and overexposed: sharp reality, sharp edges of eyelids and lips, flaking skin. Illness, rot, disease.

Ky rolled over on her hip and felt a sound roll up through her body, a sound she didn't know she could produce: a high-pitched, nasal wailing, a squeal, a sound much uglier, much baser, than a shriek. She bent her knee and kicked out, the heel of her foot colliding with the forehead of the Frances on the stairs. Its neck snapped back, its grip snapped open, and it tumbled backward, hair and dress flying. Ky listened to the thumps but didn't wait to see how it would land, or if it would die—she stood and stepped into the kitchen and slammed the basement door shut, lungs catching against her rib cage. Her face was wet. She was crying, she realized now that she was crying.

She listened with her back against the door. There was silence from below. *Stay down*, she thought, *stay down*. She tried to control her breathing, hyperventilation that grew tight like a balloon in her chest. And still she was crying. She left the kitchen and moved toward the front door, stepped outside and fell down the porch steps. She landed in the garden, a mixture of snow and mud between her fingers. A blush of bruise was widening around her naked ankle. Her face was hot, she tasted iron at the back of her throat, she had bitten her tongue, she was bleeding. She spit into the snow and watched the spot of blood tunnel downward to the earth.

I'm so sorry, she thought, and then she said it aloud, feeling the shapes the words made in her mouth. "I'm so sorry."

Her sobs had become retches. She spat and coughed, wishing she could puke, wishing she could rid herself of every organ in her body, every part of her, every cell and particle.

"I'm so sorry, Frances," she said. "I'm so sorry."

When she had calmed a little, she stood. The street was empty. Her parents' car sat parked in the driveway. It was warm, the day had turned warm, and the snow was melting down the shingles of the roof into the slanted gutters. Ky wiped dirt from her pants and went up the porch steps. She closed the front door, which she had left open in her panic. She didn't look inside.

NINE

Jeanette came to the house two days later. It had been a week since Frances had been found dead—just under two weeks, probably, since she had died. Jeanette had waited as long as she could. The U-Haul would be there Thursday to take away the furniture. The landlord would start looking for new tenants.

Jeanette's mother—her mother who was suddenly old, hair grey right through to the tips and wrinkles deep like knife cuts in her face—had arrived at the townhouse that morning with a stack of pre-made meals, making Jeanette feel, as she took them into her hands, suddenly small, child-like in her presence.

"What is there left to do?" asked her mother. She knocked slush off her boots in the entryway.

The air outside had turned warm and the snow had begun to melt, the world wet as if soaked with a hose. Jeanette interpreted her mother's question as *What can we do? What do we do now?* She sat down on the stairs with the pre-made meals in her lap, feeling the weight of the food upon her, the weight of the weeks to come upon her. The months, the years. She saw the deaths of her parents looming ahead, the surprise of old age creeping into her own reflection in the bathroom mirror. And to think: she hadn't wanted any of this. Hadn't wanted Frances, not in the way parents generally want children. Hadn't wanted the worry, the strain, a cumbersome obligation in her life. *Cumbersome*, a tumbling word, like a stone rolling around her mouth. She looked up at her mother, wishing she could open her hands in supplication, lie on the floor. *What do we do now? What can we do?*

Her hands, balancing the food, couldn't open. The food warm like a living magnet in her hands.

"Hmm?" said her mother, hanging up her coat. "So? What is there left to do? We're through the worst of it, and now's the part where we try to get on with our lives." She saw her daughter's eyes, the glassy film forming over them, the dead sag of her cheeks and mouth. "The key word here is *try*," she said gently. "We try."

She took the food from Jeanette, who hadn't risen from the stairs. "But what I'm asking," she continued, heading into the kitchen, "is if there's anything left to do. Any loose ends we haven't tied up. Hmm?" She placed the food on the counter and turned, hoping to find her daughter behind her.

Jeanette hadn't followed her into the kitchen. Still in the front entryway, she was holding her head in her hands. Yes, there was one thing left to do. She wanted to do it herself, she had to do it alone. Today, she decided, she would do it.

But the drive to Ford Crescent was longer than she remembered—it had been years since she had driven there, Frances didn't like surprise visits and rarely invited her over—and along the way she discovered that she couldn't remember the layout of the house, the rooms and hallways had mixed together in her mind. Where was the basement staircase? It was attached to the kitchen, wasn't it? But no, that couldn't be right. Where was the kitchen? At the front of the house, with a window looking out onto the road? She knew there was a window somewhere, looking out onto the road. She knew Frances's bedroom was in the basement, but even this she couldn't imagine. Something had broken inside her mind that made architecture unavailable to her memory. Doors, closets, cupboards, windows, all overlapping, floors warping upward, ceilings bending and becoming walls. She tried to imagine the house from above, tried to imagine the blueprints, and all she saw was a crosshatching of lines, dark, ink-stained patches where rooms should have been.

She thought of her mother standing in the entryway that morning. This was the last thing left to do. After identifying the body, after meeting with the funeral director, after the autopsy report, the visitation, the funeral, placing the urn of Frances's ashes on a top shelf in Peter's old study and being unable to look at it, after throwing out flowers that had already begun to wilt a day after the ceremony, after the flow of phone calls and messages and emails had trickled off like a tap twisted shut, after the food given by neighbours, co-workers, and friends had been packed away in the dark pockets of the freezer, after the obituary from the paper had been snipped meticulously out, folded, and placed in an upstairs drawer, after Jeanette had stood for long minutes in the doorway of Frances's childhood bedroom, confounded by the emptiness of the walls and corners, the prim neatness of the made bed, after Jeanette had stopped crying and gone finally numb, this was the last thing left to do. She would enter the house on Ford Crescent. She would find the basement staircase amid the maze of walls and doors. She would find her daughter's bedroom and pack up her daughter's things, decide what to throw out, what to give away, what to keep.

Years from now she would throw out more, she knew, as it began to matter less what books Frances had touched and what clothes she had worn. But for now, she would turn the pages of textbooks, run her fingers between the prongs of a hairbrush, smell the blankets on the unmade bed, and wonder, *Where has Frances gone?*

PART THREE

PURGE

ONE

After Jeanette locked up the house on Ford Crescent, and her car pulled out of the driveway and turned the corner at the end of the road, the front door opened.

Sticky, fumbling fingers turned the lock and pulled the door open.

A dim figure looked out from the dim hallway.

Before this—before touching, with numb fingers, the lock, grappling with the lock, and meeting, suddenly, open air—the figure had stared out from the living room window and watched Jeanette get into her car with a final heave of a final box into the back seat. Before that, before following Jeanette upstairs, it had peered out from the dark interior of the basement bathroom, through the crack of the almost closed bathroom door.

This figure, this body, this thing, had been in the bathroom—not in its usual place, pacing across the bedroom or lying in the bed—because it had been looking at itself in the bathroom mirror. It hadn't turned on any lights (it liked the brush of shadow on its skin), but it could still see the blurry outline of its features, the hollow pockets around its eyes, and the slits of skin becoming, more definitively, eyelids. Since it had emerged from the wall, it had grown hair: wiry, curly hair that sprouted painfully from the raw patches on its scalp, and hung in clumps down to its shoulders, touching its jawbone and hanging over its eyes. Occasionally, the thing felt bubbles breaking up into its mouth, the surprise of saliva. It liked to touch its tongue with its fingers, all the knots and taste buds, the little worm of muscle beneath its flesh. Since it had emerged from the wall, it had grown the stiff, arching cartilage of a nose. It had grown lips, sore lumps framing the cavity of its mouth. Its eyes had solidified into dull red orbs, round like peeled grapes in its head. It had begun to grow ears.

Soft as the underside of a baby's foot, it thought, but couldn't determine where this thought had come from or what it meant. The thought simply popped, independent, into its mind: the new skin forming around the ridge of its ear was as soft as the underside of a baby's foot.

This figure, this creature, this monster, stared into the bathroom mirror. It was tall, almost taller than the glass. It had to stoop to see the top of its head. Its limbs were long, limp, its arms hanging, its knees bending and nearly buckling, as if straining against the weight of its lumbering torso, against gravity itself, as if shrinking under the weight of the house sitting heavy above its head. (It still felt, to some degree, the weight of the house in its organs, its muscles, and skeleton.) Its body ached. Its skin stung when it rubbed against door frames, the paint on walls, the fabric of blankets. The soles of its feet were thick like rubber, almost without sensation, block-like beneath its legs as it swayed on the tile of the bathroom floor. When it walked, it felt as if it were moving through liquid, dragging its toes, the long nails clicking along the hallway, the body above lurching, almost falling.

And when it did fall, it fell hard, denting the walls and slamming into the floor, sending tremors through the foundation of the house, the concrete that nestled, cold and solid, in the earth. But though the monster's bones felt brittle, they didn't break. Its chin against the floor barely bruised. The impact, the hard edges of the house against its body, was a distant hurt.

What hurt was the process of growing. Hair pushing out through the skin of its scalp, flesh thickening, joints stretching. There was a throbbing in its head as if its brain were expanding, pressure building up behind its eyeballs and the roof of its mouth.

It was learning.

It had learned to use its fingers when it pushed through the wall. It had learned to use its eyes in the dark. It had learned to use its hands on the girl's body when she fell by the staircase, searching her, twining its fingers up into her ears and mouth, the sockets of her eyes, the damp space between her legs. It had learned to use its jaw on her body, how to bite at the soft part of her neck, how to suck on her lips, down her chin, her sternum to her stomach, gnaw on the bone rising up from her hip. It had learned to use its tongue in the space between her toes, in the shallow places, the arch of her foot, the bend behind her knee, suckling like a child, nosing its way beneath her armpit, sour and deep when it swallowed, the dimples down the length of her spine, the lumps of flesh that released odours when they spread, released moisture like dew on her skin. The white film, when it kissed her, that came off her teeth. The taste of her eyes. The taste of the inside of her ears. The tiny caves of her nostrils.

It took the monster a long time to realize the girl was dead.

It took the monster a long time to learn what death looked like, to learn that there was a difference between the girl's body on the floor and its own, to learn that it was, in fact, living, that it was breathing and moving and changing.

Yes, changing. The monster was changing. Growing.

It could feel its muscles filling out under its skin, tendons tightening. It was becoming more sensitive to physical sensation, becoming more aware of the world of the basement. It began to notice changes in temperature and light. Once, it had yanked open the bedroom window and thrust its head into the open air, breathing a scent of melting snow, of mud thawing, of tiny blades of grass, ice-burnt, turning green. It had seen the hedges thrashing in the wind, and the clouds above billowing like puffed cheeks, misshapen faces staring down into the backyard, looking darkly with shadowed eye sockets, then breaking apart, tearing apart to thread, wisps, long strings, veins of white.

The monster had retracted its head then, its skin pink from the cold. But it didn't feel cold—it felt warm, and something inside its stomach buzzed like a motor winding up. For the first time, it forgot the girl lying at the bottom of the basement stairs—the girl who had lain there, unmoving, day after day, whose scent and flavour changed each time the monster approached to smell her, lick her, nibble on her skin. And even though the girl was gone now, had been taken away, removed, there was still a roll of acid in the creature's gut, an empty, croaking growl, grappling up its stomach to its throat—this ache, this hunger, in the girl's absence.

But that day, when the monster had looked out the window and the outside air had slipped into the bedroom, it felt hope. It forgot the girl.

It began pacing up and down the hall for practice, teaching itself to walk without falling, learning how to lift its feet, so engrossed that it almost forgot to hide when it heard people step into the house from above. Feet stomping, the rumble of voices, the rustle of coats taken off. It hovered by the bottom of the stairs, listening.

When the basement door opened and a girl leaned into the stairwell, the monster almost didn't move, almost stood still and let her see it, but at the last moment it retreated, and in the crash of light that followed, the basement alight like fire, it stumbled to the bedroom.

From the darkness of the bedroom doorway, it watched the three girls creep down the stairs, whispering, and begin digging through the cupboards of the kitchenette. The monster was sick with hunger as it watched them laughing, bickering, gutting the drawers and shelves, their language like water bubbling, effortlessly, out of their mouths. The monster growled. With its fingertips, it tugged at its throat. It wanted to eat their words, swallow them, digest, and regurgitate them. Its stomach was sore, mouth hot with saliva, hungry for their ease of speech, because no matter how it tried, the monster couldn't produce more than a yelp, a warped gurgle sliding past its tongue. The monster couldn't speak.

When the girls approached the bedroom, the monster retreated further, shutting the closet door and tucking itself between the layers of clothing hanging in the closet. From that warm darkness, the monster listened, jumped when it heard a clatter like bones breaking, and didn't think to come out until the girls were long gone, until silence had reclaimed the house.

When the monster did emerge, it was followed by a piece of clothing: a brown plaid dress made from flimsy, scratchy material that had fallen off its hanger and attached itself to the monster's shoulder. The monster stood for a moment with the dress in its hands, looking down the long, naked plane of its body, the skin rough and falling in strips from its stomach and thighs. The girls in the basement, their skin had been smooth. The monster imagined peeling the skin from their bodies and laying it over its own. It imagined the sticky suction of that skin on its face.

It stared at the dress. The material was rough against the monster's fingertips. It wouldn't stick, wouldn't suction, but somehow it might stay. The monster pulled the dress over its head, and as it did, shreds of skin split from its body—forced off through friction, the dress rubbing—and sprinkled the floor.

The dress was tight around the monster's torso. It breathed deeply, feeling the stitches strain.

The monster ran its hands down the fabric that flared around its knees. White flakes like dandruff came off its palms. *Another layer to my skin*, the monster would have thought, if it had had the words to think coherently. *Add another layer to my skin.* The monster crawled into bed and sat propped against the headboard, its arms lying across the pillows, looking at the contrast in colour between the brown plaid dress and the pale grey of its legs.

It felt protected, hidden. It stared at the dress.

It stared for two days.

It would have stared longer, its chin hunkering down into its neck, hardly blinking, if it hadn't heard a noise by the bedroom door, the sound of a foot on the floor. It looked up with only its eyes, its head stiff from lack of movement.

A girl stood in the doorway. She was slight and dark-haired, with smooth, cream-coloured hands—hands the monster had seen searching through the kitchenette cupboards, the white fingers like feelers probing, touching, collecting, and taking away. The monster recognized the point of that cream-coloured nose, the plump swell of those cream-coloured cheeks.

It opened its mouth to speak, but instead of its voice came a rush of saliva, hunger pangs throbbing—the now-expected response to the sight of skin that looked as soft and mouldable as clay, as thick as pudding. The monster could nearly taste it between its teeth.

The monster tried to sit up, tried to stand.

The girl stumbled backward and fell against the wall. Horror swallowed her expression. She thrashed, trying to leave the room, tripping and screaming.

The monster rolled from the bed and heaved its body after the girl, limping, stumbling down the hall.

The girl was gasping, calling over her shoulder. "Frances, Frances, stop."

This word repeated: *Frances.*

The monster fell at the foot of the stairs, its legs slamming into the bottom step, and looked up in time to see that the girl had fallen, too. The monster scraped upward, flailing, numb limbs flying, the sunlight screeching against its eyes, and found suddenly the girl's foot in its hand.

Her skin was alarmingly warm, ankle bones firm.

The monster paused, not knowing what to do with its hands, not knowing yet what these hands could do. It opened its mouth—to speak?—and saw the girl's other foot rushing in to cover its vision. Pain burst open wide in its neck, and as it tumbled, pain in its shoulders, spine, and thighs, pain on its shins, the tops of its feet. A slammed door—the bottom of the stairs—and darkness again.

It wailed for a moment, but only for a moment, before it blocked the sound by biting its tongue and tasting, for the first time, the slow drain of its own blood. It listened to the girl's feet overhead, the eventual closing of the front door. Then it was alone again, it was quiet.

It raised its head, that single word familiar and pounding in its ears. It opened its mouth and said, in a croak of concentration, a dry, ripping sound from its throat, "*Fra-n-ces.*"

"*Fra-n-ces,*" it said. "*Fra-n-ces.*"

The monster dragged itself to the bathroom and spit into the sink, a mixture of blood and bile sliding into the drain as the word rolled up with one last heave from its stomach: "*Fra-n-ces.*"

It was then that the monster first found the mirror, a chunk of reflective glass on the wall that it had seen before but hadn't understood. Now it saw that its own face was in the mirror, that the face moved when the monster moved, that it had grown hair, it had grown a nose and lips. Its eyes had solidified. It had started to grow ears.

The monster saw itself, and the face it saw looked familiar. Where had the monster seen that face before? As if from a dream, half-remembered, that face hovered in the dark bathroom, its features blurry and patterned with drifts of shadow.

Where had it seen that face before?

The monster inspected its long nose, the faint spots on its cheeks that it couldn't rub out, that it didn't know were freckles. The eyes becoming almond-shaped, minutely too far apart.

It was still standing in front of the mirror when, nearly a day after the girl had left, a woman came downstairs.

Again, the monster was startled—shocked that people could enter the space so easily, that the basement wasn't somehow separate and detached from the world that the monster saw through the bedroom window. These people penetrating the house were like fingers groping, poking. *Stop touching me*, it would have thought, if it had had the words to think. *Stop touching inside of me.*

But even these non-thoughts were becoming increasingly hollow. There was an emptiness, a shade of dishonesty, in the possessiveness the monster felt for the house. Already, when it touched the walls, it felt only walls. The floor was only a floor. The monster couldn't feel the house beating, like a heart, or breathing. The house wasn't something it could crawl into or out of—not anymore. The house was inanimate, foreign, and with this foreignness came a sense of slight pulses and contractions, like birthing. A sense that the monster should be leaving. But the monster ignored this pushing, this rejection—the house was all it knew. It wondered when it would be alone again, just it and the dense membrane of the basement rooms.

The monster watched from the bathroom doorway as the woman went down the hall to the bedroom. She had dark hair. She was short, wide with strong hips, tilting as she walked, almost waddling. The monster couldn't see her face. From the bedroom, floating down the hallway, came long, extended noises of shuffling, rustling, rummaging. There were long, extended moments of silence broken by the scattered hush-shush of sobs. Finally, after what seemed a long time even to the monster, the woman came out of the bedroom, hauling a cardboard box. There were deep lines under her eyes, a slanted droop to her lips. She seemed to drift instead of walk. Beneath her swollen skin, her red and splotched complexion, the monster saw—yes—something familiar there. Something in the placement of her eyes, the length of her forehead, the point of her chin: something almost as familiar as the face it saw in the bathroom mirror.

The monster waited. The woman returned, retrieving two garbage bags, stuffed full, from the bedroom. The monster would not follow the woman, it decided resolutely. It would not.

It felt the house contracting, the walls narrowing, saw its own warped face staring back from the mirror. That word, harsh as a whisper, still seemed to echo down the stairs.

Frances. Fra-n-ces. Frances.

It would not follow her. It would not.

The woman came back one last time, to get one last cardboard box. The monster knew it was the last time because of the way she paused in the bedroom doorway, the way she paused, shaking her head, at the bottom of the basement stairs. It knew it was the last time because of the way the light clicked off, the way the basement flooded once more with darkness, the way silence crowded like static into the rooms.

The monster stumbled frantically up the stairs. *I'm not ready*, it would have thought, if it had had the words to think.

I'm not ready, it would have thought, as it watched the woman through the living room window.

I'm not ready, as it turned the lock and opened the front door.

I'm not ready, as it stepped out onto the front porch.

The monster stood on the front porch.

The woman's car was long gone. It was getting dark. But the air was warm, above freezing, and the snow was melting in soggy lumps on the lawn and in the driveway. The sky was clear—it had untangled itself, finally, from the clouds—and behind the house, although the monster couldn't see, the horizon was turning pink.

It was difficult to leave the house. It remembered its first moments of consciousness: breaking down the wall, the wild, lunatic stretching of its limbs, the first suck of air into its lungs, that dizzying feeling of space, expansion. It remembered finding the knife and cutting itself, for the first time, from darkness.

It remembered the girl lying at the bottom of the basement stairs. She was so delicate, as if folded together, made from paper. Her bones sharp against her skin. Her skin so thin like paper.

The monster walked down the porch steps. The concrete was painful, prickly against its bare feet. It went down the driveway and onto the road.

TWO

Ford Crescent stretched out like a grey elastic band from the point on the left where it began to the point on the right where it bent out of the eye and into the temple, curving away from the entrance to University Heights Elementary School before disappearing behind another property on the corner, a cluster of trees sticking up like fingers from the lawn.

The monster didn't know where the road went after it turned the corner. It didn't know that the school at the turn in the road was called University Heights, that it was named after this particular grouping of houses and streets that swooped in long crescents and avenues, tucked between Sarnia Road and Oxford Street, Western and Wonderland. It didn't know that this neighbourhood was named University Heights because of the university sprawled just a few blocks away, or that it was nestled within the larger neighbourhood of Medway, named after that larger Medway in England. It didn't know that this was all a part of London, named also after that larger London.

The monster, standing in the middle of Ford Crescent wearing Frances's dress, with curly hair and eyes minutely too far apart like Frances's, with limbs long like Frances's, didn't know that nothing had its own name—that all names were copied, cloned, and reused. It didn't know that anything had a name at all.

The monster felt the cement road on its toes. The cement was cold and hard like ice; its feet ached up into its ankles, but the monster welcomed the sensation because it was a new one, a new awakening of nerves in its feet and legs, in the soft, brainy flesh beneath its toenails. It looked back at the house, at the door it had left open, at the dark rectangle of the living room window. The monster was puzzled for a moment, confused because it still felt the pulses, the pull and push that had led it out of the house in the first place. Somewhere deep in its gut was a heaving, a *thrum, thrum, thrum*, as if a hook had slid down its throat and was now pulling back, tugging at the stomach lining, the intestines like a tail following from below. The monster looked at the house, the living room window—that single blind and gaping eye—and at the doorway with its door hanging inward like a retracted tongue. The house was a dead thing, an empty carcass, a discarded snakeskin, a hollow shell.

The woman's car was long gone, but, nevertheless, the monster followed her path down the road. With the *thrum, thrum, thrumming* in its chest, the monster walked down Ford Crescent, turned left.

⧕

The monster approached the university slowly. By the time it reached Western Road—a span of no more than four or five blocks, but long for the monster, who had only ever walked the length of the basement hallway—its legs slow and rubbery, heavy, as if filled with sand—it was fully evening and the sky had changed from pink to bruised purple, shadows swallowing sidewalks and darkening the streets. The monster's feet were numb with cold. It grimaced at the wind.

The cars were startling on the road, large and rushing, smearing lights through the air. The monster stepped back. To its right, a gas station reared up like a carnival, and behind it, a 7-Eleven's huge glass windows gleamed. Strange spheres of light hung overhead, glowing red and green. The monster found itself careening beneath these lights. It stumbled onto the crosswalk, turned to the sound of a car honking. Breaks bleated like trampled sheep, tires ripped against the road. The monster fell in the middle of the intersection, dizzy and overwhelmed, its dress flying up around its waist. It tried to stand, spinning and then running, half-crawling to the other side, to a second sidewalk, before collapsing on a patch of grass.

It opened its eyes to the dark sky wheeling behind a yellow street light and four people leaning over it, a group of students gathering, peering from beneath winter hats and the tall collars of thick winter jackets.

Their voices were muffled, rushed off with the wind. "Is she okay? Is she—oh my god—is she dead?" one student asked, reaching down to touch the monster, but retreating when it twitched, its chest heaving.

"No, look, she's breathing!" another said. "She's alive. She's breathing."

"Should we call an ambulance?"

"No, the police!"

"Did she get hit?"

"I don't know. I don't think so. Jesus, that was close."

One of the students, standing back from the rest, said, "Whatever you do, don't touch her."

"What do you mean?" said another. "What are you talking about? She's breathing. Look at her, she's going to be fine."

Another had taken out a phone, was dialling rapidly into its bright surface.

"Look at her face. Don't touch her. Something's wrong with her."

"The fuck's *wrong* with you?" asked one student, giving the other a reproachful look. He turned and leaned down toward the monster, leaned closer. "Here," he said, offering an arm. "Are you okay? Can you stand? Do you need help?"

The monster looked at the outstretched hand. *Don't touch me or I'll pull out your eyes*, it thought, not knowing where this thought—this language—came from. It reached up and grabbed the student's arm, yanking hard to lift itself from the ground. It heard a popping sound, felt it in the student's shoulder as the bone slid out of joint. The student pulled back. He started to scream. The monster wheeled around, looking for a gap in the group of pale faces, the glint of jumbled eyes. The students stared back and forth between the monster and the boy who clutched his shoulder, wailing. They were unsure of what had happened. They started to back away, thinking, as they looked closer, that—yes—there was something wrong with this woman, something deeply incorrect, something jarring and unpractised in her movements and expressions. The monster didn't wait for them to spread out and retreat. It burst past them, knocking one over, bounding free, tearing off along the sidewalk to the sound of their exclamations of "Hey!" and "The fuck?" and "Where are you going? Come back!"

It listened for the sound of their feet, but no one pursued as it raced, knees nearly chest height, into the university.

The monster dashed down a sidewalk to the right. It was wild and trembling, night wind rushing through its hair and the thin fabric of its dress. It ran through a deserted roundabout, past the university gym, the electronic *shush* of glass doors opening as it hurtled by, past a wide stretch of windows—students hunched over schoolwork in the lobby, the rapid blur of limbs and racquets in the courts below—making up the north wall. The gym was a squat, square building, as dark as the tops of trees waving behind it, and to the monster's left it could see long lines of other dark, squat, square buildings, hulking beyond the reach of street lights. The buildings were innumerable, heavy in the night sky. How could the earth hold them, all bunched up in a row? The monster imagined legs below the buildings, plunged into the dirt for stability, long roots stretching downward, whorled and knotted kneecaps flexing.

The monster turned from the buildings and trotted to the brink of a hill that dropped to a large parking lot. The parking lot was dotted with unmoving cars and tall yellow lights. There was a flight of metal stairs, and the monster moved down it, the steps cold and malleable, bending under the monster's weight. At the bottom it sat down, trying to regulate its breathing. The sound of sirens had jumped into the air from far away, but the monster didn't know they were sirens—it thought the night was wailing, crying.

Above, the sky was moonless, dimpled with clouds. It was fuzzy and grey and soft-looking, and the monster reached up to try to touch it—it only knew the distance of the basement ceiling above its head. The monster scooped its fingers uselessly through the air. It dropped its hands back into its lap.

Beyond the parking lot was an empty road, beyond this a grassy sports field. Beyond the field was unbroken darkness, seamless, rocking with the swollen shapes of trees.

The monster sat for a moment longer, rubbing its hands together. It looked at the hard knots of muscles lining its palms. When it pressed its fingers against its knees, the knuckles cracked, and, feeling jittery with the winter air filling its lungs, the monster held its hands out in front of it, tightened its jaw, and squeezed.

The skin around its knuckles stretched and popped, like old seams tearing open. The monster flinched. It relaxed its grip and inspected the gashes, gently touching the bones poking up like white pebbles from a film of gristle and a steady pulse of blood.

Somewhere deep in its body, it felt that this was painful.

Deep in its body, it felt powerful.

The monster looked up. The sirens—the wailing in the sky—had stopped. The wind, too, had fallen off. In the silence, the monster could hear far and clearly. It could hear the rumble of water, somewhere across the road and field, back in the dark swell of trees.

The monster stood, walked its aching limbs across the parking lot, and stumbled into the cover of darkness.

‡‡‡

The monster followed the darkness in between the trees, the palpable darkness it knew from the basement. The ground was softer there, spongy where the earth sloped downhill. It was fuzzy with half-thawed muck and rotting leaves.

The rumble of water expanded as the monster moved deeper into the darkness.

At night the river was careless in a way it couldn't be during the day. The core of the Thames thrashed like a frenzied snake. The monster could hear stones tumbling and groaning as it turned them, licked them, ground them smooth and stiff like worn-down teeth. Round molars lining the deep scoop of the river's mouth. Although it still didn't have language to wrap around these thoughts—language was slow, hulking and rolling like shadowy waves in its mind—the monster had begun to understand how huge the world was beyond the house on Ford Crescent. It saw that the river carried water from upstream, transported it through the forest and away. To where, the monster couldn't guess, but it sensed larger systems at work, much larger than the universe of the basement it had left. And every so often it felt, as in this moment, a blip and collision in its mind, like a key sliding into its designated lock, tangled patterns rearranging themselves deep within its brain, the stretching of its thoughts around coherence.

The monster smelled the deep brown smell of water. It stepped out onto a sandy bank.

Like the bathroom mirror in the basement, the river threw back the monster's reflection: a hazy shimmer of a face and hair, the shape of a dress, the glow of bare arms and legs. The water was almost purple in colour, still holding a hue from the evening sky. The river was whispering, talking as it rolled over itself like a blanket thrown downstairs, bundling up and folding, bubbling, tumbling, yapping.

The monster felt the river with its toes. It stepped into the current.

╫

The monster emerged from the other side of the river soaking and cold. The water had reached up to its stomach, numbing its skin from the waist down, and it was still numb as it followed a dirt path through the trees and out of the forest. If it had known the words to express the sensations rocking through its body, it would have thought, *I am tired. I am weak. I am hungry*. But the monster had only ever known tiredness, weakness—in its mind if not in its muscles—and hunger, so it plunged on unperturbed, climbing a hill out of the woods and arriving at the edge of a field.

There were no lights here. All the monster could see were shadowy lumps of willow trees.

This was Gibbons Park: a nice park, well-trimmed, with a playground, a cement bridge extending over the river. A splash pad and swimming pool closed for the winter. The park had benches stationed along its paved pathway, with convenient views of the Thames. It had washrooms and water fountains, a covered pavilion for barbecue picnics. It had a stone outcropping perfect for feeding ducks.

All was quiet except for the occasional yelp of coyotes from the bushes behind the playground. The park had a lonely feel in the dark, it was more or less unfrequented—at least on this side of the river—by the homeless men and women who often sought obscurity in the forest surrounding the Thames. Gibbons Park, a good enough distance from downtown and sewn almost seamlessly to the backyards of the Old North neighbourhood, did not tolerate the poorly constructed tents of the homeless or the sleeping bodies they held. These tents were removed like sore warts and, as far as the dog walkers, competitive cyclists, and stroller pushers were concerned, the crisis of the ever-increasing homeless population was temporarily averted, if not entirely abolished.

The monster, knowing none of this and feeling only the emptiness of the open fields, started across the park toward a dim row of houses in the distance. It passed the pool house and the drained belly of the pool, fenced in with chain link. Its eyes roamed the glow of an empty parking lot.

As it passed the playground, it heard the sound of someone breathing. The small hairs on the back of its neck bristled. It turned to look at the play equipment. Long dark shadows sat on top of the monkey bars, balanced on the teeter-totter, and sat sprawled in the sand: bodies holding very still, watching the monster, the whites of their eyes glinting in their faces, and the dull glint of something else— glass bottles between them or lying in their laps. The sharp scent of alcohol entered the monster's nostrils.

"Boo," said one of the shadows, beginning to rock on the teeter-totter. The monster jumped.

The group of shadows burst into laughter, the ones on the ground keeling over. They were men, all of them, dressed in dark winter clothing, their cheeks rosy with cold, and their hands stuffed deep into their pockets. The monster knew instinctively, from the way they sipped from their liquor bottles and leaned idly against the play equipment, that they had been not waiting for the monster, not exactly, but waiting for someone, *something*, some event or warm body to cure their lethargic discontent—and if it came, they would be ready.

"Look at your face," said one of the men, bent over in the sand. He was wheezing, having trouble speaking through his laughter. "You didn't see us, did you? Not at all? We were watching you since you came out of the woods." The man coughed, heaved a great inhale, and then belched out another bout of laughter, rolling onto his back.

The man beside him punched his shoulder. "And you thought," he slurred, "you thought she wouldn't—you thought she would—"

The monster shifted in the grass, stepped backward. It saw that these men were young, smooth-skinned and thin beneath their heavy jackets. After seeing the girls and the woman who had come to clean out the house, the monster had a basis for the concept of youth: skin supple like butter, eyes bright, muscles lean in limbs. Some of these men had voices that were high and nasally. They were tall but still filling out their shoulders—technically adults but barely more than boys.

"Where are you going?" asked the man sitting closest, the one who had spoken first, his hands resting on either side of the teeter-totter.

The monster stopped moving. The lower half of its body was still numb, and it could feel the crackle of drying blood on its knuckles.

"And where are your shoes?" continued the man. "You must be freezing."

The monster shook its head—not because it understood the man and wanted to rebuke him, but because it did not understand him at all.

"Sure," said the man, "you must be. Look at you. Those legs, that little dress..."

The other men snickered. One took a loud swig from his liquor bottle, exhaling after swallowing, something beast-like, something feral in the full and heavy cloud of his breath.

"He's right," said another man the monster hadn't noticed. He was leaning against the slide. "You must be freezing. Even we feel cold." He gestured to the group, to their coats and pants and large boots. "But we had to come out here. It's our buddy's birthday. It's tradition."

A few men whooped and drank. The first man stood from the teeter-totter and bowed, laughing. The other men hailed him, drinking again.

"That's our excuse," said the man by the slide, taking a step toward the monster. He was taller than the rest, a wiry spring in his muscles as he moved. "What's yours?"

The whites of his eyes glinted—he was smiling—but

there was something furtive behind the shadows half-covering his face: not only a leering, a hunger, but also a look of questioning.

"What brings you out," he asked, gesturing to the sky, the trees and field, "on this beautiful night? It's late, you know. It's not always safe down by the river after dark." He laughed, dry and thin.

The other men shifted and chuckled. One let out a ghostly, mocking coo that rolled, hollow, across the field. Another kicked him, and they scrapped temporarily, pushing each other on top of the monkey bars.

"But we'll take care of you," continued the man by the slide. "We'll take you home, if you like. Escort you. Where do you live?"

The monster stood motionless on the grass.

"Hmm?" said the man. "Can you hear me? I asked, where do you live?"

"I think she's mute," said the man by the teeter-totter. It was his birthday they were celebrating. He stumbled toward the monster, waving his arms. "Hello?" he called loudly. "Can you hear us?"

"You're an idiot," slurred a man from the sand. "Mute doesn't mean deaf."

"Well, maybe she's deaf, too," said the first man, wheeling around. He swayed, his arms hanging by his sides.

The man sitting in the sand smirked. "Or maybe just slow," he said.

"Where do you live?" asked the man by the slide again. He took another step forward, cocking his head. The monster could see now the long, straight nose dominating his face like a beak. His arms were folded by the sides of his body, and his shoulders were hunched forward, leaning in like a vulture's.

He stared at the monster, blinking. He was close to the monster now, within reach.

The man smiled. "I don't think you live anywhere," he

said softly—softly enough that the other men, hollering nonsense at each other, couldn't hear. "And you must be cold." He looked down at the monster's feet swathed in mud and grass, its pale, bare legs, the thinness of its dress. "You must be freezing," he said. "I bet," he said, almost stammering, swallowing, his tongue flashing out between his lips, "I bet you need warming up."

The man reached out and grabbed the monster's arm, his fingers sharp like talons against its skin.

"Come with me," he said. "Come with me."

The monster followed, pulled along, stumbling. The men on the playground yelled after them, catcalling and whistling, cackling, but the monster barely heard—the monster floated across the grass and into a clump of trees. The underbrush was thick against its legs, clinging to its shins and knees.

This surely was, this had to be, a dream. The monster, who had never slept, thought that this must be a dream. Its mind was foggy, only half-present, caught up in a reverie in which three little boys approached, reaching, saying, *Can we touch you to make sure?*

The monster shook its head, branches swiping through its hair, as the man pulled at its arm. He dragged it deeper into the woods. The monster could hear him breathing heavily, but all it could see were three little boys on a ragged section of dirt behind a school portable, staring at the monster and waiting quietly. The monster shook its head again, trying to shake the image off like water from its ears.

The man had stopped, his fingers never leaving the monster's arm, his nails digging into its skin—the monster looked and saw a drop of blood release and slip down toward its wrist. The man didn't notice. He squeezed harder.

"You want it, don't you?" he mumbled. "I know you want this."

It was clear he had never done anything like this before,

in the way his hands shook and his breathing came out raggedly—that it was premeditated only in the sense that he
had thought of it often.

"Get down," the man said. "Get onto the ground."

He pushed the monster forward with such unexpected
force that it staggered and fell, and before it could raise
itself back onto its hands and knees, the man had fallen
on top of it, heavy like a boulder, straddling the monster,
pressing its face into the dirt and soggy leaves, cutting off
its breath. The monster inhaled, choked on the musty scent
and flavour of earth, and suddenly its mind heaved.

It was back there, on the bed, in the dark and dark and
dark of the basement, cocooned in stained pyjamas and
human sweat—and whether it was itself or someone else,
the monster couldn't tell.

It surfaced back into the woods to the sound of wailing. The monster was wailing, but its wails were caught
in the muck. It tried to yell but couldn't, tried to thrash
but couldn't, its arms pinned to it sides. "*Fra-n-ces*," it
moaned—the only word it knew. "*Fra-n-ces. Fra-n-ces.*"

The man was panting, there was a sound of rustling,
leaves rustling beneath his shifting weight and his pants
rustling as he pulled them down. He reached beneath the
monster's dress. The monster felt his fingers, hot and damp
with sweat, against its leg.

"*Fra-n-ces*," moaned the monster. "*Fra-n-ces.*"

The man spread the monster's legs with his knees. He
lurched forward and pressed something fleshy, something
warm and stiff, between its legs—pressed hard and then
retreated, pressed again, pulled back.

"What the *fuck*?" he mumbled, and reached again under
the monster's dress. He felt the swell of its thighs, and,
between them, a smooth, flat plane of skin. He came up
against thick flesh, the prod of pelvic bone. His fingers

jammed at it, but found no opening.

"What the fuck?" he cried, pulling back. As he lifted his weight from its body, the monster found leverage and turned over, twisting around under the man who was now scrambling to stand. The monster's face was dark, covered in dirt. Until this moment, its mouth had remained the shape into which the man had forced it on the ground: open and painfully long, as if stuck in a scream. Now its eyes rolled forward, its jaw creaking as it closed.

"*Fra-n-ces*," the monster garbled. The word was barely a word. It was raw like the monster's skin was raw, as open and liquid-sounding as a wound. It was raw like the monster's mind was raw, hot, and bubbling. It remembered the shudder in the basement walls as its body collided with the door frame back on Ford Crescent, remembered the pop of the boy's shoulder on Western Road. It remembered its own knuckles bursting through its skin. Its own hands. It looked down at its hands.

The monster reached up and found the man's penis where it stuck, pale and still erect, out of his pants.

The man had a look of near-pleasure, a dreaminess to his expression, as the monster gripped his penis and pulled hard as he pulled away, a prehistoric strength piling into its fingers as it kept pulling and pulling until the skin at the base of the man's penis, in the dark places of pubic hair, stretched and separated with soft ripping sounds, until it was torn clean away.

The man stood, released now from the monster's grasp, and stumbled backward. Dark blood bubbled up in the place where his genitals had been, rushing down and staining his jeans. The monster saw a series of rolling contractions beneath his navel, the clenching of exposed muscle, and then the man looked down, seeing himself for the first time. He dipped his finger in the mangle of blood, flesh, and hair. The monster expected him to screech, to screech like a wounded bird and lash out, but instead he coughed wetly, as if clearing phlegm from his throat, and folded over, flopping in a heap, unconscious, on the ground.

The monster trembled all over its body—trembled and battled a tightness in its chest, a sensation of near-bursting, of energy, electrical, overwhelming, of power, and a tautness of skin in its face. Its lips stretched into what could have been a grimace, what could have been a smile—it looked at the thing in its hand, limp and slick with blood.

It stood and threw it into the woods.

The monster wiped dirt from its eyes and cheeks, wiped away the slippery traces of what it didn't know were tears. It wiped dirt and snot from its nose, dirt from its mouth so it could breathe. As the man began to stir, twitching on the ground, the monster brushed its hands down the length of its dress and walked off into the trees.

It walked far and fast, pushing onward blindly, following the *thrum, thrum, thrumming* still lurching up like a hiccup in its chest. It emerged from those dark, dark woods, rushing out into a parking lot and up a hill. When it cleared the top, it found itself suddenly in a residential neighbourhood, crowded with wide front lawns and the front faces of houses, rows of closed windows and doors. It thought for a moment that it had lost its sense of direction and come back, somehow, to Ford Crescent, drawn like a magnet across the city to the house, the comfort and closeness of the basement. But the monster looked closer and saw that these houses were different. They were bigger, grander, some with three floors towering into the sky, some with glassed-in rooms like greenhouses, some with winding stone pathways through well-tended gardens, some with balconies, some with screened-in porches furnished with long, cushioned couches, waterproof rugs, and swinging chairs.

The monster had crawled out of the woods and into Old North, a quiet, watchful neighbourhood bloated with doctors, lawyers, and tenured professors. If the monster had been spotted here, it would have truly horrified the occupants of these households; it would have been sent to the hospital or police station, the places where all visibly horrifying things are sent from neighbourhoods like this.

But nobody saw the monster. It limped down the road, dodging the glow of street lights, until it found Richmond Street. From there it moved northward, feeling instinctively—from the loudness, from the speed of its cars—that this street would disguise the monster's strangeness, that this street would wrap up its bare legs and bare feet, the dark blotches of dirt and blood staining its hands like gloves up to its elbows. This street would cover the torn features of its face and the missing chunks of hair on its head, wrap its body in the city's blurred brightness, the sheen of its hard, unbending shell.

THREE

London nights are shorter and more bearable in March than in December or January, but they're still long, with the loose, expansive feeling of a narrow rug continually unrolling—the black fabric of the night, however stiff and moth-eaten, stretching out past the limits of sight.

And so the monster was still wrapped in darkness when it passed the dead quiet of Masonville Mall and turned onto Fanshawe Park Road, still breathing in darkness when it ducked into the neighbourhoods north of Fanshawe. It cut through a deserted schoolyard, its bare feet slapping against the pavement, padding softly through the packed dirt behind a portable, and slopping through the half-melted snow on top of a hill where students played soccer in warmer weather. It continued through a field and into the public park beyond.

It was still moving in darkness when it approached a row of townhouses, white townhouses with stucco walls and charcoal roofs, the boundaries between their conjoined faces indiscernible, like melted skin.

The monster paused, sucking in its breath. It recognized a car parked on the road in front of one of the townhouses, had seen that car pull out of the driveway and round the corner of Ford Crescent. Something blanched in its brain, a contraction, a shock close to memory streaking through its body like lightning. The stucco of these houses was familiar. The uniform windows, hanging sentinel on the second floor, were familiar. Even if it hadn't recognized the car, it would have known which house to enter. The monster felt the texture of paint on the front door before it touched it.

The door opened easily—it wasn't locked. The entryway and staircase leading up to the second floor were dark. The monster stepped in, still breathing carefully, and closed the door. The sounds of the townhouse were familiar, the heat escaping in a quiet shush from the vents and the furnace sighing somewhere below. The wooden bannister felt familiar in the monster's hand. It moved up the stairs slow as a sleepwalker, quietly, lifting its knees. It moved with the silence of a child sneaking around after bedtime, an insomniac child risking a mother's wild anger for a midnight snack. The monster turned at the top of the stairs. In the dark, drifting across the carpet, it found Jeanette's bedroom door. This door wasn't locked either— it opened easily.

Behind the door, in a long rectangle of yellow street light stretching through the window and across the bed, was a little girl with curly hair, rumpled pyjamas, half-covered by the bedsheets, sleeping. At the sound of the opening door, she rolled over, sat up. Eyelids drooping, a gentle slope to her freckled nose, she opened her mouth and said—

Momma?

The monster shook its head. The figure lying in the bed was a woman, not a little girl. She had dark hair and a wide, stocky frame—the same woman from the basement in the house on Ford Crescent. The same woman with her familiar features, a familiar expression on her sleeping face.

The monster approached the bed. On the nightstand next to it was a toppled pill bottle, the remaining capsules shiny and white like scattered teeth against the dark wood. The woman, half-covered by bedsheets, was still in the clothes she had worn in the basement, a pair of jeans and a loose sweater. Her hair was matted, and a fruity scent lifted from her skin—some perfume she had rubbed on herself instead of deodorant, trying to mask, in vain, the smells of sweat and grease. Her eyelids fluttered, but she wasn't awake. She was dreaming. She mumbled in her sleep.

What was she saying? The monster leaned closer.

Two syllables, repeated over and over.

"Momma, Momma, Momma."

The monster listened, leaning so close that its breath touched the woman's face. It tried to form these new sounds in its mouth, rolling them along its tongue, pushing them out between its teeth.

"*Mom-ma*," it whispered hoarsely. "*Mom-ma*."

The woman—Jeanette, her name was Jeanette—rolled over and opened her eyes. She squinted and rubbed her face. Her legs were tangled in the bedsheets, and she took a moment to sit up, her torso swaying above her hips and her head slumped crookedly onto her shoulder.

She looked up at the monster. "Frances?" she slurred. "Is that you?"

The monster flinched at the word. "*Fra-n-ces*," it said.

"Yes, Frances," said Jeanette. She crossed her arms over her knees and laid her head against them. Her skull was like a heavy weight, a boulder she couldn't hold up. "I'm so tired," she said. "It's okay. It's okay. Just go back to bed."

"*Mom-ma*," tried the monster.

"I know. You've had a bad dream. But that's it, it's all right now. Go on back to bed."

"*Mom-ma*."

"Oh, Frances," grumbled Jeanette, slipping with ease, almost with pleasure, into that old annoyance. She swung her head back and forth, her chin bobbing as if floating in water. "Come on, then," she said. "Come with me." She twisted and dropped her feet onto the floor, raising herself to stand beside the monster and, alarmingly, grabbing hold of the monster's arm.

The monster flinched again, starting to pull away.

"Shhh," said Jeanette as she swayed. "Hold on, hold on. It's okay."

Jeanette's fingers were soft as she led the monster into

the hall. They passed the top of the stairs and opened the door to a room—Frances's room—with a rug and dresser, a mirror above the dresser, a closet, and a bed pushed up against the wall. The floor was cluttered with boxes and two stuffed garbage bags. Jeanette stepped into them as she walked, kicked them, nearly tripped over them. She steadied herself against the monster and paused, squinting at Frances's old boxed belongings through the darkness.

Her hand grew stiff on the monster's arm.

She looked up at the monster, a crease forming between her eyebrows, looked up at its missing hair and patches of bald scalp, the gashes in its skin that made up the features of its face, its long, pale limbs and long fingers, the mud on its legs and the ripped fabric of its dress.

"Frances," said Jeanette, her eyes growing large, her pupils dark. "Is something wrong? Oh god, Frances." A long, low moan tore from her throat. She had started to cry. "Frances," she said, looking down at the monster's hands, "what happened to you? You're covered in blood. Oh god, look at you. Are you bleeding? Where does it hurt?"

The monster was very still. It was careful not to move abruptly, not to bare its teeth.

"Frances," Jeanette cried. "Frances, what's happened to you?" She reached up and started pressing the monster's hair with her hands, pressing it down, trying to cover the places where it was missing. Her fingers fumbled over the monster's flayed shoulders, the tender skin around its elbows, the dried blood on its forearms and wrists. "Tell me," she said, "where are you bleeding? Where does it hurt?"

She sobbed, dropping her face into her hands.

"Where does it hurt, Frances?" she said. The words came as convulsions from her throat. "Where does it hurt?"

The monster stared at the woman, uncomprehending.

"Frances," said Jeanette, putting up her hands to touch the monster's face, then pulling away. She faltered, falling into a whisper. "What's happened to your eyes?"

The monster, unsure of what to do, breathed in and pushed deep from its stomach. "*Mom-ma*," it managed to croak.

"Yes," said Jeanette. She nodded rapidly and tried to smile. She held out her arms and said, "Yes, that's me. I'm here. I'm here now. Come lie down. It's okay. Frances, come lie down and get some sleep."

The monster walked on rigid limbs, watching the woman's face as she moved, inspecting every freckle and crease as the woman guided the monster to the bed, pulled back the blankets and fluffed the pillow. The monster sat on the bed when the woman told it to. The monster put its legs under the blankets. The monster laid its head back against the pillow, let the woman tuck the blankets around its body, pat its hair, and kiss its forehead.

It shuddered at the touch.

"Stay right here," said Jeanette. She swiped a glob of moisture from her eyes. "It's okay. I'm here now. Go to sleep."

Jeanette backed away and slowly closed the door.

The monster was alone, tucked into Frances's bed. Its head was itchy against the pillow. It didn't sleep. It couldn't sleep. It didn't know to close its eyes—it didn't know what sleep meant. But it lay still and looked out the window, out at the dark trees and the row of townhouses across the street. It lay still and listened, eyes wide, for the sounds of the woman coming back.

Maybe she would touch the monster again. Maybe she would kiss it.

The monster waited.

FOUR

Downstairs in the kitchen, Jeanette sat with her cellphone pinned to her ear. She had called her mother three times. Three times in succession, as rapidly as she had taken the sleeping pills earlier that evening. She had called her mother three times with no answer, and then she had called Peter, with whom she had left a message—she couldn't remember what she said—and then back to her mother, letting the phone ring three more times before finally her mother picked up.

"What is it?" her mother said in a hoarse whisper, thick with sleep.

"I need your help," said Jeanette, speaking so quickly that she could hardly find breath for her words. "It's Frances."

Her mother sighed. "I know," she said. "I know. Just try to go back to sleep."

"No," said Jeanette. "No, no, no." She shook her head, the phone thumping against her chin. "You don't understand. It's Frances. She's here. But she's—she's not well."

She wanted to say that her daughter had manifested somehow in front of her, that her daughter's body was rotting, it would soon fall apart. That she had an overwhelming desire to hold this body together, to carry the arms so they would stay in their sockets, prop up the head so it wouldn't fall from the neck.

She wanted to say that, most bewildering, this sensation wasn't new. She'd felt it even before Frances died. It was as familiar, as natural and flavourless, as her own breath in her mouth.

Jeanette blinked. She wanted to say, but something inside her stopped her from saying: *This is my last chance.*

There was silence on the other end of the phone.

Jeanette thrummed her fingers impatiently against the tabletop. "Mom?" she said.

"Jeanette," said her mother. "I think you're having a bad dream. Maybe it would be best to go back to bed."

Jeanette felt her pulse beating in her ears. "You're not listening," she said, standing from the chair.

She saw suddenly her stomach large with Frances as a baby, the way her skin had bulged with the child's kick. She saw the wet hair pinned to Frances's scalp in the hospital room, the tight squint of her eyes as she braced herself against the light, the length of each finger on her wrinkled hands. The smell of her skin—after a bath together, Frances so young that she would never remember—the soapy, slippery warmth of her daughter's skin.

"She's here," Jeanette gasped. The warmth in her eyes surprised her. She had started to cry again. "I don't know how—Mom, please—I don't know what's wrong with her."

"Listen," said her mother, but she was cut off by a sound of rummaging, rustling, a muffled exclamation.

"We're coming over," her father said, suddenly on the phone. "We'll be there in thirty—no, at this time of night— twenty minutes."

He didn't wait for her to say goodbye. He hung up the phone.

Jeanette exhaled, releasing breath she didn't know she had held so tightly. She had only a moment to relax, a moment to put the phone down on the table and lean against the wall, slumping, almost folding in half from exhaustion. She had only a moment to wonder if this was, as her mother had said, just a bad dream.

What had she put to bed upstairs? A couple of pillows, a sweater—air? What if she went upstairs and found nothing there but her daughter's bed neatly made, her daughter neatly absent?

A memory floated just behind her eyes: black clothing, pews of straight-faced people, a church aisle and organ music striking like an axe in her head. There had been a funeral, there had been a cremation. Someone's body had been burned. Somebody was dead.

Jeanette pushed the memory away—or rather she released it, let it fall back into the dense fog of her mind. After all, this memory could be a bad dream, too. What stopped any of it, all of it, from being a dream?

The cream-coloured underside of Frances's feet as she ran through the grass in the Nilestown backyard. The swell of her cheeks when she smiled—not often, not often enough for a little girl, so serious and remote, far off in her head. Thoughtful, pensive as she watched Jeanette from the kitchen table, from over a bowl of cereal as Jeanette left for work. The touch of her fingers, tentative, on Jeanette's spine as they fell asleep in bed, her voice so small that it might have been the wind outside, shifting by the house—

Momma?

That whisper in Jeanette's head. This was the stuff of nightmares.

Her worst nightmare was Frances as a child coming up from behind and tugging at her arm, asking her to play, or saying she was hungry and asking when dinner would be. Her worst nightmare was Frances as a child asleep in bed, her hair flared out like corkscrews on the pillow, the coo of her breath, and knowing that in sleep Frances thought of nothing, that she could finally rest. Jeanette's worst nightmare was memory, the banal momentum, now crystallized into sublimity, of every day with her daughter that she had wandered through half-present, without awareness. Unalterable, her worst nightmare was the memory of each mundane moment of Frances's childhood, slipping liquid away from her.

Jeanette thought, even now, even in delirium, *Where was I? What was I doing then?* Back when Frances was so watchful, so attentive, pausing to listen to a bird through the window, the sound of rain or a ticking clock. *Where was I? What was I doing then to miss her?* To miss the clutch of her daughter's hands on her face and the whisper—*Momma*—the pouch of her lips, the kiss she put into the air as she spoke.

All of this in a moment as Jeanette leaned against the wall, slumped with exhaustion.

Suddenly there was a knock on the front door, a banging. Jeanette stood, turned down the hallway to find Peter coming into the house, his hair in a tall, tousled mess above his head, his eyes bloodshot. He was wearing a pair of rumpled khakis and a worn T-shirt he had obviously been sleeping in.

"What's going on?" he said. And, looking down at his hand still holding the doorknob: "Haven't you learned yet to lock your door at night?"

Jeanette stopped in the hallway, her hands pinned to the walls on either side to steady herself. "What're you doing here?" she asked. The floor lurched toward her, and she squeezed her eyes shut. "What—what time is it?"

"God, I don't know," said Peter. "Two o'clock?" He watched her sway back and forth in the light coming from the kitchen. Her shadow was long, exaggerated, monstrous in front of her. "What the hell is wrong with you? Are you drunk?"

"I'm not drunk," Jeanette stammered. "What are you doing here?"

"You called me, didn't you?"

"I did?"

"You don't remember? My *god*. Come on. Put on your boots and get into the car."

"What?"

"I *said*, put on your boots and get into the car. Get your purse, too. We're going to the hospital."

"I'm—" said Jeanette, stepping backward, "I'm not going anywhere with you."

"Jeanette," said Peter. "Jeanette."

Jeanette's eyes were huge and wide. She stepped backward but stepped too high, her foot falling through the air. She had thought for a moment that she was walking upstairs, walking backwards upstairs, because that was where she wanted to go. There was something she had to do. She couldn't quite remember—some unfinished task waited for her. Thoughts curdled like smoke from the back of her brain, but when she tried to focus on them, tried to separate and force them solid, they thinned out and dissipated like overstretched cotton balls.

She stepped backward and stepped too high, stepped through the air and fell, landing on her tailbone and rolling over, gasping but not crying out, lost in a wash of pain that flooded her vocal cords.

"Jeanette," said Peter, shaking his head. He stepped across the entryway and leaned down to grab her arm. "Get up. Come *on*. Let's go."

"I'm not going," she gasped.

"What's wrong with you?" he bellowed, throwing her arm back at her. She curled up beneath him, covering her face with her hands. "You think you can just call in the middle of the night and say what you said? You think it's okay to treat people like that?" He began to mimic her, his voice high and mocking, girlish. His face was sneering, his eyes and lips scrunching up until they were ripples of skin rather than discernable features. "*She's not dead*," he said, bending over to whine into Jeanette's ear. "*Frances isn't dead. They made a mistake. She's here. You better come quickly. She's upstairs.*"

He reared back as if to kick her, as if to spit on her, but instead he relaxed and let his arms hang by his sides. His skin was deflated and rubbery, pooling around his neck and under his jaw, dark with the shadow of a beard. "You're sick," he said.

Jeanette, peeking through her fingers, thought he looked older than she had ever seen him, more weary and worn down, thin, strained. A surge of pity burned up into her chest—it was the first moment she felt that she no longer loved him.

He mumbled, "I'm going back to Germany tomorrow and I promise you'll never see me again. But someone has to take care of you. You're sick. You need help. Look at you." He nudged her with his toe and she flinched. "Get up," he said. "Get your things. We're going. *Now.*"

Jeanette shook her head against the floor.

Peter grimaced down at her, disgusted. It took him a moment to decide what to do. Whether to pick her up—flailing, no doubt, wailing, resisting, making a spectacle that would wake the neighbours and bring them to their front doors and windows, staring out at Peter as he carried her to his car, saying, *Isn't that Jeanette's old husband?* and wondering if they should call the police—or to leave her there on the floor, leave the townhouse and lock the door behind him, be gone in the morning for his flight out of Toronto, and only think of her rarely, like remembering a sore tooth when you bite down on it, like remembering the ache of an old injury when it starts to rain.

She was so distant from him now, so familiar and yet so strange, like an amputated limb. Like finding suddenly that he couldn't wiggle his toes, that he was missing a foot, a full leg, that his bone was showing through the cuff of his clothes.

He was Peter, he reminded himself. His name was Peter, and he didn't belong here. Not in this house, not with this woman. If he focused hard enough he could imagine himself walking through the streets of Berlin on his way to the university, where he would return to his research and lectures and answering of difficult questions. Even now he felt his students waiting, perpetually seated in the lecture hall and waiting. His breathing calmed, the world around him faded until it became insubstantial, holographic, soothingly artificial.

In the moment it took him to decide what to do, in that moment of silence, frowning down at Jeanette, he heard a soft noise from above. It was the soft but distinct noise—he knew the sounds of the house well; he had lived there for years—of someone moving through an upstairs room.

He looked up, turning his head to listen. He knew from the location of the sound that it had come from Frances's room. He remembered the muffled shifting during the evening hours, the thumps as Frances got ready for bed, the sounds of dresser drawers opening and closing, the closet door shutting, the rustle of her blankets being pulled back, the click as she turned out the light.

"Jeanette," said Peter slowly. "Is there someone upstairs?"

Jeanette whimpered on the floor, shaking her head again. "I already told you," she said. "I already told you."

Peter heard another sound, a sound of objects being pushed around. He moved back into the front entryway, to the bottom of the stairs.

"Jeanette," said Peter again. "Who else is here?"

Jeanette didn't answer. There was a dead silence from the hallway. Peter could see her feet, small and motionless, illuminated by the kitchen light.

He looked up the stairs into the dark upper floor. "Who's up there?" he called sharply, alarm making his voice bite. "Hello?" he said. And then again, louder, a near-growl as he leaned forward, shoulders hunched up to his ears: "Who's up there?"

He started up the stairs.

FIVE

"Who's up there?" said the man's voice, close outside the room. "Who's up there?"

The monster didn't answer.

It had been standing there, less than a foot from the bedroom door, for what seemed like a long time, trying to hear what was going on downstairs. Even if it couldn't understand the words, it was trying to hear what was happening to that woman.

Before this, the monster had lain quietly in bed, where the woman had left it. It was patient, waiting, wide awake. When it heard the woman talking below, a low murmur through the carpet and floorboards, the monster had pulled off the blankets and forced itself to its feet. Its legs swung over its ankles like a boat rocking in waves. Exhaustion rolled up in cold pulses to the roots of its hair.

The monster found its face in the mirror above Frances's old dresser. This face was vastly different from the face it had seen in the basement mirror on Ford Crescent. Its lips were fuller, less flat and torn. Its eyelids could now entirely cover the orbs of its eyeballs, and the eyeballs themselves were paler, thicker, less gelatinous and more defined. New hair, short and spiky, had begun to sprout from the bald patches on its head.

The monster felt safe, tucked into the room just as it had been tucked into bed. It bent down and opened one of the boxes on the floor. Inside, placed haphazardly amid a mess of paraphernalia, was a shoebox. The shoebox was held together by an elastic band and labelled in black marker: *Frances*. The monster wasn't surprised, somehow, to find images of its own face in the shoebox—or, of a face that was similar to its own, with minute alterations like those found in an identical twin. The same length of nose and lips, the same shape of eyes and jawline, as if it had been formed with the same idea in mind. The monster found this face on plastic cards pressed snugly in a folded piece of leather: Frances's old wallet with Frances's old ID, a wallet still swollen with half-used gift cards, twenty-dollar bills, a pocket of change. The monster found this face in a small black booklet—a Canadian passport renewed the year before and empty of stamps.

Beside the shoebox, perhaps displaced by the photographs and ID, was a pair of beige shoes, trailing white laces like limp, ineffectual tongues. The monster picked up these shoes, turned them over in its hands, and knocked on the hard, rubber soles with its knuckles.

It sat on the edge the bed and slid the shoes onto its feet. They fit perfectly, the way skin fits over a face.

The monster picked up the shoebox again, eager to study the photographs that presented, from multiple angles and perspectives, the face reflected back at it in the bedroom mirror. That was when it heard the bang of the front door downstairs and the man's voice, tough and gravelly, vibrating through the house. The monster stood in its new shoes by the bedroom door, holding the shoebox in its hands.

"Who's up there?" called the man, his voice now close outside the door. "I can hear somebody up there."

The monster didn't hesitate. It had learned, from the men in the park, to move quickly. It remembered the man in the park pushing its face into the muck—it remembered the heat of the man's blood in the divots between its fingers.

Shoebox in hand, the monster went to the bedroom window, fiddled with the lock until it snapped, and threw up the glass. The screen came apart easily, tearing like spiderwebs along its arms. The monster thrust its feet out into the night. The winter air was cold, wrapping around its ankles and sliding up its legs as it sat on the windowsill.

Before it could move further, the bedroom door opened and the man stood in the doorway, a dim figure looking in from the dim hallway, the light from the foyer downstairs softly framing his silhouette.

They looked at each other. The monster saw something familiar in the man. His eyebrows, dark and heavy above his eyes. The tight, concentrated twist of his lips as he stared at the monster from across the room. His long, slender arms tense, muscled. He was like a blur from a dream, clipped and pasted into consciousness.

The monster had the desire suddenly to speak, but words were still shapeless in its head. It had the desire suddenly to howl. It tightened its grip on the shoebox, its grip on the windowsill. It saw something familiar in the man and found that it was trembling, fear rushing like wind through its limbs.

Then it remembered the men in the park again, the man who had led the monster into the forest. It remembered the sensation of the man's skin tearing—like clay, stretched and tearing. It remembered the heat rocking through its body as it stood above him, the exhilaration—yes, the exhilaration so intense it was close to nausea—and the knowledge that this power would make the monster sick the moment it began to enjoy it.

But the monster wanted to enjoy it.

It looked down at the shoebox, bent beneath its fingers. It thought about how easy it would be to lift its legs and come back into the room. It thought about how easy it would be—the man's skin tearing like clay.

The monster looked at the man from where it sat in the window.

#

Peter looked at the monster.

He thought, *What is that thing in the window?* He didn't see his daughter there. The similarities—in the curl of the monster's hair, the oval point of its chin, the turn of its shoulders away from him as it hung half out the window— were monstrosities. They were vile. Something close to vomit came up in his throat. The thing in the window was ill, obviously contaminated, dirty, diseased. Its skin was rotting, its limbs hanging loosely at the joints, as if about to fall off, disassemble. Its eyes were lifeless in its face.

But still the thing stared at him. Peter stepped backward, retreating out of the room, and the moment he moved, the monster leaned forward. It slipped out the window, hurtling through the night until it hit the ground, hit the walkway. Above, Peter heard a snap, perhaps of a bone breaking, and rushed to the window to see the monster fumble for the shoebox, which had fallen to one side.

"Frances?" he said.

But the thing was already hobbling away along the line of houses. The thing had already rounded the corner and disappeared into the compact darkness surrounding the playground and clumps of trees. And Peter was already blinking to clear his head, was already coughing to clear his throat of that name he had uttered so inexplicably, was already backing away and closing the window, was already calling to Jeanette, saying, "Why did you leave this window open? Are you crazy? It's freezing out there."

Anything could get in, he thought, shaking his head, trying to remember why he had come upstairs in the first place. There must have been a breeze. He must have felt the cold creeping down into the entryway. He scowled. It was idiotic to leave the windows hanging open—anyone could get inside.

#

Jeanette's mother and father, turning onto the townhouse's road, saw movement in the beam of their headlights, and each thought it must be a raccoon lumbering through the shadows, an overlarge raccoon scaling the fence beyond the playground and rolling over it to the other side.

╫

The monster's thoughts were sticky, thick with repetition as it limped down Fanshawe Park Road toward the parking lot surrounding Masonville Mall. Every cement block of the sidewalk looked the same. Every street light—yes, hadn't the monster seen that street light before, looming up against the fence? That same street light, not on this night but a different night, a different night in a different body. Hadn't it studied the dimples of the bark on that tree, examined the liquid consistency of litter melting into the grass?

The monster had the distinct sensation of moving backward, retracing its steps. It felt the *thrum, thrum, thrumming* in its chest. Its leg, bending painfully beneath its body, injured from the fall, made the monster hobble, nearly hunchbacked as it heaved itself across the parking lot and onto Richmond Street.

It clutched the shoebox under its left arm and limped onward, drawn like a riptide downtown.

SIX

In the early hours of Saturday morning, before the sun leaked grey into the sky, a boy with mud-coloured hair and a deep mud colour within the shadowed sockets of his eyes crossed Richmond Street. He was jogging to clear the way for an oncoming taxi, hands pushed into his jean pockets to keep off the cold.

He wasn't really a boy. He only looked like one from a distance—he was, in fact, twenty-two years old. He was tall, his limbs slim and long down to his fingertips and toes. His chin was sharp, and he had an edge to his cheekbones. His elbows prodded stiffly against the fabric of his jacket. His eyebrows hunched above his eyes, bending inward as if trying to link together, as if trying to create a roof, some sense of symmetry or coherence to his face.

He wasn't a bad-looking man. His friends at Fanshawe College, before he dropped out, had thought him striking and intense. But he could never be fully handsome, not with his sourness wedged like a needle behind his expression or a scowl bending the corners of his mouth. He had lost the softness that had lingered in his face and body throughout childhood. Any roundness of thought and movement—any gentleness, lightness, or courtesy—had sloughed off him like a wet skin.

Jasper had grown up.

He hopped the curb and strode across a parking lot swamped in yellow light, heading for Victoria Park. He puffed out hot clouds of breath in front of him. His shift at the bar had been long, beginning at seven and not finishing until three o'clock in the morning, a full hour after closing time was announced and the students that crowded the place had shambled out onto the sidewalk. It had been hot in the bar, and loud, and Jasper felt a pulse beat in his arms and hands. His hair crackled with sweat and hair gel as it began to freeze in the open air. There was an ache behind his eyeballs and a slow but regular throb in the centre of his skull. It was late—or was it early? He hardly knew the time, he almost wanted to laugh—he was tired. The high from the joint he had sucked back just outside the bar and then flicked in a glowing arc across the sidewalk hadn't kicked in yet.

Despite his exhaustion, he wasn't ready to go home. Not yet. He wasn't ready to climb the flight of stairs to the second floor of the house on Central Avenue, to his cramped studio apartment. He wasn't ready to see the yellowing walls, bare except for one window looking out onto the street, or the fake hardwood on the floor that crackled in the cold weather, or the mattress in the corner that functioned as his bed. He wasn't ready to face his kitchen, the black mould that smelled of sewer water continually seeping out between the tiles lining the wall. He wasn't ready to sink into the patched leather of his couch and watch YouTube videos on his phone until sleep came—maybe he would move onto the mattress, and maybe he wouldn't, but by midday he would rise to pull the window's curtain closed, a terrible heaviness bearing down into his lungs. He would urinate, drink from the oily faucet in the bathroom, and then sleep again, this time deeper, until he had to get up for his next shift.

He wasn't ready to start this routine, to put in motion this cycle. Just as he had been doing for the last two and a half years. His life—the habits that formed his days—seemed to roll autonomously onward, tearing rapidly out of reach and out of his control.

Jasper often found himself surfacing as if from a deep sleep and witnessing, as if from a distance, his own motions and gestures. At work, mid-sentence with a customer, Jasper would note the way he smiled, how it felt, his lips stretched painfully across his face in hopes of a larger tip. While riding the bus to the grocery store, he would observe the way he stood to get off at the correct stop. He regularly found himself drifting further from some essential part of himself, relaxing steadily into the sensation of floating that dominated his consciousness, leaning into this sensation like leaning back into a low chair.

And yet, amid this feeling of falling, this slipping away from the someone or something that he used to be, there was still a part of him scrambling upward. He curated various avenues of rebellion against the route his life appeared to be taking. Sometimes he scratched himself with his fingernails until he bled, until the skin of his arms went numb. Sometimes he imagined being choked to death, imagined it vividly with his eyes closed, the bulge of veins in his neck, the warmth and twitch of his body in someone else's hands. Sometimes he watched porn until his stomach hurt.

His first and most important avenue of rebellion, however, was the folded wad of cash in his jacket pocket: his tips from the night, carefully counted before leaving the bar. He would take half of this money and place it in a shoebox beside his mattress. The shoebox lid barely fit now—he had saved nearly three thousand dollars. He didn't know what he would do with the money, he hadn't thought that far ahead, but he kept it close, visible. Solid, material reassurance that things could get better than this.

His second avenue of rebellion, well-frequented, was the moment in which he now stood: this moment of hesitation and delay before heading home. It was his habit to stop in Victoria Park and smoke a final cigarette or joint after work. He did this no matter the cold chafing the backs of his hands or the emptiness he felt in the space before daybreak. He liked the feeling of the rolled paper, warm and acidic between his lips. He liked to look out over the park and the intersecting roads beyond, the slow revolution of late-night traffic. He liked the darkness of the grass between the pathways. He liked the quiet. He liked the long huff of breath in his chest.

Jasper moved quickly. It had been a particularly busy night at the bar, a particularly good night for tips, and he was hoping it would be a particularly peaceful night for smoking before sleep. The weather was cold, but not as cold as it had been the night before, or the night before that. Some of winter's tension was letting up, loosening, making Jasper's steps lighter as he walked, his thoughts a little softer in his head.

He had barely stepped into the park, however—had barely crossed the first section of grass and headed toward the picnic tables in the centre—when he spotted the figure sitting under the pine tree.

It was a dark night, the sky mottled with clouds, but in the white lights lining the paths, the pine tree looked tall and skeletal, silvery as if dusted with snow. The figure was difficult to discern, though it was less than fifteen feet from him.

The figure was a woman.

She was a woman—he could tell that much at least. She was a woman because she had long hair, scraggly and falling over her shoulders. She was a woman because she wore a dress, her bare legs sprawled loose and pale out in front of her—strange to be wearing such a short dress on such a cold night, but this he attributed to her being homeless. Newly homeless, he decided, when he stepped closer and saw the stark cleanliness of her beige shoes. She was a woman because against the front of her dress, against the dapple of silver light spilling through the pine boughs, was the round swell of breasts.

By this time, by the time he was able to see the slope of her chest, he had moved closer to the tree and was half-kneeling, peering through the branches, his head beginning to swim pleasantly from the weed he had smoked on the other side of Richmond Street.

The woman's ankles were slim, the bones pushing out like knuckles beneath the skin. Jasper wanted to reach out and touch them, wanted to pluck the ankle bone from her leg like a marble and hold it dismembered in his hand. And without thinking—his thoughts moved slow and slippery behind his eyes—without thinking, like a child who reaches out in a store to grab a toy, Jasper actually did reach out toward that patch of skin, her ankle, above her little shoe.

But as the pine needles touched and scraped along the back of his hand, the ankles pulled away and disappeared into shadow. Jasper blinked, frowning, his brows furrowed and confused, as if he had forgotten himself, as if he had lost some thought he had been extending with his hand.

The woman stared at him, her knees tucked up beneath her chin. He couldn't see her face. Her nose was pushed deep into the space between her knees and her forehead was covered by long drifts of hair and shadow.

"I'm sorry," said Jasper, retracting his hand. "I didn't mean to scare you."

The woman didn't respond.

"Listen," said Jasper, "you must be cold. You must be freezing. Come out—" He swallowed a throatful of saliva that had gathered on his tongue as he looked at the line of her thighs beneath her dress. "Come out from under there."

The woman didn't move.

"Come on out," he said, pushing his hand once more between the branches of the tree. He felt each needle as it passed along his skin, like the scrape of light fingernails. He thought suddenly of his mother, who, when he was young, when they were still living in the townhouse in London, would rub his back before sleep. He remembered it, lying on his stomach in the bed as her warm hands lifted his shirt and her fingernails scraped lightly like pine needles across his skin.

The woman stared at him.

"Come on," he said. "It's okay. I—" He stuttered on the word. "I won't hurt you."

Jasper's hand was close enough now to touch her knee-cap, and he almost did, almost flinched forward and put his fingers on her leg, her lack of resistance an invitation to him. But at the last moment he pulled back—surfacing far enough from the murky cloud of his mind—to glance behind him into the park, to feel the cold on the back of his neck and wrists, to see himself as someone else might see him. A man, stinking of weed, trying to coax a homeless woman from beneath a tree in the middle of the night.

"Okay," he said, shoving his hands into his pockets and jumping out of his crouch. "All right." He nodded at the woman. She was little more than a shadowy smudge now that he stood above her. His jaw was tight as he moved away across the grass.

He began walking. The cold settled deep between his shoulder blades as he fiddled with his last joint, pre-rolled and tucked into the corner of his pocket. His breath floated out in a warm, white cloud in front of his face, his lips beginning to feel chapped and sore, all the slow and tired sensations of the night leaning into his body.

There was a rustle behind him, the soft shift of clothing, the drag of knees. He turned and saw the woman standing upright beside the pine tree.

"Hello?" he said. "Have you changed your mind?"

She began to walk toward him.

✝✝✝

The first time Jasper had sex was at a college party, before he had dropped out of school. He and a girl he had met twice kissed drunkenly on the couch before moving into his friend's bedroom, locking the door, and proceeding to have rough, uncoordinated intercourse. He hadn't lasted long, and she had screeched at him to fuck off when he tried to bite her ear—something he had hoped would be sexy, but which he had apparently done too aggressively, judging by the line of blood running down the back of her cheek and under her jawline.

Her expression while leaving the room wasn't quite disdain, not quite a scowl. It was a look closer to bewilderment, closer to horror in the way her eyelids hiked up into their sockets and the muscles around her jaw tightened, in the way her skin turned white around her lips and her body rushed for the door. It was an expression he had seen on his mother's face many times when he was young, after his father had come home for a weekend or two. His mother wore that expression while they sat around the table eating breakfast: a kind of shocked exhaustion that lingered in the lines around her eyes and lips throughout the day, re-emerging while she brushed her teeth before bed. It was the expression she wore all the way down the hall to her bedroom as Jasper's father followed her.

Fuck you! Jasper had yelled at the girl as she left the room, not really sure why he had said it. He knew he had hurt her in other ways, besides biting her ear—clawing at her as he tried to take off her clothes, moving too rapidly inside her, moving even as she swore and tried to push him away, moving faster as she became still beneath him, scrunching shut her eyes.

Fuck you! he had yelled again as she slammed the door.

He was confused by her anger. Even if he had hurt her, at least he had touched her, shown her intimacy, a form—however brutal—of physical affection. He exhaled heavily, the euphoria from his orgasm still rolling over him. And the next time he had sex, he closed his eyes and imagined that first girl's expression as he came, eyelids peeled back and lips pulled into a tight O.

"Hello?" he said. "Have you changed your mind?"

She began to walk toward him. Her limbs were rigid, thrown forward stiffly across the grass, her right hip bucking upward with a slight limp. This Jasper attributed to the woman sitting so long under the tree in the cold. She moved as if she had just woken from a deep slumber, as if she were still half asleep. She was robotic but also clumsy, dragging her feet, lurching forward and peeling back, her strides long and then short, wide, as if the practice of walking were new to her. Jasper wondered if she was drunk.

He swallowed. It would be easier if she was drunk.

He pulled the joint out of his pocket as she drew near him, and he began turning it between his fingers. He needed something to do with his hands. The woman was tall, lean—almost too lean, he noticed as she came closer, her face almost gaunt, her collarbones poking out above the top of her dress. *Homeless*, he thought again. *She must be homeless.* Her arms were long and pale, legs long and pale, so much skin touching the frigid air. *She must be homeless and in shock*, he thought. Newly homeless—he looked again at her clean shoes—and in shock. She must be stunned somehow, inebriated, or else she would be shaking horribly from the cold, her teeth clacking, arms looped around to hug her body. Instead she stood calmly, stopping five feet away from him, her hands at her sides, head tilted down so her hair hung and covered most of her face. Jasper didn't wonder at the stains on her arms and dress. The earth was sloppy with mud and newly melted snow. She must have tripped. She must have fallen down.

Before putting on the shoes? he thought, and in the same moment discarded the thought.

In her hand, the woman held a dented shoebox.

"What've you got there?" he asked, fiddling with the joint between his fingers. He thought of the shoebox sitting beside his mattress in his apartment, stuffed with cash.

The woman didn't answer, didn't look at him.

He coughed uncomfortably. "So," he said, "you changed your mind? My place is just up the road." He gestured over his shoulder, pointing toward Central Avenue.

The woman didn't answer him, didn't act as if she had heard.

"It's warm there," he said, tucking his chin down into his collar and blowing out air.

That wasn't exactly true. His apartment was never warm in the winter. The walls were old and thin. He had a space heater that only half heated the room, and when he stood by the kitchen counter, he could feel a draft against his toes. But it was better than out here in the open air. Jasper stomped his feet, trying to force blood back through his ankles.

"Well?" he said.

The woman didn't move.

He held up the joint and dug the lighter out of his pocket. "We could smoke?" he suggested. It was what he had come into the park to do, after all. It might bring the woman closer.

She lifted her head slightly, watching him as he flicked the lighter into life.

He sucked at the end of the joint, breathing deeply and then exhaling. He looked up. The sky was fuzzy in the darkness, cloud cover absorbing the white lights of the park. The tops of the pine trees were like the jagged teeth of a lower jaw. He felt the wind slide from the back of his neck to his throat, along his Adam's apple, and down into the collar of his jacket. The clouds swirled heavily, gradually, the white light from the park folding into their layers like the milk his mother used to fold into cake mix on his birthday. He took another long draw from the joint, the paper warm and acidic between his lips.

When he levelled his gaze, the woman had moved closer.

"Here," he said, holding out the joint.

The woman stared at his hand, but didn't reach forward to meet it.

He shrugged, pulling his shoulders back up against his ears. He had begun to stop caring so much what she did or didn't do. He sucked once more from the joint and then ashed the end, tapping the paper lightly with his fingertip.

"You know why I like this?" he said. "Smoking, I mean. You know why I like it?"

The woman was quiet in front of him, watchful.

"It slows things down," he said. He was looking at the sky again, away from the woman. "Even now, when I'm talking to you, every word takes longer to say. And it's good. It feels good. Let's say I'm walking down a road. It's a long road to begin with, and now it takes me longer. It's a plain road, but now it's not so plain because I can feel more. I can see more because everything's slower. My thoughts come slower." He watched the clouds moving in the wind. "My thoughts come slower into my head," he said, "and the thoughts mean more because there are less of them. And you know what? You know what it is? It's like being a kid again. I can remember what it feels like to be small and not have as many thoughts in my head. Not just remember, but really feel it. What it feels like to walk down a long road for a long time and forget that it's plain, that it's a plain road and there's nothing to see. I can remember all of a sudden. I can feel—"

Jasper felt a tickle at his throat. His chin dropped. His eyes veered away from the sky and landed on the woman now standing directly in front of him, her face still half-covered with hair, the rest plunged in shadow. Her hand reached out, her arm straight, erect, in order to touch his neck.

"Hey," he said slowly. "Hey." He didn't step away.

Her fingertips drifted across the spiky, half-trimmed hair under his jawline and the soft, downy skin below. It was a strange gesture, to be sure, but it was the first gesture she had made besides walking across the grass. And although she hadn't said anything, although she had hardly looked at him, he took this gesture as confirmation, confirmation of their consensus, their silent communication—silent on her part, at least—a gesture confirming they were both thinking the same thing, had the same idea in mind.

He realized—now that the woman was this close, as his breath pulled up into his throat and a pleasant chill ran down his back—that there was something familiar about her, something he couldn't quite place. It was something in the curve of her face, the shape of her shoulders, the length of her arms. He couldn't see her clearly. The night seemed to be growing darker, blurry—or perhaps this was simply the effect of his eyelids beginning to close, from the weed or from exhaustion.

He leaned into her touch, thinking again of his mother lifting his shirt to rub his back before sleep. He wondered why he was thinking of her, why now, here—he hadn't seen her in years. Maybe this woman reminded him somehow of his mother—maybe this was the familiarity he felt. He leaned into her hand and her fingernails slid by his ear, her fingertips touching his neck, her touch making him dizzy. Her elbow hitched up onto his shoulder, his arms groped forward to find her waist, breathing in, trying to breathe into her hair—

He drew back at the smell of her, coughing. There was something rotten in the odour that came off her body, something rancid and putrid and sour. He stepped away, lifting the joint to his lips to disguise his movements, but also to put a familiar flavour in his mouth. The joint was barely lit, and he sucked at it dryly, looking at the woman out of the side of his eye.

Her hand had dropped. She seemed unaffected, unperturbed, stood in the grass as if nothing in particular had brought her there.

Jasper decided for certain the woman was drunk. Drunk or high or both. Or—his mind flipped through each possibility in succession, pulling the thoughts from his slow and sticky consciousness like pulling gum from hair—or disabled. Maybe she was disabled.

Stupid bitch, he thought, the words rising to him, compulsively, out of nowhere. He swallowed them back down into his stomach, swallowed them along with his weed-flavoured saliva and the stench from her skin that still lingered in the mucous of his throat.

He looked at her standing in the grass.

"Fuck it," he mumbled aloud.

He took one last drag from his joint, tossed it down, and clamped it beneath his shoe. Then he walked toward her, one hand already extending to slide around her hip.

Jasper had never done well at school. He had never cared enough to do well, had never found any subject important enough to try at—at least, that was what he told himself. In elementary school he had been what some called imaginative, what others called distractible. The teachers disliked him. He would do strange things when he got tired or angry, things that seemed to happen without his conscious involvement, like spitting on the floor, or throwing bits of broken eraser and pencil at the windowpane. Once, while a teacher was trying to drag him from the classroom, he got hold of the chalkboard eraser and patterned her skirt with dusty chalk marks. When she bent down to brush them off, he stuffed the eraser in her face.

Once he brought in a BB gun and pretended he was going to kill— He didn't know who. Everyone, probably. The teacher, mainly.

In high school, in Toronto, he cared even less than he had in elementary school. He took applied classes, and his teachers made frequent appointments with his mother about the possibility of him failing and what they could work on at home to improve the situation. Then his mother stopped coming to the appointments, and his teachers stopped making them. Jasper supposed his mother was disappointed. At the very least worn down, exhausted. The new job that had brought the two of them to Toronto had fallen through in the first three months.

"It was bullshit," she told Jasper. "They hired me with no real position to fill."

In truth, she had lied about her qualifications, her education, and her boss had found out.

She went back to serving, and Jasper didn't see much of her. They lived in a one-bedroom apartment with a balcony that showed a close-up view of another apartment building. Jasper liked to lie on the pullout couch and watch people across the narrow stretch of air between buildings, people who had forgotten to close the blinds or didn't care, people watching TV or making dinner or getting undressed. People talking on the phone, entertaining guests, staring at computer screens. He began to wonder what his own life would look like from a distance, pushed into a lit-up, tiny box.

It would look like this, he thought, gazing up at the living room ceiling from the pullout. They were near the top floor of the apartment building and the ceiling was blotchy with stains from past water leaks. *It would look like this.*

Jasper never failed a class. He wasn't that stupid, in the sense that he knew if he failed he would have to take a class again, and that if he failed enough times he might have to stay in high school longer. So he didn't fail. But he supposed his mother was still disappointed. He supposed this because they didn't talk much.

That was why, when *it* happened, he decided not to tell her.

He expected that, inevitably, she would find out. She would come home unexpectedly—a short shift at work—and see his face. Or would encounter a fellow parent or teacher from school who would mention the incident as if she already knew, and she would question, confused, and discover—

She would delete the old messages on the answering machine so new ones could come through, from the principal, vice principal, the mothers of the other boys.

She would answer the phone one morning.

She would just know, somehow, in the way that mothers know. She would notice the way Jasper slept late and buried his face in the blankets on the couch.

She would hear his silence. She would.

It happened like this. At a party. At Rebecca's party, at the house her parents rented. Jasper wasn't officially invited, but his friends Michael and Jeff were, so he tagged along.

They were only recently his friends—guys he knew as acquaintances from gym class and homeroom. Jeff was round in his body and face, with narrow eyes, permanently rosy cheeks, and big hands. Michael was slim, wiry, taller than Jasper and broader in the shoulders. He had an open face, eyebrows raised as if he had just remembered something important, and hair that stood straight up from his forehead, the strands separated and stiffened with gel— pointed like porcupine quills.

Jasper hadn't paid much attention to either Jeff or Michael until Michael approached him one day at lunchtime, looking skittish, and invited Jasper to smoke weed with him behind the school. They slunk outside and past the back fence as the bell rang, taking turns smoking a joint and coughing. Less than ten minutes had passed before Jeff showed up and threw his heavy arms around them both.

"Where'd you sneak off to? Huh?" he said to Michael, who scowled and pushed him away. "I've been looking all over for you."

Jasper met up with them on weekends after that, mostly to smoke and drink and play video games. He found Jeff and Michael excessively boring, almost brutish, but he was too bored by himself to decline Michael's invitations. Better to be bored and high on someone else's couch than be bored and sober at home.

And it wasn't a problem, wasn't something he felt he should avoid—those long hours during which they rarely looked away from the TV screen, Jeff stuffing his hand into a bag of Cheetos while laughter cracked like cannon fire from his mouth, Michael snickering and shifting as his hands sweated on the controller. Jasper could tell he sweated because of the wide, damp circles Michael's palm would leave on his shoulder whenever he shoved him sideways onto the couch after winning a game. It wasn't a problem. Whether those long hours in front of the TV happened or not, Jasper didn't care. It was a way to fill time until school started again on Monday, and school was a way to fill time until the weekends when he would sit and get high and play video games. Each day spilled into the next, rolling together, blurring, until Grade 11 was nearly complete and the final year of high school loomed heavily in Jasper's mind.

But before he could worry too much about the final year of school, there was Rebecca's party.

He tagged along behind Jeff and Michael, taking four shots from his mickey before he had even entered the house, and then four more just inside the front door. Someone handed him a beer, and then suddenly he looked up to find that he was in the basement with Michael and they were alone, and Michael was undoing his pants.

Michael was undoing Jasper's pants. Jasper was lying on the floor with his arms spread out like wings on either side of him. His head was very heavy. He couldn't remember coming downstairs. He couldn't remember walking down the stairs into the basement. Maybe Michael had carried him there. He stared for a moment at the basement ceiling, noticing how it was painted the same colour as the ceiling of his apartment above the pullout couch, how it had similar dark splotches, stains from past water leaks. He imagined for a moment that he was back home, waiting to fall asleep. That he had managed somehow to leave the party and get himself back home.

Jasper felt Michael's fingers on his cock, trying to tug it, limp, from his underwear. He looked down to see Michael lowering his face into his crotch. Jasper didn't think. His knee came up to meet with Michael's nose. He blinked and then he was above Michael, staggering, kicking him in the chest and legs. Michael's nose was crooked. His face was full of blood. Jasper zipped up his pants and went upstairs. He left the house without talking to anyone, vomited on the front lawn, and woke the next morning in his clothes on the couch, his hair tousled, mouth sour and dry, but otherwise fine.

But otherwise fine. He was otherwise fine.

The party was on a Friday night. He spent Saturday recovering from his hangover on the couch. On Sunday he walked around the block three times, feeling cooped up and suffocated, and then tried to do his homework, an unusual guilt building up like a ball of acid in his chest. He kept waiting for the phone to ring, for someone to press the buzzer in the lobby below. He thought about skipping school on Monday and then thought better of it—he was two days of missed school away from being suspended.

On Monday, in homeroom, Jeff and Michael didn't look at him. Michael's nose was still crooked, and faint bruising had spread across his cheeks and eye sockets. The skin around his nose looked swollen and sticky, like Play-Doh. Jeff and Michael didn't look at Jasper and they didn't talk to him after class or approach him during lunch break. This was a good thing, Jasper decided. He didn't want to look at them or talk to them either. He would find something else to do on the weekends.

But on his walk home—they knew his route—they were waiting for him.

"Hey, Jasper," said Jeff, as he turned a corner, and before he could move, Jeff grabbed him by the back of his neck and dragged him behind an apartment building, throwing him down on the pavement beside a Dumpster. As Jasper tried to scramble to his feet, Jeff produced a mini baseball bat, small enough that it could fit in his backpack. Something long and black hung from Michael's hand. A sock. Inside the sock, weighing it down, was something small and hard, what Jasper later found out was a gym lock.

They beat him until he started to scream. They beat him until he stopped screaming and bile worked up like a worm through his throat and he looked down into the gravel and was certain this was how he was going to die. He felt numb—they must have broken his spine. Then Jeff reeled back to kick Jasper in the forehead, splitting his skin and knocking him unconscious.

When Jasper woke, the colour in the sky looked the same, but Jeff and Michael were gone. He couldn't stand. He called for help—a broken, mewling sound that he was surprised came from his own mouth—until someone heard him and peeked around the side of the building. From a distance, that person called the police.

The police and then the hospital staff wanted to contact Jasper's mother, but she didn't own a cellphone. By the time they got hold of the phone number of the restaurant where she worked, the person who answered said she wasn't there—her shift had ended early and she was on her way home. When they called the apartment, no one answered, and they couldn't leave a message because the answering machine was full. Was there anyone else they could contact? No. Jasper promised to tell his mother himself. Of course he would tell his mother. Why wouldn't he tell his mother?

There were two hairline fractures, not quite splitting the bone, one in his jaw and one in his eye socket. Three of his ribs had been broken. He had a minor concussion and bruising—and somehow this was the worst—bruising and swelling all over his face, making him bloated and purple, unrecognizable in the mirror. His lips were fat and squishy, full of liquid. A bandage, hiding the tape that pulled together his split skin, covered his face from the eyebrows up. He was a warped version of himself, a figure in the mirror that moved when he moved, breathed when he breathed. He was monstrous. He was disgusting.

But he hadn't broken his back, as he had thought. The doctor said his injuries were mostly superficial. He was lucky.

They kept him for a couple of hours and then sent him home in a cab with a prescription for painkillers that he never filled because he couldn't afford them. They assumed he would press charges with the police. When he arrived at the apartment, it was late, and dark, and his mother was already asleep in her room.

Later that year, in the summer, Jasper decided he would go back to London for college. It was the last place he remembered being happy.

―――

She hadn't said a word, but she didn't resist him.

The woman walked beside Jasper, brushing against his jacket, and his pants felt suddenly tight, restrictive—all of his clothes felt suddenly restrictive—as he realized she was coming with him back to his apartment. A warm pulse ran down the inside of his thighs. The woman hadn't said a word, but when he placed his hand on her lower back and guided her toward the edge of the park, she came easily, willingly, her feet dragging only a little, her toes catching only a couple of times in the grass and making her stumble. He caught her when she stumbled, laughing, breathing through his mouth so he wouldn't smell her, the world rolling up like a wave as he stumbled, too, stumbled beneath her weight and then lifted himself up again, holding her, steadying her. The woman's breath came out in short and choppy huffs. She was laughing—he imagined she was laughing, too.

"Fuck it," he had said, looking at her standing in the grass. *Stupid bitch*. The words pushing up from inside his stomach and into his head. His fingertips tingled. He would put her in the shower, he decided. He would put her in the shower and wash her, make her clean. She looked like she hadn't showered in weeks. He would wash her hair and her body, her face. His hand gripped her waist tighter as they walked, and he pictured her body, an amalgamation of all the women's bodies he had ever seen. The park drifted away behind them. They coasted through a set of lights and headed up the road, the woman huffing, almost wheezing, and Jasper feeling the front of his jeans rubbing on him he walked.

The woman was walking stiffly. He wanted her to hurry. He wanted to pull her along, drag her, but his own feet weren't working beneath him. His head was full of static, the white fuzz on a dead TV screen. In the yellow glow of street lights, he looked down and watched her large, bumpy shadow move along the road, her shoes clopping, limbs rising and falling, shadow stretching. Jasper felt the tops of the trees moving above him. The sky above him, he knew, was moving through night into morning.

When they arrived at the outdoor staircase leading up to the second-floor apartment of the house on Central Avenue, he turned to the woman, who was staring down at her feet. He thought of telling her, *We're here, this is it, my apartment*, but realized what a waste of words it would be. He grabbed her wrist and began pulling her up the stairs.

The woman followed him, her shoes clapping on the steps.

At the top, he fumbled for his key, which was tucked beneath his wallet in his jacket pocket. It was dark on the landing. The wind flew through the trees, wound around his neck, and lifted the woman's hair. He couldn't see her face, but in the shadows he could see her lips moving, twitching, jerking upward as if trying to speak. He felt her hand moving, spider crawling into his sleeve and along his forearm. He jumped at her touch, his tongue pulling back into his mouth, his throat hot.

The key stuck in the lock. He turned it, and the door popped open.

He pulled the woman inside, roughly, rough enough that she tripped on the door frame, dropped the shoebox she was still holding in one hand, and fell into his arms, her nails scratching through his jacket sleeve to his elbow. She grunted, coughed, her mouth still moving against his neck where it had landed. But it wasn't a kiss, this movement. Her lips twitched rapidly—he was certain she was about to speak. Her body pressed against his crotch, and the dark room expanded around him, his brain throbbing. He forgot for a moment where he was, how he had gotten there with this woman leaning against him, her bare arms papery and cold in his hands. He forgot for a moment that he had wanted to clean her, strip her down and wash her, before he really touched her. Here he was, touching her, pulling her arm from his jacket sleeve so he could place both hands on her skinny breasts, swooping down her rib cage to her stomach and waist, stepping toward her, against her, his leg dragging up between her thighs. They hit the door and slammed it closed, the room snapping into full darkness.

Jasper felt an inexplicable sob roll up through his throat in this darkness where the woman couldn't see him. He thought of her fingers on his neck in the park. He couldn't remember the last time he had been touched by someone, the last time someone had initiated touch. And in the background, there was still familiarity in the woman, the feeling of coming home.

He reached up and lifted the woman's face from his shoulder. He kissed her. He strapped himself onto her moving mouth and pushed his tongue between her lips. Her jaw fell open—in shock, in submission, he didn't know—and he met with her saliva, a foul, dark flavour rushing through his mouth. She tasted sour and earthy, somewhere between bile and the iron undertones of blood. His tongue, thrust up against her teeth, felt something soft and granular release from the pockets beside her gums: soil—yes—he could feel that it was soil, mud coming up out of her mouth. There were other things, too, rolling forward onto his tongue. Mud and hair, large tangles of hair, and the sharp curve of what felt like a fingernail.

Jasper yelped, spitting, pulling backward. He slammed against the wall directly behind him and wiped at his lips with his hands, swiped at the woman he knew was standing in front of him, felt the hard scrape of his fingernails make contact with the skin of her face.

He felt sober for the first time in hours.

The woman was not homeless, or disabled, or drunk. No. The woman was not anything he could imagine.

No explanation came to him.

He lashed out, striking the woman and pushing her away as he tried to pull hair and dirt from his mouth, spewing saliva and blood onto the floor.

The light switch, he thought. *The light.* He scrambled sideways, reaching over his shoulder to turn on the light.

SEVEN

Jasper and Frances were sitting on the steps of Frances's back porch, the wood bending softly beneath their hips and bare feet. It was late afternoon. The sun fell through the treetops and over the playground. The thrum of cars on Adelaide Street behind the fence, angry as a disturbed beehive, had begun to subside as rush hour dropped away. The air was still warm. It was still summer.

It was the summer moving into the autumn that would become the winter before Jasper left. Neither of them knew this yet. All they knew was that it was late afternoon, school was starting up in a week, and their mothers would soon call them in for dinner.

I'll be an astronaut, Jasper was saying, waving his hands around in the air for emphasis. You'll be waiting for me back home, crying boo-hoo while I'm up there stomping around on the moon.

Yeah, right, said Frances. Fat chance. She laughed at him.

Behind them, in the townhouse, her father was still packing his things. His flight to Germany would leave the next morning. Her mother had stopped talking, was frying meat and vegetables silently on the stovetop.

Frances laughed at Jasper. It was nice to sit, shoulders loosened, and laugh with him.

I could! said Jasper. I could be an astronaut!

I know, said Frances, but fat chance I'd be waiting around down here for you.

What, you'd forget about me?

No, dummy, I'd be up there with you! I could be an astronaut, too, you know.

Now Jasper was laughing. I know, he said. But would you want to?

Frances shrugged. She stretched her toes out onto the grass at the bottom of the porch steps and wiggled them. I don't know, she said. I don't know what I want to be.

Aw, come on, said Jasper. You've got to pick something. I already said I'll be a deep-sea diver, an architect, *and* an astronaut. You know what? Maybe I'll be a lawyer, too. It'd be nice to walk around all day in a tuxedo, looking important and saying whatever I want.

Frances giggled. I don't think lawyers wear tuxedos, she said.

Jasper smiled, his crooked teeth pushing out from behind his lips. Well, I could, you know, he said. If I wanted to.

I know, Frances said.

But, come on, you've got to pick something.

Why do I have to pick something?

'Cause that's the game!

I didn't know we were playing a game.

Frances.

Okay, fine. There is one thing I could be.

Well, what is it?

I can't say it out loud.

Why not?

'Cause then it might not come true.

Like a wish?

Yeah, like a wish.

Jasper stared for a moment at the ground. Then he threw his hands in the air. Aw, come on! he said. You've got to tell me!

No way! said Frances.

Are you kidding me?

I'm not kidding you.

Aw, come on.

You'll go blabbing it everywhere.

I will not!

You will.

I won't.

Well, then—promise.

I promise.

Just like that? You mean it?

Jasper nodded. I mean it.

Frances scrunched her lips together, wrinkling her forehead. She looked for a moment like she would stay that way, face pulled inward, eyebrows tucked together, arms crossed. Then she leaned over and put a hand up to Jasper's cheek, cupping her mouth, and whispered into his ear.

Jasper listened, lips pinched seriously. When Frances pulled away from him, he turned to look at her, eyes squinted, looking at her whole face and body, her blush rising up to the tips of her ears, and he saw her, all of her, for the first time—maybe for the only time.

He nodded. You'd be good at that, he said. You'd be really good at that.

Their shoulders fell against each other. They leaned against each other, sitting on the back porch, looking out at the late sunlight turning the blades of grass dark green. They didn't wonder what it meant, this leaning. They didn't name it.

They stayed there until their shadows stretched and spilled out into the yard, one amorphous lump, like conjoined twins lying in the grass.

EIGHT

Jasper found the light switch. He turned on the light.

The woman stood a foot away from him, her jaw hanging open. Looking at him.

"Frances?" he said, but the moment the word left his mouth he knew that it was wrong. It tasted wrong passing over his tongue.

Jasper hadn't seen Frances in person since he was eleven years old, but he had been to her funeral, had seen her premature graduation photo propped on the table at the front of the church. He had seen her photo—the same photo—in the online obituary. He had seen her photo again and again on social media, gazing out from his Facebook home page or Instagram feed, posted and reposted by his college friends. They identified with her, perhaps, or they simply felt for her. The rumour was that her body hadn't been found for a week. Jasper had temporarily closed his accounts so he wouldn't have to look at her.

He looked now at the woman standing in front of him. Her hair hung ragged over her face. Her dress was torn. In the full light of the entryway he could see that the stains creeping up from her hands to her elbows, the stains he had thought came from falling in the mud, were in fact dark red, were in fact crusted blood. Her left leg, he now saw, was bent sickly to the side, and the edges of her eyelids and mouth were red and puffy, as if torn.

Still, she looked undeniably like Frances.

But she was also undeniably *not* Frances. There was something essential missing from behind her eyes, something vacant, almost cross-eyed, in the way she looked at him.

She wasn't Frances. She wasn't a woman at all.

There was something inhuman in the figure standing in front of him, something that kept it genderless, despite its hair and clothing and the tentative push of breasts against its dress. There was something in the figure that exceeded gender, spilled out from it, overwhelmed it.

"*Frances*," said the thing standing in front of him. It spoke rapidly, its jaw snapping up to form the word. Jasper flinched at the gravel in its voice. He looked at its body, unable to believe that just a moment earlier he had touched its breasts, pushed up against its legs.

"*Frances*," said the thing, the *creature*, again.

That he had kissed it, put his tongue in its mouth.

"*Frances*," said the creature, the *monster*.

That he had wanted to wash it in the shower, bring it to bed. That he had sobbed when he touched it, because it had been so long since he had been touched in return. That the monster had let him sob, had heard him.

His hands came up, unthinkingly, to its throat. "Get out," he said, but he didn't let go. He pushed the monster back until it slammed against the opposite wall, his thumbs digging into its trachea, feeling its breath hitch and disappear. The monster's smell filled his nostrils and he wanted to cough, to vomit. He waited for that bewildered expression, the expression from his first sexual encounter, to appear on its face, for its eyelids to peel back and its mouth to pull into a tight O. He waited for it to become human in his hands.

The monster stared at him, its throat bucking, but otherwise unresponsive.

If he had looked down, he would have seen its fingers curling into claws.

"What are you?" he said, pushing harder into the skin above its collarbone, pushing his entire weight against the monster's neck. He would push until it squirmed, until it tried to scream. He would push—yes—he would push until it became human in his hands.

"Who are you?" he said.

"*Fran-ces*," the monster wheezed.

Jasper realized, still pushing against its neck, that *Frances* was the only word the monster had said. He wondered how much the monster could understand, wondered how many words filled its head. And if this word—*Frances*—was the only one it knew, then how many times must the word roll, from moment to moment, through the dark space behind the monster's eyes? The monster appeared thoughtless, staring at him, beginning to grow bug-eyed beneath his hands. What were thoughts, Jasper wondered, without words to shape them? What was experience—the slow bulge of emotion and images surfacing like large fish from underwater—what was memory, what was contemplation, without description?

What was action, Jasper wondered, what was motivation, without any words for explanation? What drove someone, something, that didn't even know enough to say that it was driven?

Instinct, Jasper realized.

It was like an animal, instinct welling up in the black currents of a mind, like heat rising. The monster's motivation was the same as its impulse to breathe. Its movements were natural, necessary, uncomplicated. Without words, without the clutter of thought, its actions were simple, almost automatic, unadorned.

The monster reached up and grabbed the sides of Jasper's head.

NINE

"*Who-are-you*," the monster said.

It put its thumbs into Jasper's eye sockets and pushed until he let go of its throat.

"*Who-are-you*." It grabbed his wrists as they pulled away and bent them until they snapped and crumpled, twisted, by his sides.

Jasper started to squeal, a high-pitched whine that didn't quite rise into a shriek. He turned and tried to dash into the interior of the apartment.

"*Who-are-you*," the monster said.

Words had begun to slop through its head. Words as familiar as memories, rolling in and jumbling, this boy's face, frightened as he tried to get away, his face rolling in with a slippery wash of memories, memories breaking like waves and settling. The image of a boy with mud-coloured hair standing at the top of playground equipment, pointing down and saying, *Would you tell?*

If the moon was falling to Earth, if it was going to fall right on your house, would you tell?

If a crowd of eagles swooped down and pulled out your hair with their claws—

If the ocean rose up and covered the whole world—

Would you tell?

Tell what? the monster asked. *Tell what?*

I can't say it. You just have to know. It's like a promise.

I wouldn't tell, the monster had said.

No, not the monster. A little girl. A little girl, watching the boy rocket down the slide and pound through the stones lining the space around the play equipment, had said: *I wouldn't tell.*

The monster grabbed Jasper, one hand on his face and the other on the back of his skull, and turned his head around to see his eyes.

Would you tell?

I wouldn't tell.

Not even, not even, not even.

Jasper looked suddenly calm, his arms hanging uselessly by his sides.

The monster blinked through the memories spilling across its vision.

Would you tell?

Tell what?

I can't say. It's like a promise.

It's like a promise, the boy had said, but he had never explained what it meant.

And a little girl, years ago, had promised. She had promised and remembered the promise, deep down like an empty skull inside of her, the promise she had made on the day she discovered she wasn't real. Her hands in front of her face, her hands in the dark weren't real. She couldn't see her face in the dark. Her body on the bed in the basement was numb, she couldn't feel her legs or her arms, couldn't feel her feet as they paced across the room. She couldn't taste the taste of water in her mouth, couldn't feel the oily slick of paint as she touched the wall. She couldn't hear her voice because she wasn't screaming. She had never tried the door-knob—the door had never been locked. None of it, nothing had been real. She couldn't move because she didn't have any muscles, she couldn't talk because she didn't know how, she had never learned. Her fingers, she felt them, they were falling out of her knuckles. Her tongue she had cut from her mouth. Her feet from her legs. Her hands from her wrists. *But how could she cut off her tongue, Grandpa, if her hands were gone?* It was an important question that she was asking her grandfather. *How could she cut out her eyes?*

How could she cut off her head? Somehow, she had cut off her own head.

Tell—what? The boy had never explained.

But now she understood, she had always understood: the boy was lying.

Frances had always been real.

But how could she say aloud that he was lying? He was her first and very best friend, and the worlds he had created were enchanting, and the instructions he gave her were easy to follow—it was an easy world, at first, to live in.

There is something so soothing in floating, something so safe in dreaming. It's so simple to lie back and unroll yourself into an invisible body, to unroll your invisible toes into a bed that's inviting.

How can you wake yourself from dreaming? thought the monster. *It's as difficult as dying.*

Jasper looked at the monster. It was a look of resignation, lacking fear, an old and tired look, years of hurt flooding his eyes. His mouth opened and bowed into what might have become a sob.

He didn't have time to speak. The monster struck him in the face—one, two, three times. He fell backward, his arms with their broken wrists reaching up and weaving through the air, as if searching for an embrace. The monster followed him to the floor and hit him again, again, again, until his skull bent inward, dented from the monster's fists, dimpled like a golf ball, until he had stopped squealing, stopped breathing, and blood had begun to bubble in his ears.

The monster hit him until the skin of his face tore and started to come off in long strips, long strips that the monster stretched and pulled away, grappled with and ripped until there was no face left to see, no features or details that would make him recognizable, that would allow someone to call him Jasper, to know him.

When the monster had finished, it held the skin of Jasper's face in its hands and looked around the room. The walls were fuzzy and soft. The monster's vision had blurred with adrenaline. It didn't know, for a long moment, where it was or what it had done.

Is this a dream, it wondered. The sharp edges of the world had fallen away. The furniture had begun to smear into the floorboards. The kitchen appliances and light fixtures bled into one another.

Was this dreaming? All of this—dreaming? How could it tell the difference? Half the memories in the monster's head weren't its own, but they stuck with the thickness of wax behind its eyes. It tried to blink them away. The memories remained a silkscreen across its vision.

The boy lay on the floor beside the monster, his neck bent to one side, his arms splayed open. The skin on his face was gone, his cheeks and forehead a red mess of flesh and muscle, his eyes white and wide without eyelids, his eyebrows and eyelashes gone, his teeth bare, remnants of cartilage soft beneath the bone of his nose.

The monster still held in its hands the skin that had made up his face. The monster looked at this skin, surprised at how stretchy and thin it felt, how delicate, like dough. It brought its hands together and mashed the skin into a ball, squeezing and rolling until every part of it was red and bruised-looking, until the monster's hands and the skin from Jasper's face were the same colour, a bluish-grey beneath the blood.

It remembered the boy in the snow back behind the townhouses, lying in an oversized winter coat. *I'm so cold.* And the hunger brought on by him leaving.

The monster remembered him with his knees tucked up under his chin in his bedroom. *Is he gone?* Something terrible waiting for him below, pacing through the townhouse kitchen. Something terrible like a monster below.

The monster mashed Jasper's face together in its hands. It mashed his face until the skin tore again and pulled apart between its fingers.

When Jasper's flesh had gone cold and his body stiff, the monster placed the remains of his face onto the floor and stood. From the kitchen faucet, it drank water, drank until it vomited in the sink and then drank more. It found crackers in the cupboard, bread, milk, and eggs in the fridge, which it devoured raw, one after the other. It found pickles and ate until the jar was empty. It licked the vinegar from its skin.

The monster ran the faucet and washed its body until all the blood had disappeared down the sink.

Outside the window, the sun was rising. Yellow streaks from the east stained the clouds a soupy orange.

The monster went to the corner of the room and fell down onto the mattress. It didn't bother with the blankets. It slept.

TEN

The monster dreamt that it was an old woman.

It had blinked, and then it was dreaming. But it didn't know it dreamt. It was sleeping, but didn't know it slept. It had blinked and suddenly, somehow, it was old. Everything between young and old disappeared in that blink, like water thrown on a flame, a dark splotch spreading across its memory.

It looked down at its hands and they were wrinkled, translucent like wax paper and soft. It looked down at its feet and the flat, thick yellow toenails scooping down into the skin. Its body was deflated. Its breasts were long, its shoulders curved inward, and it could feel the bumps of its spine rising like a wave against the skin of its back. Its head was heavy on its neck. Its body was heavy beneath it, every limb weighted like a sack full of sand.

It looked up and saw it was looking in a mirror, and in the mirror its face was old. The monster touched its face, trying to pull off the skin. It dug its fingernails in, but its flesh only stretched, wouldn't tear.

The monster gave up. It was tired. Besides, its hands were as old as its face and covered with the same wrinkled skin, and it would have to tear all of this off, too, all of it, pulling off its own hands with its hands. It was tired. It was old and wanted to sleep.

It looked at its eyes in the mirror and wanted to say they were the same. The same as what? It had trouble remembering anything before the blink. But yes, that's right, its eyes in the basement had been bloodshot and sloppy, nearly dripping out of its face, slowly hardening, and this, it knew now, was the growing. Like a child it had been rapidly growing, like a fetus placed outside the womb but still growing. And screaming. With no words, but still screaming.

It looked up in the mirror and found itself screaming, its jaw dropped low, skin waggling, soft hair on its head, white, trembling. Bellowing. Deep from its bowels and gut roiling—a scream.

‑‑‑

The monster woke to the sound of an alarm ringing. It was three o'clock in the afternoon, light slanted through the window and onto the opposite wall, and an alarm was ringing.

No, not an alarm. A phone. Jasper's phone was ringing in his jacket pocket, pinched beneath his body still lying in the entryway.

The monster waited for the ringing to stop, and then it sat up on the mattress and looked around the room. It was a small apartment, the walls drab and smudged in daylight. The air smelled stale. The monster wrapped its arms around its legs and tapped the soles of its shoes against the laminate flooring.

Beside the mattress was a shoebox the monster hadn't noticed before. It lifted the lid. Money, wads and wads of small bills, pushing up out of the box. The monster touched the inky paper with its fingertips. It couldn't tell how much money was in the box, it couldn't possibly estimate. It was still learning. But each moment brought new memories, a new heat and stretching in its brain, a hum like the vibration of bees.

There must be enough money for a plane ticket, it thought. It had woken with this thought—*airplane*—although it had never seen one before. It had woken with the words *Europe* and *Germany*, with a desire for flight, the notion that it had to get far away, that there was something yet left to do.

The monster stood and went to the closet. Inside was a backpack. It unzipped the flap and placed both shoeboxes— both the one holding the money, and the one it had brought and left lying by Jasper's body, which held the pictures of Frances and her identification—neatly at the bottom. It filled the rest of the bag with clothing it found on the floor: two pairs of socks, pants, and a sweater. On top it placed the half-empty box of crackers from the cupboard, and Jasper's phone, which it had fished from his jacket pocket.

As it zipped up the bag, it looked at its hands. The open wounds on its knuckles had closed. The skin on its hands and arms was flawless now, smooth. New. Its leg had healed too, the bones realigned. It stretched its arms above its head and felt the muscles flex.

All of this must have happened while it slept.

The monster stood and pulled the backpack onto its shoulders. Its shoes were soft, less than a whisper passing over the floor.

It left the door open.

ACKNOWLEDGEMENTS

As with any project that spans years, *Tear* would not be the book that it is without the sacrifices and steadfast support of many people in my life. The person to whom I owe the most gratitude is Aaron Schneider, my professor, mentor, and friend, who believed in this story when it was nothing more than a novella proposal for a fourth-year undergraduate thesis course. Aaron spent innumerable unpaid hours editing and shaping the manuscript. He was the first person to take my writing seriously.

Thank you to the team at Invisible Publishing for taking a chance on this book and treating it with such care and attention. To Leigh Nash, for her precise editorial eye and ability to make the best and most difficult decisions. To Norm Nehmetallah, for picking up and championing *Tear* as it launched into the world. And to Bryan Ibeas, for his sharp edits, unflinching and honest opinions, and invaluable humour.

Thank you to Lily and Seva Ioussoufovitch for reading the first draft in its long, convoluted entirety.

To the writers and artists in London, Ontario, who welcomed me into their community and counted me as one of their own even after I had moved across the country. To "WPB" Kevin Heslop.

To Christopher Keep, who influenced so many of my early literary ideas concerning the Gothic and the strange, who taught me about the Brontës, Mary Shelley, Henry James, Vernon Lee, Sigmund Freud, Jacques Derrida, and Mark Fisher.

Thank you to my family: to James and Ben for listening to my stories and asking for more; to Matthew for keeping me honest and permitting me to read Stephen King aloud for long hours in the living room; to my dad for his "monster stories" before bed; and to my mom for trips to the library, full bookshelves in our home, and for transcribing my writing when I was too young to even know the alphabet.

Thank you to Nic, who experienced with me every moment of frustration and despair, every small and unexpected triumph. For pulling me again and again out of my own locked basement, thank you.

INVISIBLE PUBLISHING produces fine Canadian literature for those who enjoy such things. As an independent, not-for-profit publisher, our work includes building communities that sustain and encourage engaging, literary, and current writing.

Invisible Publishing has been in operation for over a decade. We released our first fiction titles in the spring of 2007, and our catalogue has come to include works of graphic fiction and nonfiction, pop culture biographies, experimental poetry, and prose.

We are committed to publishing diverse voices and experiences. In acknowledging historical and systemic barriers, and the limits of our existing catalogue, we strongly encourage writers from LGBTQ2SIA+ communities, Indigenous writers, and writers of colour to submit their work.

Invisible Publishing is also home to the Bibliophonic series of music books and the Throwback series of CanLit reissues.

If you'd like to know more, please get in touch: info@invisiblepublishing.com